By BRYAN ELLIS

The Red Thread

Published by DREAMSPINNER PRESS
www.dreamspinnerpress.com

The Red Thread

BRYAN ELLIS

Published by
DREAMSPINNER PRESS

5032 Capital Circle SW, Suite 2, PMB# 279, Tallahassee, FL 32305-7886 USA
www.dreamspinnerpress.com

This is a work of fiction. Names, characters, places, and incidents either are the product of author imagination or are used fictitiously, and any resemblance to actual persons, living or dead, business establishments, events, or locales is entirely coincidental.

The Red Thread
© 2016 Bryan Ellis.

Cover Art
© 2016 Brooke Albrecht.
http://brookealbrechtstudio.com
Cover content is for illustrative purposes only and any person depicted on the cover is a model.

ISBN: 978-1-63477-723-0
Digital ISBN: 978-1-63477-724-7
Library of Congress Control Number: 2016906156
Published September 2016
v. 1.0

Printed in the United States of America

This paper meets the requirements of
ANSI/NISO Z39.48-1992 (Permanence of Paper).

This novel is dedicated to my family and friends,
especially Renee Ellis, the greatest mother
anyone could ever have and the best friend
any man could ask for.
This book is also dedicated to my oldest brother, Brett Ellis,
who sadly passed away before his time.
I know he'd be proud of me.

ACKNOWLEDGMENTS

I HAVE to thank so many people for this novel. First and foremost I must thank my family and friends, and also my boyfriend, Alex Maccaro, who were all there for every step of the process with me. My closest friends, Amanda and Alanna, were also big helps with inspiration. No matter what, all these people stood by me and believed in my dream, and for that, I can't thank them enough from my heart.

I must also thank Dreamspinner Press for believing in my work and helping to make my dreams come true.

CHAPTER ONE

THE DAY I realized I was depressed, I was seven years old. I was sitting in the playground of my elementary school, and all the kids around me were running around, playing. I listened to their laughter, and I watched them have fun. Then there was me. I sat alone on the swing. I stayed away from everyone else. My teachers thought I was merely shy, but I knew even at that age I was sad. For as long as I've known, I've been a sad person. I didn't really have many friends as a kid. I mean there was this one girl. Her name was Alison—Ali for short—but she moved away. I never spoke to her again after that. It was my fault. She sent me a few letters after the move, and I just never responded to any of them. I don't know why I never did.

I wonder what she is up to in life now.

But other than Ali, I've been mostly alone my entire life. Well, that isn't totally true. I do have a couple friends, but I also have my books. They have always been there for me throughout everything. I'm one big stereotype. A depressed person who reads books. Even my therapist probably thinks I'm incredibly clichéd. I guess the scars on my wrists would prove that point as well. To add to my painfully depressing life, I tried slashing my wrists about eight months ago and then proceeded to spend the next seven months in a hospital dealing with my "internal struggles," or at least that is what the doctors called it there, and now I've been seeing a therapist every week since the moment I left that bleak place one month ago. Geez, when did my life become *Girl, Interrupted*?

But I'm so glad to not be in that hospital anymore. Damn, was it an awful place to be in! Seven months was way too long of a stay. The other patients were incredibly moody, and the doctors were both strict and way too nice at the same time, which I didn't even know was possible. I felt a mixture of being smothered and fear. I mean, I may have emotional issues, but at least I'm just sad all the time.

Now, in this very moment, I stand in the small local bookshop in town—The Book Revue. It's a tiny shop, one I had always adored growing up. The moment I turned sixteen, I applied here. And now here I am three years later and still employed. I take in my surroundings, as books are piled high on the shelves around me. Not a lot of people are sauntering about. Ever since they opened up a Barnes & Noble here in Wilshire, people just stopped shopping here. And now The Book Revue is becoming a bit of a relic. It'll be like Blockbuster.

I look around the tiny bookshop, which has become a salvation to me in this past month, and I breathe in that old-book smell. That wonderful scent that fills your nostrils when you take in the aroma of a book. The only other great scent is that of a new book. The few people who inhabit the small building sit in their far-off corners, each person with a book in their hands and some a steaming cup of coffee by their side. No one has even walked up to me in the last half hour. I sit behind the cash register and pull out my tan canvas bag, which I keep underneath the desk. I unzip it and pull out a small book—a thesaurus. I open it and randomly turn to a page. I look down, and the first word I notice is *sullen*. I shut the book and put it back in my bag. What a good word sullen is.

Sullen; adj.

surly, sulky, pouting, sour, morose, resentful, glum, moody, gloomy, grumpy, bad tempered, ill-tempered; unresponsive, uncommunicative, farouche, uncivil, unfriendly.

Antonyms: cheerful.

Yes, I decide I like the word. One of my small obsessions is my old, torn-apart thesaurus. I've had it nearly my entire life. It once belonged to my mom back when she was in college. When I was about six years old, I did what many children did. I snooped through my parents' bedroom. At the bottom of a dresser that once sat in their bedroom but now is long gone, I set my eyes on the dark red book with the cracked spine and dog-eared pages. Seeing that book was what I imagine love at first sight being like. I took the book, and it has been with me ever since.

I love to learn new words and to expand my vocabulary. It makes me feel smarter than I actually am. Who doesn't love an elephantine word every once in a while? Elephantine. How is that for a good word? Every day I try to look up a word, and then I try to use it later that day.

For example: Jesse Holbrooke, myself, is a sullen man. It's also a true fact. My therapist, Dr. Barbara Wheeler, says it's bad to lie.

When I first started talking to doctors in the hospital, I had a habit of lying to them. It's a problem that manifested as a young boy. I would lie to my parents all the time.

Oh, how are you, Jess?
I'm fine.
Are you happy?
Of course.
Why aren't you smiling?
I'm tired.
Why did you try to kill yourself?

Okay, that last one, even I couldn't really find a good lie to cover that one up. I've honestly spent my entire life lying to everyone. Whenever people asked me how I was doing, I would just answer, "I'm fine," because I figured that is what you are supposed to do. No one wants to really hear about the intimate details of your life and mind, especially when you're as crazy and fucked-up as me.

"Excuse me, I'd like to buy this book."

A young man's deep voice brings me out of my recollections. He's an attractive man, probably in his early twenties or so. He has a giant smile that might be a bit too big for his face, but it's a nice smile.

"Sure."

I ring up his book and tell him it'll cost $7.50 with tax. He hands me eight singles and says to keep the change. This is probably the most interaction I get from people. I only really speak to a few others outside of my family, including my boss, and he didn't even show up today. I don't think he cares much about this store, or at least as much as I care about it. It's not that this place is so perfect, but it has become a home away from home for me. An escape from everyday life.

The customer leaves, going through the door, and the little bell dings that annoying ding. I hear it once again, as my boss *finally* walks through the door. He's an older man in his forties, with graying hair and light stubble. He walks up to the cash register. It's nice of him to show up, since neither of my two coworkers are coming in today. I'm basically on my own.

"Thank you for opening today, Jess."

"Yeah, no problem, Peter."

My boss's name is Peter Jackson. No relation to the director. Don't even mention the name to him because he'll get pissed off. It happens way too often. We've lost customers that way. It's kind of funny. Pathetic, but funny. He grumbles as he walks past the cash register and heads to the back room, leaving me alone once again. I look around to see that only two customers remain. One is sitting cross-legged on the floor with a book of poetry, wearing a pair of oversized Ray-Ban's, looking something like a pretentious hipster. The other person is an elderly man, fast asleep in our most comfortable armchair. That's Roger. He comes in a few times each week to nap. I always let him. I kind of feel bad for him. I don't think he has anywhere to go. Over the years, he has come in every day wearing the same pair of jeans and a green threadbare army jacket. When winter comes, he still wears the same jacket. I wonder if he even has a family.

Peter comes back out onto the floor, his breath reeking of Jack Daniel's. He always drinks the same thing for breakfast, lunch, dinner, and for snacks in between. Probably brunch too.

"That *vagrant* is still here," he says in his deep, gruff voice. When he speaks, he always sounds as if he has swallowed a handful of pebbles that scratched his throat on the way down.

Peter calls Roger a vagrant. Peter is also an asshole. I don't think Roger is anything of the sort. Peter has never even spoken to him. He just always sees him asleep. The way Peter criticizes Roger, he makes it sound like there is nothing worse than being homeless.

"He's tired," I say.

"What? Speak up!"

"I said he's tired." Everyone tells me I speak in a really low voice. It sounds loud to me, but apparently everyone thinks I talk like a middle-aged nun in church. Peter gives me a look of disdain, one I've grown very accustomed to. I'm safe from his firing hand, though, because without me his shop would fail. I am the one who is here most of the time and takes care of it. I'm the one who actually cares about this place. If I didn't work here, he'd lose more money than he actually is.

"Is anyone else coming in today?" Peter inquired in that annoying voice of his.

"Why are you asking me? *You're* the boss."

Sometimes I don't think he realizes that he's the one who owns this place, not me. If I had the money, though, I'd take it right out of his hands. I could probably turn this into a really cool vintage bookshop.

Peter shrugs. "Don't talk back to me, kid."

"I'm nineteen years old."

"Whatever."

In his mind I'm no older than a prepubescent boy who is still trying to catch a peek of his hot babysitter changing. But me being the spiteful bastard I am, I refuse to tell him that no one else is coming in today because he should act like a damn boss.

"Go sell something."

He walks away, disappearing into the back office, aka his hideaway from society. What gives him the right to disappear when I'm forced to confront my problems and get help? When I was found in bed with my wrists slashed open, I had passed out from blood loss. In the moment before I did it, I didn't think I would ever wake up. Opening my eyes and seeing the blinding white light of the hospital surprised me. I left behind a note for my family. I was so ready to say good-bye, but here I am. Funny how life works. There are so many people out there, young children even, who have so much to live for. And some of them could become doctors or teachers or might change the world in some way. Some of those people will die of disease or will be murdered. But then the nobodies—me, for example—who have nothing to live for and bring nothing of benefit to society, are the ones who end up living, even when they don't want to. It's a cruel joke. If there is a God, in my humble opinion, he's an asshole too.

The rest of the day seems to pass by in a blur. The shop never really gets busy, but a few more stragglers find their way inside. Most of them are regulars. They greet me as they all come in, and I'm polite as usual:

"Hello."

"Hello, Jess. How are you today?"

"Fine. Yourself?"

"Not bad."

It's the same monotonous routine that happens just about each day. When it's time to close, I find Peter in his office passed out. I shake his shoulder, but he does not respond. I shake him harder, and he finally comes to. He tells me to fuck off, but after that he gets up, throws me the keys, and says not to fuck up before he leaves. I am probably better at closing down the shop than he is. I lock the doors and bring the shades down in the windows. I count the money in the cash register, only a little bit tempted to take some for myself, which I don't. It's normal. Who wouldn't be tempted? It's like the money is saying "Take me and run away." It's the little devil that sits on my shoulder. I do what any sane person would do: push the devil away and close the register.

The walk to my house is a short one. It's a cold autumn night. It's late October, a week and a half before Halloween, but you can feel the incoming winter. I zip up my sweatshirt and push the hood over my head. I put my hands in my pockets, and I keep my eyes cast toward the ground. The wind is bitter as it smacks me across the face, brutally reminding me I should drive to work. I do have my license. I just choose to walk. I hate driving, to be honest. Before anyone asks why, I have no reason. I just do. Walking allows me to keep my thoughts in order, which sometimes is a bad thing.

When I walk into my house, I hear my parents in the kitchen. Silence reigns, and as I enter the room, a thick, awkward air envelops each and every corner.

"Jess. You're home," my mother, Christine Holbrooke, greets a little too cheerfully. "I started dinner. It's spaghetti, and I'm making meatballs as well. Your favorite."

She's a real June Cleaver.

"Thanks, Mom. I'll be right back."

"Take your time. Don't rush. Dinner will be done in ten minutes."

I turn around to head toward the staircase.

"Did you hear your mother?" And as usual, there's my father, Holden Holbrooke, who feels the need to forever chime in. People always ask me, and yes Holden Holbrooke is really my father's name. It's quite unfortunate. Who would name their child that?

"Yes, sir."

I continue up the stairs, and I lock my bedroom door behind me. I sigh as I take in my bedroom. Books overflow from the shelves, and piles upon piles rise high upon the walls. Posters and pictures, which I have printed from the Internet, are taped to the walls above my bed. They are of writers I look up to, musicians I adore, or even movies I love. A majority of the clutter on my wall is horror movies posters.

My bedroom is, to put bluntly, perfect. I get to go to sleep every night with my favorite things looking over me as I look up to them.

I take my peacoat off and throw it over the back of my swivel chair, which sits in front of my laptop. I have spent many long and forlorn (my word of the day two months ago) hours in that area.

The smell of cooked pasta and meatballs drifts through my door, and the scent is just too strong for me to ignore any longer. My stomach growls, quite loudly I must say, and I don't fight the hunger off any longer.

AT THE table I sit next to my mother, as Dad sits on the other side. A fourth chair is at the table, but it lies empty. My older sister, Clara, always sits there, but she is away at college and excelling there. Last time we spoke, she had a 4.0 GPA. I told her I was proud of her, and I know my father is. He has always shown his favoritism toward her. Growing up, Clara was always *his* girl. Me… I was just there. I was the accident child. I know they won't admit it, but it's true. I've heard my parents talking late at night, when they thought I was asleep. At the time, they didn't realize I didn't really sleep.

People probably think this is part of the reason I'm depressed, but the truth is, I was depressed way before this. This was just another needle stuck in my flesh.

"Aren't you going to eat, honey?"

I look up. I must have spaced out again. I look down at my food, which has gone uneaten. I take a bite, and it's delicious, but sometimes no matter how hungry I am, I can't bring myself to eat. I force a few bites down, though. I look up to see her compassionate smile… and I try to smile back. I really try, but sometimes it just hurts to smile.

"Are you in one *those* moods again?" Dad asks.

One of those moods. I really fucking hate that phrase. Before my suicide attempt, every time I was upset, he always called it one of my moods. And every time he said that it just pissed me off more and more. He still hasn't taken a hint that I really hate it when he says that. He acts like I can help the way I am. If it was that easy, then I wouldn't be medicated more than a Beverly Hills housewife.

"I'm fine," I answer.

I stare down at the knife and run my fingers over its jagged edge, each point like the strings of an instrument. I push deeper and watch as drops of blood form. As I move my hand away from the blade, the blood trickles down my finger. It's the proof that I'm a living human being. I look back down at the knife, and I push the blade, and I watch the knife spin on the table, slowly, but I push it again. Faster and faster it spins, like a child's top, and my eyes never stray away. I watch it spin closer to the edge until it falls to the floor with a bang.

I look up to see my parents' scrutinizing eyes. I shrug, and I pick my knife up off the ground.

"Whoops."

I take a couple more bites and then push my chair in.

"Are you done already?"

"Yeah. I'm completely full. Thank you, Mom, for dinner. It was delicious."

"I'll put it away in case you want more for later."

I give her another forced smile, and I thank her before exiting the kitchen to head toward my bedroom. It's a waste to save that food. I already know it won't be eaten—by me at least.

In my bedroom, behind my locked door, I fall onto my bed, wrapping myself into a cocoon of blanket, hoping to emerge as a different person in the morning.

We can all dream.

CHAPTER TWO

I'VE BEEN asked many times in my life: *What does depression feel like?* Well, for one thing, it's torture. To describe depression, it's as if everything hurts. It hurts to move. It hurts to smile and laugh. It hurts to think. It just hurts to be awake. Every time I'm awake, it's as if I'm battling through to make it to the next morning.

I once told my therapist that my mind is a broken record player. Dr. Wheeler asked what I meant. I responded back the best way I could:

"What I mean is that my mind is a broken player. There are all these thoughts racing through a million miles per hour. Each one is worse than the last. Some say 'you're ugly' or 'you're worthless.' Some say 'you should just kill yourself.' These thoughts keep racing through my head like a record on repeat. Except, I can't stop them. I can't press the mute button, because the mute button is broken. So I try to lower the volume, but the volume button is broken. Instead the volume gets louder and louder… until finally I can't hear anything else. It drowns out the entire world until it drives me mad, and I can't do anything about it. No one can hear this record except for myself. It is my own personal curse."

I remember the way she stared at me. I could see in her eyes as she took everything in to analyze, like the good doctor she is.

"Jess," she said in a sympathetic voice, "do you still hear those voices?"

I remember the way I sighed. She totally didn't get what I was trying to say. I had to explain to her I wasn't schizophrenic. I wasn't hearing voices. It was just what my mind screamed at me every moment of my life, telling me everything I knew and secretly feared.

A person's own mind is their worst enemy.

The vibration of my cell phone pulls me out of my mind. I bring the phone up to my ear.

"Hello."

"Yo, what's up? It's Tommy."

Thomas Riley always feels the need to greet a person on the phone like he thinks he's some kind of badass. Tommy—don't ever call him Thomas to his face; he gets very pissed off if you do—is a skinny, pale redhead. Let that image sink in. Now you can see why it's hard to see him as a "badass."

"Hey, Tommy. Not too much. What are you doing?"

"I have Alex in the car. Look outside your window."

I walk over to my window and look down to see an old red convertible, with the top up, sitting outside. I look down, and I see twenty-year-old Alexander Young staring up at my window. He gives me a large smile, and I answer with a small wave.

"Get your ass into my car. We're heading out tonight."

"Where are—" I'm met by a dial tone before my question even finishes. I grab my light blue zip-up hoodie and throw it on over my T-shirt. I zip it up and put the hood on over my head. As I run down the stairs, I hear my dad ask where I am going. I tell him that I'm going to spend the evening with Tommy and Alex. I hear him mumble something, but I have a feeling it's about his hatred for Tommy, which is quite intense. Tommy is someone you need to have an appreciation for. Patience is the key to being friends with Tommy Riley, and my dad has little, if any at all.

I jump into the backseat of his car, pushing aside the empty beer bottles, cigarette boxes, and McDonald's bags.

"Look who's out of the loony bin."

He's about as understated as a garbage truck in the early morning.

"Tommy, I've been out for a couple of weeks now," I respond.

I've been out of the hospital for just under a month, and now he's finally coming to see me.

"Sorry, life has been hectic."

Alex turns back toward me. "It's good to see you again."

Alex, on the other hand, has seen me quite a few times since I've been home. Alex is a good friend, but I wouldn't exactly consider either of them my best friend.

"You too."

I look out the window as the scenery passes by, a bit too fast for this to be safe driving. Everything flashes by underneath the dim glow of the streetlights. A tree here. A building there. It's all so monumental, yet insignificant at the same time. All these *things* are here now... but in years, they will all be gone. No one will remember what was here when it is nothing but dirt and rubble.

Even all of us. No one will remember any of us. We're like cartons of milk. We all have our own expiration dates. In the scheme of everything, we're like all of these material items—*nothing* in the end. There will come a time when no one will even know my name. No one will cry over my family or me because it will be as if we never existed. It really makes me think what the point of it all is. That's the ignorant thing with society. Everyone is so damn desperate to be remembered, to be immortalized. That's why everyone posts his or her entire life online through Facebook or Twitter. This is society's fucked-up way of each person writing their own damn autobiography. But really, none of it matters.

We're just dust in the universe, waiting to be blown away.

The car finally comes to a stop, forcing me out of my dangerous mind. Tommy turns around, grabbing a six-pack of beer from the floor by my feet.

"What are you thinking about?"

"That we are nothing."

"Cool. Now let's drink, boys."

Tommy's answer to everything in life is to drink it away. The first time he ever got drunk was when his father went too far with his punishment. Tommy was fourteen and was covered in bruises. His lip was split, and he wanted anything to stop the pain. He stole a bottle of Jack Daniels from his father's liquor cabinet, and he drank himself into a stupor right behind the high school. That was the first time I ever saw Tommy so frightened. He was like a pathetic puppy that night. I snuck him into my bedroom, so my parents wouldn't see how drunk he was. He was gone by the time I woke up. Sadly that wasn't the last time his father beat him.

Tommy grabs the beer, and I look up to see the abandoned warehouse. Tommy and I have been coming here since we were freshmen in high school. The first night we ever hung out, he took me here. Alex started joining us when he moved here from Michigan in the eleventh grade. It's funny. We technically shouldn't be friends. Tommy is very loud and eccentric. He gets into a lot of trouble. And I'm not any of that. I pretty much keep to myself and would rather blend in than stand out.

Our personalities juxtapose one another, but we have remained friends all
these years because in our own way, we're like kindred spirits.

We sit behind the warehouse on the old couches we brought here
one night when we were about sixteen, maybe seventeen. My memory is
a bit hazy sometimes with certain details. We found them outside a house
late at night and spent an hour and a half dragging both couches behind this
place. They are damp from a recent rainstorm, but we sit down anyway.
Tommy opens a can of beer first and downs half of it in a moment.

"Slow down, man," Alex says, worry in his eyes.

"Yeah, okay, Dad," Tommy quips.

I'm the last one to grab a beer. I open the can, but I don't take a
sip right away. The smell reaches my nose, and it makes me want to
throw the can down to the grass and let the liquid seep into the ground.

"So did you meet any guys at the loony bin?" Tommy really
likes to call the hospital the *loony bin*, for some reason I can't explain.
I guess he finds it funny or something.

"Not really. Everyone was as crazy as I was. I don't think I
should date someone equally crazy."

"You're not crazy," Alex mutters. It's just low enough for me
to hear.

I look up and give him a small, somewhat painless smile.

"What about you, Tommy? Any girls in your life?"

"Every girl turns him down," Alex laughs.

"Fuck off, Alex. I'm single by choice. Just not my choice,"
Tommy states as he brings the can of beer to his lips. In the light of the
moon, I can't help but notice Tommy's light green eyes. His dark red
hair is cut close to his head. Alex smirks, and I just sit there, holding
my beer in my hands. It still lies untouched.

Alex eyes me. "Hey, you okay?" he whispers, so Tommy
doesn't hear.

"Yeah, I'm fine."

I bring the beer to my lips, and I grimace as the abhorrent liquid
slides down my throat.

"Don't be such a pussy, Jess."

Why must Tommy always call everyone a pussy? I think he
thinks it makes him seem tough. Honestly, it just sounds like a boy
acting like a man to me.

I watch as Alex takes a sip, and I follow suit, this time taking a longer gulp than before. A part of me hopes that the longer sips I take, the quicker I can finish off this beer. I finally finish, and when Tommy offers me another, I decline.

"Good. More for me." Tommy beams with a smirk.

He lets out a long belch, much to Alex's dismay. He's always been a refined man.

"Classy," I utter.

"Shut up," Tommy hisses at me, saliva spitting out between his clenched teeth. He's also a lightweight.

He grabs a beer and tears into this one as well. Alex and I look at each other, and I can see the worried look in his eyes already. Alex is still on his first beer. I watch as Tommy smiles and laughs. He looks so happy and free, as if nothing can touch him. He's on the top of the world, and nothing can hurt him. I want to feel that way.

I take another beer.

"That's the spirit," my redheaded friend screams in my face. Tommy looks as if he wants to dance.

The one thing I like about being Tommy's friend is that he doesn't care I'm depressed. He treats me just like a normal guy. My family walks on eggshells with me, and so does everyone else in this damn town. Even Alex acts like I am about to break if he doesn't look after me every single moment we're together. But not Tommy.

I open the beer and take one long swig. The warm liquid is just as bad as before, but this time I am prepared for it. By the time I finish another beer, it feels as if I'm floating. I can feel everything I'm doing, but it's as if I'm not actually in my body. I guess I'm a lightweight.

"I have more beer in the car," Tommy slurs, "should I get it?"

"Why not," I say, trying to get my vocal cords to work right. Even trying to form a word is becoming difficult.

"I'm done drinking for the night," Alex states.

"Good. You can drive, then."

I watch as Alex rolls his eyes. "Fine." I can hear the uneasiness in his voice. He's never comfortable when Tommy drinks. And now, combined with me drinking, he has to deal with both of our fucked-up selves. I feel the seed of guilt plant itself in my gut.

Tommy stumbles back with another six-pack of beer. When did he go back to the car? The two of us tear into another six-pack, and we manage to finish it off between the two of us. I hear Tommy laughing as he falls to the ground, which only causes him to laugh more.

I'm not laughing, though. Why aren't I laughing? Shouldn't alcohol make me feel good? Instead I just feel worse. I look down at my fourth beer and lay it on the ground, only half-empty.

"I think I'm done," I whisper. I don't think anyone hears me, but soon Alex is by my side, and I shiver as he puts his warm hand on my back.

"Are you okay?"

I simply nod, having trouble trying to find the words. I look up at the sky. Not one star can be seen through the clouds and pollution. Where are the stars? I want to see the stars.

"Stars...."

"What?" Alex asks me.

"The stars… they make you realize how little you truly are."

I don't know what I'm even saying, but it's like I can't control a thing I'm doing. This must be what an out-of-body experience is like, or as close to one as I'll ever get to.

"Jess, what are you trying to say?"

"The universe is so big and so vast. Our planet is huge to us, but in the galaxy it's pretty small, and then our galaxy is like dust compared to the rest of the universe. The universe is so immense. If our own galaxy is so tiny, why do we matter? Why do we exist? There is no point for us to be around. We're so small and meaningless."

And then I don't know what happens. I feel tears work their way down my cheeks. I taste the salt as they slide over my chapped lips.

Alex pulls me into a hug.

"It's okay, Jess, it's okay. I'm here."

He rubs my back as I keep my arms to the side. They kind of just dangle there like limp noodles.

"Why am I crying? I want to be laughing like Tommy."

Alex and I look over to see him passed out asleep on the ground. That causes us to smirk.

"Well, he's not laughing anymore. Alcohol is a depressant, and it's just having a negative reaction with your medication. I'm gonna drive you and Tommy home."

He helps me up, putting an arm around my waist and helps me into the passenger seat of the old red convertible. I wait there, laying my head on the glass as he carries Tommy into the backseat and lays him there. I never realized how strong Alex is. Tommy's snoring overtakes the car, and I can't help but slightly laugh. He sounds like a trombone.

Alex sits behind the steering wheel of the car, and I jolt as I feel the car jerk into motion. Alex drives very slow, making sure to stay under the speed limit. He turns on the radio, keeping the volume low. It's an oldies station. The Beatles are playing. I love the Beatles. When I was little, my dad used to fix cars for a hobby. I used to help him, but every time we would fix up some old car, he would grab his radio and play a Beatles CD. We would get greasy, but we had fun. Then he'd take me out, and we'd get some bad fast food that probably clogged up our arteries. Those were some of my happiest memories with my father as a kid.

Dad and I lost that bond. I just think he didn't know how to act with me anymore because of my increasing depression as I grew older. I became an alien to him, the son he didn't want. Dad doesn't even fix up cars anymore. It's like he lost his enjoyment for cars when I lost my enjoyment for life.

With my head still pressed against the glass, I close my eyes, and I listen to the soft melody of "I Want to Hold Your Hand" and wonder what it would be like for someone to hold my hand right now.

CHAPTER THREE

I WAKE up in my own bed, with no memories of how I got here. Tommy would say this is the sign of a good night, but for me I would much rather remember what I did with my life. My curtains are closed, and a water bottle sits beside my bed. A Post-it note is stuck to it.

For your hangover.
Drink lots of water.
—Alex

I grab the water bottle, and as the warm liquid seeps through my body, I can't help but drink more. It feels so good, almost like I haven't had water in years. I put the bottle down, completely empty, and wipe my lips with the back of my pale, bony hand.

I stand up, my bare toes on the soft blue carpet. I drag myself to the window and prepare myself to look outside. I pull apart the curtains, and the sun blinds me, burning into my retinas like a laser.

"Fuck me." I can't help but spit out. "Shit."

I quickly close the curtains, and I curl back up in bed. I look over at the clock to see that it is still pretty early. I don't have to open at work today, so I can just relax a bit more. I close my eyes and bring the blanket over my head.

I really have no memory of going to sleep. I'm guessing Alex put me into my bed. I don't even have a memory of taking my antidepressants last night. I'm supposed to take them every night right before bed, and then I take another antidepressant in the morning. Plus there is my medication for anxiety and then another for sleeping. I could open up a pharmacy right from my own bedroom. Skipping one night won't hurt. What's the worst that will happen, I'll kill myself? And I wonder why no one finds my sense of humor funny.

After taking my morning pills, I finally drag myself away from my bed and find myself under the hot water of the shower. The water is soothing as it flows over my skin. I wash away the stench of alcohol, and dirt spirals down the drain. After my shower finishes, I wrap my soft cotton towel around my skinny waist. The mirror above the sink is foggy, so I wipe my hand across it only to find my pale face staring back at me. I put my black-framed glasses on, and I look at the young man staring back at me from the mirror. His skin is so pale, he could almost pass off as a corpse, and his hair is dark, almost black. His face is thin, and his body is emaciated. I can see the ribs peeking through the flesh. Along the sides of his body and arms are tons of little scars. Past cuts he has done to himself. Cuts he did to stop the thoughts in his head. They put those thoughts to rest for a tiny bit. But instead of defeating the darkness inside, it just quenched its thirst, and it wanted more blood.

My sapphire-blue eyes stare back from the mirror, the same eyes my mother has. For all my life I've heard how beautiful my eyes are. I should thank my mom someday for giving me one nice thing.

"Jess, are you okay? You've been in there for a while," a concerned voice asks from the other side of the locked door.

I sigh. "Yeah, Mom. I'm okay."

I finish drying off and brush my teeth. I walk back to my bedroom, keeping a hand on my towel so it doesn't slip down my too-skinny waist. By the time afternoon comes, I'm dressed and I'm on my way to work. Mom asks if I need a ride, but I just tell her I'll walk.

Walking there I try to ignore the stares of the townspeople. Living in Wilshire can be hell. It's an incredibly small town, one of those storybook-looking towns where everyone knows each other. This also means everyone knows one another's business, aka my suicide attempt. Ever since I got out of the hospital, I have had to deal with the stares and the whispers. It's like I'm some freak show for the entire town to judge and laugh at. Sometimes it drives me so crazy. I want to just give them the show they want and scream for all of them to burn in hell, if there is one. I'm saved from their unnerving stares by the sight of the bookshop. It's tucked away in between a café and a barbershop.

The bookshop is already open by the time I get there. I walk in to find one of my coworkers already there, Laurie Thompson. She's a cute, mousy girl, around eighteen. Her dark, curly brown hair is kept back in a ponytail, and she wears a pair of oversized glasses on her nose. Her sweater is a bit too big for her, and her skirt goes down to her ankles.

"Hiya, Jess," she says in a sweet voice.

"Hey, Laurie. How are you today?"

"I'm well. Peter is in his office."

I'm sure with a bottle of whiskey at hand. I walk to a wooden door in the back corner of the shop and knock.

"What do you want?" I hear Peter shout in an exhausted voice.

"It's Jess. I clocked in. What do you want me to do?" I say through the door.

At first I'm only met by silence, but then I hear him respond, "Laurie is ringing. You can make sure the shop is put together."

I walk away from the door to leave him to whatever he was doing before. If he wasn't such an asshole, I might feel bad for the poor schmuck. I walk up to the cash register to find Laurie is already back there. She has a book in her hands. We are two of only three employees that work at The Book Revue. The other employee is a girl named Jill Sawyer. She's a college graduate who is living back at home. Yeah, the system really fucked her over. She has a degree in English, but instead of a job, she is left in debt. I went to college for English too, but I had to leave school during freshman year for my extended hospital stay, and I just haven't gone back.

I take my beige canvas bag off my shoulder, and I lay it on the floor underneath the cash register.

"I'll guard it with my life," Laurie attempts at a joke. A for effort, at least.

"Thanks, Laurie."

I look around the shop to see no one around. "Busy day today." I am met by Laurie's cute little giggle.

I grab a metal cart, already stacked with books, and I roll it through the small building. I place each book carefully on their shelves. When I see a book out of order, I pull it out and add it to the cart so I can make sure it's in the right place. I notice that a lot of the books have pages torn or folded over. Damn people. Everyone is so used to electronic reading that no one knows how to take care of a book these days. You need to show them care. Books are fragile.

The familiar bell of the shop door jingles. I hear Laurie welcome them. I don't hear a response back to her. Most of the customers don't really respond when you try to talk to them. I tend to ignore many of the customers, so I can just focus on what really matters here—the books.

I continue pushing the cart through the small aisles, and I finally come to the nonfiction aisle, my least favorite. I'm not the biggest history aficionado. As I roll the cart around the corner, I notice that there is a young man in the section. He sits on the floor, cross-legged. He holds a book in his hands. As he hears the sound of my cart, he looks up, and I can't help but stop dead in my tracks. The cart comes to a screeching halt. He has light brown hair, which falls into a pair of gray-blue eyes. His skin is not pale like mine, but not quite tan either. He gives me a small lopsided smile, and I feel my heart pound like a jackhammer in my body.

"Hey," I force myself to say. I even manage a small smile.

He doesn't respond. A blush rises to his cheeks as his smile widens.

"What are you reading?" I ask.

Instead of responding, he just shows me the cover of the book. It's a book about the art of violin. I wait for him to say something, but he just continues to stare at me. It looks as if he wants to say something, but he can't find the words. I open my mouth, but nothing seems to form. His face continues to redden, and the smile drops. He sighs as he looks down to the ground.

"Well, um, if you need anything, I'll be around," I add to the lack of conversation. He looks back up and gives me a small smile. I wonder if he can't talk?

He nods, and I continue to roll my cart away, totally ignoring if any of the books on my cart belong in this section. When I turn the corner, I chance a peek to see that he is still watching me. I'm tempted to run back and ask him for his hand in marriage, but I figure that might be too forward. I'll just stick to my creepier form of flirting, which involves plenty of staring with a bit of stalking.

When he pays for the book, I can't help but notice how tall he is. He is at least six foot tall. No, he has to be even taller. He's like a giant overlooking all us tiny people. I might also notice how well his biceps fill out the sleeves of his tight T-shirt. Along with noticing his good looks, I am grateful to see someone actually buying a book from here. Too many people come in thinking they found just some random place to hang out. I hate how people don't seem to buy books. They come in and peek through our books, but no one ever seems to buy them.

My heart finally returns to a normal pace as the door closes and the quiet man with the beautiful eyes is gone. Laurie turns toward me, and she has a wide smile.

"He was just so…." Even she can't find the words.

"Yeah" is all I manage to respond.

THE DAY goes by in a blur, and yet that strange, silent man never leaves my mind. When I walk home, I lay my hoodie and messenger bag on my bed. I eat and then I get into the car with my father, who got home from work right before dinner. It's Wednesday night, which means it's therapy night. Most people go out drinking at night, and I go to the doctor on Wednesday. I know how to party.

Dad waits in the waiting room with the newest mystery crime novel he is reading. They're his guilty pleasures. No matter how bad they are, he eats them up like dessert.

In my doctor's office I sit down on the sofa in front of Dr. Barbara Wheeler, an older woman in her midfifties, with her jet-black hair tied back in a neatly tied bun. Not a hair is out of place. She wears a light gray sweater with a long floral skirt. With her cheekbones and good complexion, she is one of those women who you know was beautiful in their day.

"How were you this week, Jess?" she speaks with a slight English accent.

"I was okay."

"Only okay?"

"Yeah. For me, that is damn great."

My therapy isn't like how it looks in all the movies. Dr. Wheeler doesn't hold a notepad in her hands and take notes, nor does she put me under hypnosis. She just sits there and listens. For forty-five minutes, it's all about me, and to say that is unnerving would be an absolute understatement. I can say I know what it's like to be put under a microscope, because that's what therapy is like. You are sitting there as a person you hardly know anything about studies you and analyzes you.

"How is the medication affecting you? Is there any change in mood?"

"It's helped," I respond. "This new medication made me a bit sick at first, but my body is getting used to the Prozac. It's not affecting the Trazodone or my other meds."

"That's good. Do you find that it is helping you more than the medication you were on before?"

I shrug.

"Is that a no?"

"It's about the same, I guess."

"So tell me about your thoughts and feelings for this week, Jess."

Dr. Wheeler speaks with a soft, caring voice. She is a good doctor, but I just have trouble communicating. I tell her what she wants to know, and the session comes to an end. I pay her with a check, and she tells me to have a good week. I tell her to as well. But when I walk back out into the waiting room, there *he* is.

The beautiful stranger. Twice in one day?

He looks up as I walk out, and he gives me the same lopsided, wide grin he gave me earlier today. He's even holding the violin book in his lap. Our eyes meet, and it's as if an electric charge is exchanged between the two of us. I don't know if he feels it, but it's sending jolts throughout every single one of my bones.

"Ready to go, kiddo?" Dad asks, and I look over to him.

I can't find the words, so all I do is nod. The moment the stranger and I had is over. He looks back down toward his book, and I zip up my hoodie. Dr. Wheeler walks out of the door.

"Adam Foster, you ready?"

The young man looks up and nods, following Dr. Wheeler to the office.

I watch as the door shuts behind him. I can now put a name to the stranger's face. Adam Foster. I am overcome by two emotions: the desire to see him again but also the urgent need to never see his face again. Just seeing him is putting me through a whirlwind of emotion. Getting to know him might lead to my death. I was already sad, but if someone broke my heart… what would be left of me?

CHAPTER FOUR

I'VE NEVER actually thought about relationships or boyfriends before. Well, I have, but never about actually having one in reality. It's always been a nice thought, but I always figured never for me. That happens to sane, happy guys. Not guys like me. For me the idea of a relationship has been nothing but stories. I read about them, and I hear about them, but it'd never actually happen in reality to a guy like me. It's merely fantasy.

My parents seem happy together. But all this happiness can lead to something much more painful. I've seen what heartbreak has done to people. Alex's ex-girlfriend Nikki broke his heart last week. He's been curled up in bed and walking around in a daze. His heart was shattered, and he looked as if he was about to keel over and die at a moment's notice. I'm already unhappy, why would I want to be even more unhappy? Love is like a bomb, ready to explode at a moment's notice.

For as long as I've known I have never been happy. People look down on me for being sad. Ever since I got out of the hospital, the people in this small town stare at me like I'm some kind of pariah, but are any of these people truly that content with their own lives that they can look down their noses at me? Is anyone truly ever happy? Or is it just a myth, some lie we're all told to believe? Maybe my parents aren't even happy? Maybe they are just buying into a societal norm that doesn't actually exist. Society tells us all these things we should do. Society tells us that as long as we buy that nice car or that new iPod, we'll be happy. It's all so superficial. We might think we're happy, but we're really not. We're just enjoying whatever new materialistic item we find. But that's not happiness. Even love is superficial. It's an idea we trick ourselves into believing so that we can be happy. Happiness is the biggest lie we tell ourselves.

I listen to the wind as it blows outside on this sleepless night. The branches, with the dying leaves, scratch along my window. The shadows of the branches stretch out along my walls like the fingers of a monster in a horror film. I stand up, wrapping the blanket around my body and stride over to the window. I look out at the night sky and look up at the moon shining high above, only half-full. I watch the leaves fall off the trees as they dance in the wind.

I throw my blanket to the ground, and I pull on a pair of dark skinny jeans over my briefs, and I pull on a tight sweater. I slowly sneak outside of the house, careful not to wake my parents. I lightly close the door and pocket my key. I zip up my hoodie and tug it over my head, and I start to walk. To where, I don't know. I just let my legs take me wherever they want to go.

The night is cold, and the wind is brisk. I find myself in the old children's park I used to spend time at with Ali, before she moved away. As kids we used to just sit on the swings, and I'd close my eyes and dream of flying. It was a time when I dreamed that in my future I'd be happy. I wish I could go back in time and tell that little kid he was wrong. It just got worse in the future.

I wonder if Ali ever thinks of me.

I sit on the swing, and I close my eyes, and I kick off the ground. I feel the bitter wind numb my cheeks, but I ignore it. I just allow myself to go faster, higher with each swing.

Higher and higher I soar. I imagine myself letting go of the creaky chains, but instead of being met with the ground, I'm met with the air. I'd just soar high above the town. I'd just float away, end up in some strange town, different from my own. No one would know who I was. I'd change my name and start a new life. Would I be happier? Probably not, but I like to pretend that in my nonsensical fantasy, I am happier wherever I end up.

The crunching of leaves catches my ears, and I open my eyes. I'm pulled back to reality as if I fell out of the sky and just hit the ground. The swing comes to a screeching halt, and I look up to see who's there. The streetlights are too dim to make out who it is, but I see the slight outline of a man.

"Hello? Who is that?"

He doesn't answer. I feel the faint notion of fear quiver through my spine. I watch enough horror films to know how these situations end up for skinny guys like me.

"I said, who is that?" I try to hide the fear in my voice, but I know that my question came out shaky instead of with the confidence I want to pretend I have. I feel like I'm the victim in a slasher film, just waiting to get stabbed to death by Jason Voorhees with his machete. And here I am just calling out who's there instead of running. If I am going to die, I want it to be by my own hands. I don't like the idea of not controlling my own life.

"D-d-d-don't worry, i-it's me...." The stranger comes into sight.

Three times in one day? This is impossible. Is this fate, or am I dreaming? I don't believe in fate, so I must be asleep in my bed. I slightly pinch my leg, and when the stinging pain shoots through me, I know I'm awake.

"Oh, hi," I say in my usually awkward manner, followed by silence, because nothing else comes to mind.

Adam comes into sight and motions his head toward the swing next to mine. I shrug and say it's fine. He sits down beside me, and he pushes off the ground. We start to swing in silence.

Well, this is interesting.

"So, what are you doing out here?" I'm the first one to break the silence on this weird moment we're having.

"Just w-w-w-walking," he stutters. "How about you?"

I nod. "Yeah. Me too. I couldn't sleep."

"N-n-neither c-c-could I."

"Are you cold?" I ask.

"I'm okay. W-w-why do y-you ask?"

"You're stuttering, so I thought you might be cold."

I stop my swinging and look over to see his cheeks grow red in the faint light of the streetlights and underneath the half-moon. He looks away.

"It's n-not the c-c-c-cold."

Oh. Shit.

"I'm so sorry. Damn, I didn't know."

Adam lets out an awkward laugh. "I-it's fine. You d-d-didn't know."

The seeds of guilt, which have been planted inside me, begin to grow. The vines plant themselves into the cores of my body.

"I'm sorry again," I apologize once more.

Adam gives me a small, embarrassed smile and just waves my apology off, as if what I said was no big deal. Meanwhile the seed of guilt has now turned into a full-blown tree in my stomach.

I want to change the subject, but not a thought comes to mind, so I do the most reasonable thing I can think of.

"I have to go," I tell him. "Good night."

He gives me a smile and tells me good night, and I rush home as quick as I can, hoping to leave my mortification behind me, for it to just stay in the playground.

Sneaking back into my house is as easy as it is to sneak out. Once my parents are asleep, they are asleep. Not even the apocalypse could wake those two up. I make my way up to my bedroom, and I grab my medication. After stripping down to my underwear, I down three small white round pills. Trazodone is great for falling asleep. Not so great for depression, to be honest.

A COUPLE of days later, and I haven't seen Adam again. I don't know whether I'm happy or saddened by that. It's funny how I can feel so many opposing feelings at once, each battling one another out.

On Saturday morning I wake up to the sounds of a car pulling up the driveway. I wipe the sleep from my eyes, and after opening my curtains, I see a small silver car sitting outside. The motor is turned off and a beautiful twenty-two-year-old woman, with wavy light brown hair, steps outside. She holds a suitcase in hand, and a duffel bag hangs off one shoulder. Clara Holbrooke, my older sister.

I quickly dress, and I make my way downstairs, just in time to see my dad bringing her into a tight hug. He and my mom kiss her and gush over how much they missed her. Finally Clara turns her attention to me, and she pulls me into a tight hug. I close my eyes and wrap my arms around her thin waist.

"I didn't know you were coming home this weekend."

"Well, I'm done with midterms, and I wanted to come home for the weekend, and besides I missed you, little brother."

"Yeah, you too, big sister."

I help her bring her bags to her bedroom, which is right next door to mine. Her room is much livelier than mine with her light pink walls and beautiful paintings covering the walls. Each painting is of a different cottage or landscape, many by an artist named Thomas Kinkade. She's always loved art.

"So how is school?" I inquire of her, as she opens her first bag. I take a seat in her swivel chair, which sits in front of a small white desk.

"School has been amazing so far. I'm so sad that after next semester, I'll be finished with my undergraduate degree." I listen as she goes on about her school and how much she loves the campus. I like how happy she gets when she talks about it, so even though I've heard it all before, I still let her go on. As she continues to beam away about her love of the school, her smile just continues to grow wider and brighter.

She comes to a stop, and she turns toward me. I see the seriousness in her eyes, and I know what she is going to ask.

"Have you been... okay, Jess?"

I was only waiting for the moment she'd ask. She's never been able to last longer than a half hour before asking me how I'm feeling.

"I'm okay."

"Really? Have you had any of your... *dark days*?" She grabs my hands and holds them in her smooth, pale fingers.

Clara nicknamed my bad moments the *dark days*. Even though I've always been sad, I've had my moments where I just slipped into something worse, something darker. It's like something so dark, so unholy takes me over and I just can't control it.

"Not while I've been home again," I respond.

She gives me a sad smile. "I'm sorry I wasn't able to visit more at the hospital."

"It's okay, Clara. I understand. You had school and work and life. You can't put everything on hold because of your psycho baby brother."

"You are *not* a psycho," she berates. "If you *ever* say that again, I'll be sure to give you something to be upset about."

She might even mean that too. She became a bit of a legend in our old high school. When she was in her senior year of high school, she found her boyfriend (I can't remember his name) had been cheating on her. Right in the middle of the hallway she walked up to him, and she punched him right in the face, making sure to spill blood. She ended up breaking his nose for the whole school to see. After that day, no one would ever mess with my dear, sweet sister again. She wasn't even expelled. Just a few days' suspension. That was what she got for being friends with all the teachers and the principal.

She mocks a punch, and I pretend to flinch, and the two of us break out into laughter; mine isn't even faked. Clara has always been one of the few people to bring out the lightness in me. It's like she can puncture all the darkness in me, to get to the goodness trapped underneath. I guess that makes me the damsel in distress trapped in the tower and my sister the knight in shining armor.

"So what is your word of the day?" she goes on to ask, apparently trying to change the subject.

"Beguile."

"What does that one mean?" She has a small smile on her face. I think she already knows what it means.

"To be attracted to or mesmerized by something or someone."

"I like that word. Beguile, it's pretty."

There is a small silence, and then Clara asks the other question I was waiting for. There are three questions she always asks me:

1. How are you?

2. Have you had any *dark days* recently?

And 3....

"So are there any guys in your life?"

Ding! Ding! Ding! We have a winner. What do I get for guessing the question she was going to ask next? Absolutely nothing.

"Nope."

I decide not to tell her about Adam, because honestly what is there to tell? I met a cute guy with a stutter? I may or may not have accidentally stalked him? Yeah, there isn't much to really say now, is there.

"I know you're going to meet someone. I can feel it in my bones. You're too good of a guy to not have that happen for you."

At twenty-two, she still believes in fairy tales and happy endings. It's why I love her. Sadly, my eyes have been opened to reality. I'm nineteen, and I still haven't had a serious relationship—or even found a guy who somewhat cared about me. The closest I've ever gotten to having romance is by reading about it in a novel.

"This is real life, Clara, not a fairy tale."

She sighs. "I know... but I still like to believe it happens."

"Is there anyone you have your eye on?"

She just gives me a small smile. "No. I spend so much time studying that I kind of lose track of dating or having a social life. It's a bit much. You know I've never been very good at juggling these two areas of life with one another. This past month I haven't seen one friend at all because I've been in the library or my dorm room the entire time studying or working on my projects and essays. I just never have time for dating."

That makes two lonely, loveless losers (I do love alliteration) in this family now. Clara kisses my forehead and says she is going to finish unpacking. I don't know why she bothers. She's only going to be home for a couple of days. I get up and head back to my room. With nothing to do, I grab a book off my nightstand and open it to where I left off. It's a novel about a young man suffering from depression and is contemplating suicide. Most people like books to escape from life, and while I do love that, it's nice to read a book I can relate to. I sometimes want a book about someone like me. It won't let me escape, but it will show me that there are at least other people who know what I'm going through. The truth of the matter is that unless a person has depression, they don't know what it is like to actually be depressed. So many people think it's so easy to just get over it. My dad used to tell me "just take a deep breath, and stay calm," as if that was the answer to all my problems. If that is the secret cure to depression, then everyone must be a fucking moron. I'm going to give you a hint; it's not the cure we're all looking for. My parents didn't really take any of it seriously for the longest time. One would think that a perpetually depressed child would be a cause of alarm. Not to my parents. They just thought I was a very emotional child. Yeah, I'm emotional all right—emotionally unstable.

I put the book back on the nightstand. Sometimes reading just doesn't stop my thoughts. If there were one thing I wish could end, it would be my never-ending thoughts. Sometimes they're just torture. My own mind has this cruel idea that torturing me is fun. It's waiting for the moment that something strikes and brings back the darkness. The medication does a good job of keeping the darkness away, but how long can it stay like that? Like any war—and I fight this war every day of my life—the enemy will find a way to get inside. It always waits for the right moment to strike, and when it happens, when this outside force gives my mind motivation, that is when my mind will attack. It will pull me back into the darkness, and if it happens again, I honestly have no idea if I will ever escape.

When I got away before, it was barely an escape. All I remember is taking a razor blade to my wrists. There was so much blood. It just kept spilling all over my arms and my clothes. It was all over the carpet and my bed. It had even gotten on my walls. It looked like a morbid painting. I became faint, and everything went to black. I was so ready to say good-bye to everything. I left behind the note, and I thought it was over. I was getting ready to never see light again.

When my eyes opened, I was surprised. At first I thought my ideas on atheism were wrong and there was a heaven after all. Then I saw the hospital. For a quick second, I thought, *Shit. I'm in hell...* but that was wrong too. It was worse. I was in a mental hospital. My wrists were bandaged up, and tubes were stuck into my pale flesh. I looked undernourished. The doctors told me I had passed out for two days. I lost a lot of blood. Mom and Dad came running into the room. Mom was crying. She apologized repeatedly and told me how she should have paid more attention to me. She felt it was her fault. That was the first time I felt guilty over what I did. I didn't think of my family or anyone else. Clara took a short leave of absence from school to come see me. She hugged me close and told me she loved me. Like Mom, she said sorry for not being there for me. I told her the same thing I told our mother: it's not their fault. I'm just an incredibly sad person.

Dad, on the other hand, took a more standoffish approach. He said it was good to see me awake, but he didn't say he loved me. At first I saw anger in his eyes, but then I realized it wasn't anger. It was disappointment. I had disappointed him, and that I will never forget. To this day, I still feel as if I'm just one big, embarrassing disappointment to my father. My mother has smothered me ever since. I love her, but she stopped letting me breathe, and my sister tried to act as normal as she could. Clara is too compassionate to truly look at me differently. She is so motherly that she became more of a second mother than a sister to me sometimes.

When the doctors discovered my other scars, they wanted to keep me in for testing and to get mental help. I ended up staying there for an arduous seven months. I stayed in a special ward for suicidal teens. I hate being in my own mind, so why would I want to be with other people like me? I'd much rather read about them than actually talk to them. They all seemed so despondent and far off. There was one guy;

his name was Jake, and he was crazy. Every day he would show off his scars. He was covered in scars everywhere. They were on his legs, his arms, and his chest. They were even on his damn face. I think he was proud of his scars. It's like he wanted to be there in the hospital. I had a theory that he was happy to be depressed in some fucked-up way. He was sent home before I was, and the last thing I heard about him, he'd found gasoline and matches. He'd set himself on fire. He apparently just couldn't take being in his body anymore.

Tommy couldn't bring himself to visit me. I think he was scared of me. When it comes to being scared, Tommy doesn't like to admit it. He feels it makes him look pathetic. Alex visited me quite a few times. The hospital made him uncomfortable, but the days he came were sometimes fun. We would walk around the grounds outside or he would just bring new books for my stay there. He always had words of encouragement, telling me he knew I would be out soon. He always told me I wasn't crazy and that I was strong and brave. I'm still not sure if I believe most of that. I'm neither strong nor brave. Those are just the things you're supposed to say to a sick friend, and sick I was. I'm still sick. I might always be sick. The key is just to learn how to deal with my sickness and to stop those malicious voices that tell me all the negative things about myself or command me to do all the heinous acts to myself. I need to learn to finally mute the record, so to speak.

CHAPTER FIVE

ADAM STILL hasn't come back to the bookshop. Every time the bell would ring I would find myself looking up at the door, but it was never Adam. It has now been a week since I last saw him on the swings that late autumn evening. I still haven't told a soul about him or about our three bizarre encounters in one day. I haven't been able to get his face out of my head, especially those icy blue eyes. They were so light and had a grayish hue to them. His eyes reminded me of the ocean during a storm. As I stand in the bookshop, I have the door in view, and I wish more than anything to see him walk through the door, so I can look into his magnificent eyes and drown in them once again.

It's a slow day as usual, and hardly anyone comes through the door. Jill is working today at the cash register, and I'm working my way through the aisles just to make sure everything is where it should be. Roger is in today. He's asleep on one of the chairs. Peter is too hungover to even realize that Roger is in here. Jill and I let Roger sleep, feeling sympathy for the man, who must be cold from the autumn nights. I really do hope he finds a warm place to sleep at night.

The jingle of the bell resonates through the quiet little shop, and my head instantly turns toward the door, feeling hopeful, my heart pounding and my mind praying to see his face. To my chagrin, I see that it isn't Adam. Instead it's a woman with gray hair and a body made mostly of fat rolls, and her "skinny as a rake but totally not anorexic"—or so she says—daughter coming in. The woman is Mrs. Rattree, pronounced the way it looks, Rat-Tree, and her daughter is Charlotte. Their eyes turn toward me, and I watch as they whisper to each other. I look away, trying to ignore them, but I can't escape their staring eyes. I catch Mrs. Rattree staring down at my arms, and I look away from her prying eyes. I dig my fingernails in my skin, feeling itchy all over. Mrs. Rattree continues to stare, as does her bitch of a teenage daughter. And trust me, I know she's a bitch; I graduated with her. I want to look away. I want to not care, but it doesn't work that way. I wish for them to leave, but they don't move. I just watch as their lips move, with their fake stage whispers, but I hear every word.

"Did you see his scars?"

"Yes, Mom. They're disgusting."

"How could such a young man destroy his body like that?"

"Who knows? I'd never do that to myself. It'd ruin my skin."

"If you did that to yourself, I'd lock you up like him."

I hear their low cruel chuckles, and I continue to scratch away at my arms, underneath their scrutinizing eyes. My body feels like it is on fire. I feel the heat rise to my cheeks, turning them bright red. I continue scratching, but I can't get rid of the itch. I dig deeper, but the itch is still there. Their voices sound in my head like an alarm. *Disgusting.* Jill looks up, and I see the anger flare behind her dark brown eyes. Her slanted bright blue bangs fall into one of her eyes.

"Is there anything I can help you with?"

"Oh no, dear." Mrs. Rattree sounds incredibly fake, with her faux politeness.

"Okay, then you can get the fuck out."

Mrs. Rattree acts offended, and she shoos her daughter out of the store. Jill gives their retreating backs the middle fingers, both of her middle fingers. She turns back toward me, and all the anger leaves her body. I see the pity and the sympathy. I don't know what is worse: the snide remarks or the pity. Both make me uneasy.

"Damn bitches. Are you okay, Jess?"

I simply nod, not able to find any words. Jill jumps over the counter in a swift dancer-like maneuver and stands in front of me. She takes my hands and pulls them apart to stop me from scratching. The heat in my body begins to die down, and I realize that my hands are trembling.

"Do you need to go home?"

I shake my head. What use will that do? I'm going to have to deal with people like this every day. This is what my life has come down to.

"Okay. Well, I'm here for you, okay?" She runs a hand through her wild, messy hair, which falls down to her chin.

I nod once again.

"Damn, Mrs. Rattree really lives up to her name. She's a real rat."

I know she is trying to make me laugh, but not even a smile forms on my face. I slowly walk away and continue my trek through the bookshop. I quietly fix all the overturned books and place anything out of order back where they need to be. Pain begins to shoot through my arms. I've left many long, thin scratches, some having drawn blood.

"Shit."

I roll my sleeves down, and I try to ignore the pain throughout the rest of the day. Jill and I are alone in closing down the shop that night, and she offers me a ride home, but I decline. I need the fresh air. Walking home, the cold air helps cool down my arms, and I try to forget about today, but I just can't.

Those stares. Those words. The laughter. It's all too much. It could drive a person crazy.

Crazier.

I feel the tears slip down my cheeks, and I don't even bother to wipe them away. I just let them fall. Who's around to judge me now? I pull my hood over my head. I keep my eyes cast toward the sidewalks, letting the tears continue to roll down my cheeks.

"Are you o-okay?"

Shit.

I look up to see Adam's soft blue eyes. I nod, afraid to speak. If I open my mouth, my quiet tears may turn into loud sobs.

"Are you s-s-s-sure?" His question is full of compassion, but I don't notice an ounce of pity. That brings a bit of warmth to my body, but not like earlier today. Earlier, I was burning alive inside my own body, but now I'm warm and comfortable as if I am sitting beside the flames, not cooking within them.

I nod once more. "Yeah," I brave, saying it anyway. No sobs come. Some miracles do happen. I did say I wanted to see Adam today, but I really did not want to see him like this, with a tearstained face. Embarrassment charges through my body like lightning, and I am mostly sure my cheeks are the same shade as the red fire hydrant standing right next to me.

His cheeks are a beautiful rosy pink, similar to his full, light pink lips. As my eyes dash toward his lips, a desire to grab him and kiss him overcomes me. The thoughts of his body next to mine, keeping each other warm, his lips on mine, are too much to handle. I feel my cheeks burn even brighter, like they are on fire. But my desire turns into fear, as I realize what that could lead to.

"Don't b-b-be embarrassed," he states. "We all c-c-c-cry. I c-c-c-cry at s-s-s-s-sad movies. I even c-c-c-cry at children's f-films s-s-s-s-sometimes."

He has a lopsided grin on his face, and I can't help but let out a small laugh. At the sound of my laughter, his smile seems to grow the slightest bit wider.

"Thank you, Adam."

He stands closer to me, and I can already feel the warmth of his body radiating off onto mine. Who needs a quilt when you have this?

"D-d-d-do you want, want to t-t-talk about it?" he asks sympathetically. It's his turn to face away from me, embarrassed. I wonder if he has to deal with assholes talking about him as well. He can't hide his stutter, while I can at least try to hide my scars or my insanity. I mean, everyone in this damn town knows each other's secrets, so I can't escape them... but at least I can try. Adam can't do that. His pain is out there for the entire world to see and destroy.

He turns back toward me, and I find myself staring at his lips once again. He doesn't say a word, and I realize he's still waiting for me to answer his question.

"It's just been... a bad day, I guess," I finally answer.

I need to get a grip. He's just a guy. He's just an incredibly cute guy with a stutter that somehow makes him even cuter.

"I'll b-b-buy you c-c-c-coffee."

"No, Adam, it's okay. You really don't have to."

"I insist." He has a giant goofy grin on his face, and how can I say no to that?

"Okay, yeah. Make it tea, and you have a deal."

"T-t-tea it, it is," he replies with a certain cheeriness to his tone.

We walk in silence before he finally asks, "So w-w-where are we g-g-going?"

I stop in my tracks. "I thought you were leading the way?"

"N-no. I was f-f-following you."

The two of us stare at one another, and we can't control the laughter that follows. It is loud and happy. One would think we were crazy if they saw us walking down the street. Well, in my case I am, but looking at us we seem like two regular loons who belong in the mental hospital. And in my case, return to the mental hospital.

"The only place that would be open now would be the diner."

"Lead the w-way."

I do a one-eighty spin, and I start walking, looking back at Adam. We walk for about ten minutes before we come to a small building, shaped like a rectangle. The diner is more window than wall. We enter the diner, and are met by the blinding fluorescent lights. The walls are painted a light mint-green color, with black-and-white checkered floors. The diner looks like something out of the 1950s, hence the name, Vintage Diner.

The diner is basically empty. Only one other person is inside, a frail, wrinkled man who sits alone with a plate of pancakes and a cup of coffee. Adam and I walk to a table, sitting beside one of the many large windows. I always like to go for the window seats.

A waitress walks right over to the table, hardly giving us a moment to look at the menu. She probably wants us out of here just as much as she wants to be. She's probably in her midfifties, with bottle-blonde hair and a voice that sounds like she's smoked a pack a day for the last fifty years. I just order a cup of tea, but Adam orders a bacon cheeseburger with a side of fries. I look at him, raising my eyebrow.

He closes his eyes as he smiles, almost looking like an anime character. "I'm s-s-s-s-s-starving."

"I am still full from dinner," I lie.

"Oh I c-c-could always eat. When I was a k-kid, my p-p-p-parents used to s-s-s-s-s-say I had a healthy appetite." His eyes close and he turns his head downward, as if he is remembering a sad memory.

We sit there in silence. I look out the window, at the almost empty parking lot.

"D-do you c-c-come here often?"

"Is that a pickup line?" I joke.

His cheeks grow red. "N-n-no. I w-w-w-was j-j-just asking." He turns away.

"Relax. I'm only kidding, but not really," I respond. "I used to come here more often, when I had trouble sleeping." BM. Before Medication.

"Why, why did you s-s-stop?"

"I—"

I stop midsentence, not wanting to tell him the truth. Probably the best way to a guy's heart is to *not* tell him about your seven-month stay in a mental hospital. Now that's a real keeper, right there.

"It's complicated," I finally answer.

Adam doesn't pressure me any further, and I'm beyond thankful. Too many people force me to talk, so it's nice to find someone who allows me to talk at my own pace. The waitress comes back with my tea and Adam's coffee. I sip in silence, letting the hot liquid soothe my insides. I keep my eyes focused on the inside of the teacup, almost afraid to look up. What must Adam be thinking of me? He's probably thinking how pathetic I am to be walking alone at night crying.

"I've never seen you in Wilshire before," I mention, trying to get the subject away from me. "It's a pretty small town, so I feel I would've seen you before."

"I m-m-moved here a c-c-couple months a-a-a-a-ago."

So he moved here when I was still in the hospital. I wonder if anyone told him about me? Gossip seems to travel fast in Wilshire.

"Oh, do you live with your parents?" I ask, trying to escape the embarrassing thoughts of him finding out the truth. "No one ever really moves to Wilshire. Most people just try to get away."

"N-no. I live on, on m-m-my own."

"Really? I would love to live on my own." Now would anyone trust me on my own? Probably not. My friends and family would be worrying too much that I'd off myself. When I started college, I stayed in Wilshire. I didn't have the money to dorm or go away, so I just attended the community college in town.

"Have y-you ever th-th-thought about l-living on your own?"

"Yeah, a lot actually, but too many factors have worked against me, so I'm still biding my time in my parents' house. So how do you afford your house?"

Adam laughs. "It's a t-t-tiny apartment, b-b-but it's home t-to me. I am w-w-working, and my uncles are helping m-me out. They live here. You d-d-didn't t-tell me your n-n-n-name."

If his uncles live here, how come I've never seen him before, never even for a visit?

"It's Jess Holbrooke. Why don't you live with your uncles?" I really am asking a lot of questions. He must think I am interviewing him or something.

"I-I like b-b-being on my own. They helped me find my apartment. I j-j-just wanted to l-l-live where I, um, knew, knew someone. I c-came to this t-town to visit them, and I f-f-fell in love with W-Wilshire."

I nod and sip my tea. The waitress, whose name I've already forgotten, finally walks over with Adam's burger. His eyes widen in delight, like a child being allowed to open his Christmas gifts. He thanks the waitress, and she answers with an "Uh-huh" before walking away.

He takes off the bun and picks off the onions and the pickles, and then takes a huge bite out of the burger. He moans as he swallows.

"This is the b-b-best b-burger I've ever had." I can't help but laugh as he takes another huge bite.

"Enjoy."

He devours the burger and closes his eyes with a giant smile on his face. He runs his hands through his light brown hair, letting it fall wherever it wanted to. I feel the urge to run my fingers through it too, but I push the desire away. There is no point in me getting attracted to someone.

Adam starts eating his fries, one after another, nonstop. I've never seen someone eat like that before. How is he so skinny?

I sip my tea. It's no longer hot. "So are you in school?" I ask.

"I w-was. I g-graduated in May, moved here in July, and I w-want to go b-b-back to get my master's d-degree. I'm t-t-taking s-s-s-s-some time off. I have a d-d-degree in elementary education."

Wow. He is definitely on a better track then I am. I couldn't even finish freshman year of college, and here he is with a degree and plans to go back to school. I look down at the table staring at my now empty teacup. How did I fail so hard in life?

"Are you in s-s-school?"

I shake my head. "Not anymore."

"Why n-n-not anymore?"

To tell the truth, or to not tell the truth. That is the question.

"It's complicated." So I wuss out and go with neither. At least I'm not lying. I'm just avoiding the truth. Loophole.

Adam nods and doesn't pressure me any further. He finishes off his fries as I sit there staring at the table. He looks up at me and smiles, and a blush rises to my cheeks as my heart pounds a tiny bit faster. I look away from his eyes.

"So, I guess I should go home. It's getting pretty late," I state, not being able to take the beating of my heart anymore. I can't let myself feel like this.

"I-I-I can w-w-walk you?" He sounds like a young child asking for permission.

"You don't have to," I tell him. I don't want him to do it because he feels he has to.

"D-do you not, um, want me t-t-to?" I see the pained expression, and I instantly feel bad.

"It's just I don't want you to feel like you have to."

"I w-want to," he says with a hint of desperation in his voice. A smile is plastered on his face.

I nod. "Okay, sure."

I go to grab my wallet, but he shakes his head, pulling out his own wallet, paying the bill and leaving a tip.

He follows me out of the diner. We walk in silence. I listen to the sounds of the light breeze. After fifteen minutes of walking in silence, we come up to the doorstep of my house. I look up to see Adam as he towers above me.

"So…."

"So…," he responds right back.

"I guess I should go in now," I state. I really don't want to go in. If I could, I'd stay out here all night with Adam. I just want to talk to him and get to know him. I want to hold his hands. I want to kiss those lips, which look so soft and perfect.

Then the thought of him breaking my heart flashes through my mind. Falling for someone can lead to me being hurt, and I want to avoid that at all costs. I take a step back from Adam, trying to will the electricity between us away.

I turn around, but as I unlock the door, Adam grabs my shoulder.

"W-w-w-wait."

I look up into his compassionate eyes and wait for him to respond, but I feel as if I cannot breathe as he looks into my eyes. Someone could really get lost in those oceanlike eyes.

"Can, can I g-g-get your n-number?" he lightly asks, turning away. Geez, even his embarrassment is adorable.

I can't control the smile that forms on my face, a real, honest smile. I quickly nod, and he pulls out his cell phone. I type my number into it along with my name, and I save it. Texting won't hurt, right? It can be fun. As long as nothing goes beyond that.

"Text me," I tell him, before closing my front door behind me.

Before I reach the staircase, I feel the vibration of my cell phone.

I had fun.

Another vibration.

Oh, it's Adam Foster. :)

I can't stop the smiling, as a welcoming warmth overtakes my body, and I feel the beating of my heart speed up, just from the simple reading of his name.

Hi, I respond back. *I had fun too. Are you still walking home?*

He doesn't take long to respond. It feels as if it only takes a few seconds.

Yeah, but I don't live too far from you. Maybe twenty minutes?

That close? Where do you live? I text back.

I walk upstairs and lightly knock on my parents' door.

"Come in," my mom answers, still awake.

I open the door to find her reading in bed.

"You're home late."

"I hung out with friends after work."

"Oh was it Tommy or Alex?"

"No, a new friend," I answer, feeling my phone vibrate in my hand.

I watch my mom smile. "Good. I'm glad. Good night, Jess. I love you."

"Good night."

I crawl up onto my bed, kicking off my shoes, and I read my newest text.

The better to stalk you.

He texts me back right afterward. *I was trying to be cute and funny but I failed and came off creepy and weird. Awkward.*

I laugh. I won't lie—I found it endearing.

You're a real dork, aren't you? I text.

I've been told that many times. Bow ties are cool after all. If you get that reference, I might have to marry you.

Sadly I don't get it. No marriage in my near future, then.

Sadly no? Sorry.

Nooooooooooo…………………… It's a Doctor Who reference. It's my favorite show. You NEED TO WATCH IT, JESS! YOU NEED TO WATCH IT NOW!

I silently laugh to myself at his geeky textual outbursts, enjoying the fact that I'm actually smiling.

I don't think you used enough exclamation marks, but I've never heard of the show.

There is a moment of silence. And this is when his barrage of texts begins.

Sorry… what?

You

Have

Never

Heard

Of

Doctor Who???!!!

Sorry… I type into my phone and send to him.

It's okay. I accept you for your flaws : P Maybe I can introduce you to Doctor Who?

I am overcome with something, some emotion…. Is it the myth of happiness? I doubt it… but it's something warm, and it feels good. I could get used to this feeling. I mean, I guess as long as I don't let it turn into anything more. Harmless, friendly flirting isn't too bad? I just have to remind myself of what it is.

Soooooooo… is that a yes?

Yeah. I'd like that, I finally respond.

Yay! Perfect! I'm happy now :) I could dance!

I giggle to myself at the thought of his dancing, which I imagine is quite adorably dorky… adorable I guess you could say. I like his childish charm, as I find it quite exhilarating. So far I like everything about him.

How old are you exactly?

I'm 22!

Could've fooled me, I joke right back at him.

That is mean! I'm quite mature for my age… okay, even I don't believe that. Good night, Jess! Sweet dreams :)

Good night, I respond, overwhelmed by his absence already. I really don't want to say good-bye. But he wants to see me again. Adam *wants* to see *me*. Why, I don't understand, but right now I won't think about it. I refuse to let anything take me back into my dark place. Right now I feel like I'm shining so bright the sun has nothing on me.

I grab my laptop and do a quick google search. What the hell is *Doctor Who* anyway? Shouldn't it be Doctor Whom? Google tells me it's a show that has been around since basically the dawn of time and is about a nine-hundred-year-old alien who travels through time and space and is only known as The Doctor.

Um, okay?

Yeah, it sounds kind of weird. I'll probably stick with horror films and books. I turn my computer off, let out a yawn, and finally get ready for bed. My antidepressants and sleeping pills go down smoothly, and before I know it, I'm lying in bed, and I feel sleep coming on.

I WAKE up to the sounds of vibrations on wood. I groggily grope the nightstand to grab the manufacturer of the noise, my wicked cell phone. Who the hell is texting me? If it's Tommy, I swear I'll punch him in the....

Oh, it's Adam. It's okay, then.

*Good morning! :) I hope you have an amazing day ^___^*

He really does love his emoticons. He doesn't exactly use them sparingly.

Good morning, Adam.

I look over at my clock. It's only 8:57 a.m. Couldn't Adam have texted me a bit later... like maybe closer to the afternoon? He's probably one of those morning people. I hate morning people; they're the worst. They're always so happy and chipper when they wake up, unlike me. When I wake up, I'm more akin to one of the walking dead.

How did you sleep?

Why do I imagine him sitting there like a cute little child getting really excited as he texts? Maybe it's just the image I'm hoping for. I picture him sitting on his bed in his pajamas wrapped up in his blanket. His light brown hair is a mess, and it falls into those icy blue eyes, and he has his dopey wide grin as he has his phone in hand. Even though it's only a fictitious image, it still brings a smile to my face. How does Adam do this? Without even trying, he manages to make me smile. I only just met him, and he already brings me such joy. I guess that is what happens when you start talking to an attractive guy.

I slept okay. WHY are you up so early?

I like the mornings, silly!

I knew it. He's one of those morning people.

You're weird.

And proud, he shoots right back.

I'm going back to bed. Good night!

Don't you mean good morning? : P

Good MORNING!

I plug my phone back into the charger and settle under the blankets once more, with a smile still on my lips. As I try to fall back to sleep, my heart is pounding too fast, and Adam's face just won't leave my mind. Dammit. I grab my phone.

I can't fall back asleep. Thanks a lot.

It's my pleasure! :) What are you doing today?

I'm working at the bookshop, why?

What time are you working?

12—6. It's not a very long shift.

Good to know!

Why is it good to know?

Thank you, Jess!

Why are you being so mysterious?

Who's being mysterious? Me? NEVER! :)

I don't know if I should be scared or excited. I still don't know too much about this guy, but I hope to know more soon. With my luck he is probably a psycho murderer.

I put my phone down and get dressed, pulling on my nicest skinny jeans and best button-up shirt. If he is coming by the shop later, which I have a feeling he might, I want to look good for a change. No hoodie and T-shirt today. I tie my beaten-up black low-top Chuck Taylors, and when I walk into the kitchen, my parents are shocked to see me up. I see the look on my mother's face; she looks as if an animal just talked.

"You're up early for any reason?" Dad inquires.

"Just woke up early."

"Huh," he grunts, sounding like a caveman. He's always been sophisticated like that.

Dad gets up and says he has to start heading to the office, or he'll be late. My dad works in a small cubicle at an insurance office. It's not the job he dreamed of, but it's where he ended up. He's worked there for my entire life, but when I was growing up, when we would fix cars together, he would tell me of his dreams to open up his own car shop. Cars were always his life. In our basement the walls are still covered with shelves upon shelves of classic model cars. Any automobile connoisseur would tell you it's quite impressive. Although, it's nothing compared to my collection of books. My bedroom might as well be a library.

I sit down at the kitchen table, and Mom sits down in front of me. She sips a mug of coffee and lets out a sigh.

"This is good."

"It's the same coffee you drink every day, Mom."

"So are you up for any special reason? I know you said before you just woke up early, but you *never* just wake up early. There's a better chance of your sister failing a class."

"Now *that* is impossible." My sister is back at college, and I miss her terribly. Whenever she is home, it just feels right having the whole family together again.

Mom laughs at my sarcasm, pushing her long, dark brown hair behind her ears. The same blue eyes like mine stare back at me. Her skin, like mine, is pale and smooth. My mother is plain, yet she is still quite beautiful. She never did much care for dressing up or wearing too much makeup. She likes to keep to herself and stays out of the gossip in this town the best she can. I'm glad, because I would hate for her to hear what the town thinks of me. The Mrs. Rattrees of Wilshire would kill my mother. If there is one way to hurt her, it is to hurt one of her children.

One of my fondest memories of her has to be when I was in elementary school. I was beaten up by a group of young boys who were pretending to be badass. They thought they were in a gang, but never in my life have I seen a gang of sixth graders. Neither have I seen a gang in Wilshire. Wilshire isn't exactly the badass capital of the world. Yeah, we have some deplorable people, but that's every town. The people here are usually harmless. It's their biting words you need to watch out for. But these sixth graders I guess were trying to start something new in Wilshire. They failed. You can thank my mom for that. They beat me up for being a weirdo, and they called me faggot, but at the time I didn't even know what that word meant, nor did I know I was gay at that age either. I just figured every young boy was attracted to other boys. After beating me up, I went home all bloody.

My dad wasn't home, but my mom was. I saw the anger boil up in her body. It was like watching a volcano preparing to erupt, and my mom erupted all right. She marched to each one of those kid's houses and told their parents what they did. I went along with her, and to see their parents' reactions was exquisite! Most kids don't want their parents meddling in their business, but when you're just a scrawny little sixth grader, there isn't much you can do. Yeah, those kids bothered me until the day I graduated high school, but they never physically attacked me again. Their gang never came together, and instead they just stayed three lousy assholes. They didn't go to college, and none of them have jobs.

I guess I shouldn't say much, since I'm a psychotic college dropout. I'm not one who can judge others. I have a reason for the way I am. They had no reason or excuse. They were just assholes.

Even when I came out, my mom took it so well. In most movies, television shows, or books, coming out is this huge, painful process. It involves lots of tears and fighting and your parents coming to terms with who you are and how you can't control it because you're born that way, blah, blah, blah. It's always that clichéd bullshit. I know it happens a lot in life, but it didn't to me. My mom just smiled and said she knew. She knew? I asked her how. Her only response was that a good mother always knows. It might also be because when I was only four years old, she caught me trying on her one pair of high heels she kept around for special occasions. That could have given it away too, but who knows. Clara was the same. She hugged me and told me she loved me. Dad just remained silent. I was only fourteen when I came out. I was fairly young, but I knew. My parents used to tell me I was quite mature for my age. Maybe that's why I'm so depressed. I was mature enough at a young age to know how the world truly is: a piece of shit rock that fucks everyone and anyone over. It's not something young children should realize.

"So are you going to tell me who you're planning to see today?"

I look up, my eyes wide. How did she know?

"What?"

"Who is the boy?"

"How did you know?"

"I notice things. I'm your mother, not a wall ornament. I saw your smile last night, and I see that you're dressing up to go to the bookshop today. I like it when you smile. You have a beautiful smile, Jess. I just wish the world got to see it more often. This boy must be special to be able to pull that smile from you. What's he like?"

I watch my mom as a smile blooms on her face. It's so beautiful and full of love. There are laugh wrinkles around her mouth, showing a lifetime of happiness.

"His name is Adam," I finally respond.

"That's a nice name. I like Adam. Tell me about him."

"There really isn't much to say. We've only hung out a couple times. He seems nice, I guess. But it's really nothing. We're just gonna be friends."

I downplay my attraction toward him. I don't want her to get her hopes up for me, for what might end up just being nothing. Or is it me who doesn't want to get my hopes up for nothing? I just really don't want to go back to my dark place again.

"You shouldn't be afraid of getting attached, Jess." It's like she can read my mind.

My mom kisses my forehead, and she leaves the kitchen. I'm left to ponder what she says. Why shouldn't I be afraid? If I just let myself get attached to Adam, then when we end, it might send me back to my dark prison.

I make myself a cup of tea and silently sip it, wondering if I'm doing the right thing with Adam. What if I really do begin to like him, what then? Do I allow it to happen, or should I stop it now before it becomes too much for me? But I'm only thinking about myself. I'm being selfish. What if I hurt him in the end? I'm only thinking about me getting attached, but it could happen to me. What if I actually succeed with killing myself, and then he'll have to live as that guy whose boyfriend offed himself.

Maybe I'm getting too ahead of myself. I should probably go on a date with this guy first. I pull my thesaurus out of my bag, which hangs off the back of my chair, and I open it up to a random page. I close my eyes and slide my finger over the smooth page… and I stop.

Beautiful; adj.

Synonyms: Attractive, pretty, handsome, good-looking, alluring, prepossessing; lovely, charming, delightful, appealing, engaging, winsome; ravishing, gorgeous, stunning, arresting, glamorous, bewitching, beguiling; graceful, elegant, exquisite, aesthetic, artistic, decorative, magnificent, cute, fair.

Antonyms: ugly.

Which word to choose here? I've had beguile before, and beautiful is too simple of a word that everyone knows. I like winsome. Yes, winsome is a very good word. As in Adam Foster is quite winsome.

I return the small book to my bag and grab my hoodie. I leave the house, locking the door behind me. It's still too early to go to the bookshop, so I just walk through town, taking in the warm autumn day. The leaves crunch beneath my sneakers. I look down at the ground, going out of my way to step on each crunchy leaf. I smile at the sound.

I do my best to ignore the stares. When will I not be the talk of the town anymore? I pull my iPod out of my bag, and I crank up the music so that I am in my own little world. No one else matters. No one is even here, except for me. I'm alone on the sidewalks, my Converse crunching the leaves. I don't even know where I am walking; I just let my legs go.

Soon, I find myself at the local bakery. I walk inside to be overwhelmed by the different smells of cakes and cookies and pastries and pies. Each one smells better than the last. I close my eyes and just take in everything. All the different smells come together to create something delicious to the senses.

I get in the short line, mostly made up of elderly people on this bright morning. As I get to the cash register, I am met by an elderly Asian woman with a bright smile.

"Hello, Jess! How are you? I haven't seen you in a while."

"Fine," I tell her, like I tell everyone else, "I guess I've been pretty busy."

I used to come here a lot as a child with my mom and sister, but as I got older, I stopped coming here as often, but when I do show up, Mrs. Chen still greets me like I was just here the other day.

"What can I get for you today?"

"A cup of English breakfast tea," I tell her. One cup a day just isn't enough for me. "And also a blueberry muffin!" I add right afterward.

My biggest weakness, other than tea and books, are blueberry muffins. I'm not big on sweets, but I love blueberry muffins, especially Mrs. Chen's.

She brings over a small bag and a steaming Styrofoam cup of tea. She hands it over, and I pay her the money, remembering the price by heart. I'm a tea junkie, searching for his fix. I live off tea like I live off air and sarcasm.

I wish her a good day, and I take my tea and muffin to a nearby park. It's empty, while the kids are at school and the parents are at work. I put my iPod back on, and I sit on the bench. It's a sunny day, and I feel the warmth on my skin. The tea burns my warm hands, but when I sip on it, it feels good as it fills me up.

I take a bite of the muffin and look around at the scenery. Multicolored leaves fall to the ground around me. With my music playing and a hot tea in my hands, this could almost be considered heaven. I pull a book out of my bag and open to the page I left off at.

I don't make it very far before a tap on my shoulder interrupts me. I look over to see Mr. Samuels. He's an elderly man in his early eighties with thinning white hair and a large gut that sticks out. I watch his lips move, but I don't hear a sound. I am almost tempted to leave my music playing, but that would be considered rude, or something like that.

I pause the music only to hear him talking about how beautiful the day is.

"This weather is so lovely. I do love the autumn. Don't you, Jesse?"

He also will only call me by my full name, for a reason I don't know. Countless times in the past I told him I prefer Jess, but he just ignores it, and I just stopped telling him.

"It's okay, Mr. Samuels."

"I can't wait for the winter, though, when the snow covers the ground like a white blanket. It's beautiful. Oh, do you hear that, Jesse? Oh yes, don't you hear those lovely birds chirping. Chirp! Chirp! They must be so happy."

I look around, but no birds are in sight, nor do I hear any. Mr. Samuels is also senile. He's great company, because you never know what he's going to say next. I know all the children in town make fun of him, but he's a nice guy. He's weird, but he's nice. But then again, I'm the town lunatic, so I should not say anything.

"Oh to be a bird, it must be so freeing. I used to dream of being a bird, Jesse. Did you know that? I could just fly away and go anywhere I would like. I would find new trees to live in and make friends all over. I would be a beautiful bird with bright blue feathers."

"That's nice," I respond. "I guess." I never know what to say to him.

"Or maybe a penguin... but they don't fly, so maybe not. I'm glad you're home, Jesse. The town isn't the same without you. Are you better?"

Am I better? I don't even know the answer myself.

"I'm working on it," I finally answer. I'm working on it.

"Oh that's good. You should come around for tea sometime. It's awfully lonely."

"Sure, yeah, I will."

"Good. How is your sister, Claire?" For years Clara and I have told him her name is Clara, but he still calls her Claire, so we just stopped correcting him.

"She's good. Still in school."

"That's good. I must go. Good-bye, Jesse."

He gets up and walks away, chirping under his breath. He has a point, though. Being a bird would be freeing. I would travel everywhere if I were one. To have the ability to fly must be the most freeing and wonderful thing ever. I wonder if birds appreciate it, or do they take it for granted? Just like how us humans take walking for granted. We have two legs that can take us anywhere, yet the majority of us stay planted in one place, never seeing what is out there in the world.

I finish off my tea, and I start walking toward the bookshop. I clock in, and Peter is actually on the floor. Not literally on the floor, although that has happened before. I came in one morning, and he was just passed out on the sales floor, reeking of Jack Daniels and wearing yesterday's clothes. Trying to get him to move was quite aggravating. He's a rather large man.

"Hey, Peter."

"Jess, you will be ringing today."

That is all he says before leaving for his own prison: his office. I often wonder why he drinks so much. It's like he can't live unless he has a little buzz going on. What happened in his life to make him this way?

Jill and Laurie enter the shop, and I greet them. The entire staff today, wow. As the day goes on, Jill sits around while Laurie walks through the store trying to find things to do. It's pretty dead throughout the day.

"You're dressed nicely today," Jill remarks, lightly tapping the collar of my button-up. She sits on the desk by the cash register.

"Thank you," I reply, my voice low and my eyes on the ground.

"Be confident."

"What?"

"You talk like you're afraid of the world. You shouldn't be. Look someone right in the eye, talk loud, and be brave. If the world bites, well, then you bite it right the hell back."

I nod. "Okay."

The day goes by rather slowly. Thankfully no Mrs. Rattree to deal with today. I think Jill scared her off for a little while. Some people stare while others whisper. Usually if they do talk about me, it's not with me in sight, which I am glad for. I want to pretend like I'm not the town pariah.

Then the little silver bell jingles above the door, and I hear the sound of heavy footsteps clomping away on the hard floor of the shop. They stop right in front of me, but I don't look up. I have my book open in my hands, and I pretend to be focused on the scene unraveling in the novel.

"Hello, J-Jess."

That adorable stutter is enough to have me slam the novel closed, the sound echoing through the mostly quiet shop. I look up to see Adam, with his light brown hair nicely styled and wearing a nice button-up shirt, with a plaid bow tie. He wears a pair of black, thick-framed glasses over his eyes. He looks good in glasses. I don't know how he did it, but he somehow became even more adorable. I use that word a lot to describe him, but it is the word that fits Adam best. If a small animal turned into a human being, it'd be Adam.

"I like your bow tie" is the only thing I can say. No other words seem to form in my brain. It's like it is just a thick fog, and nothing can be formed. Not even a syllable. I look over at Jill, who has a smirk on her lips. She jumps off the desk.

"I'll leave you two alone." She walks through the maze of bookshelves, and I silently thank her. I turn back to Adam. Alone at last.

"Thank you. It's b-b-busy today," he jokes, with a smirk playing upon those soft pink lips.

"Yeah, ha-ha…," I say with the most awkward laugh anyone has ever heard. If Adam is adorable in human form, then I am awkward in human form. Adorable meet awkward. His smile begins to disappear, and my heart drops.

"Are, are you, um, o-okay?" he asks.

"Yeah, I am. Don't worry."

What the hell am I doing?

"You, you s-s-s-said you w-were working, s-s-s-s-so I wanted to s-s-s-surprise you." He has a giant grin on his face, like he is so proud of himself. He really is just a tall dog, probably one with floppy ears too.

"Oh yes, I'm so surprised. Incredibly." The sarcasm is dripping from my voice.

"I-I was t-too obvious?"

I nod. "Slightly."

He pouts his lips, and never in my life have I wanted to grab a person and kiss one like I do now. He licks his lips, and I can't tear my eyes away from them. I can only imagine them tasting like heaven. No, they're probably better than heaven, and unlike heaven, I actually know that Adam's lips exist.

"I g-get too excited s-s-s-s-s-s-sometimes. It's a p-problem of m-mine."

"It's fine," I reassure him. "I still like that you're here."

His smile somehow becomes bigger, and joy radiates from his entire being, and it's all from me. I have to admit I do like being the cause of that dorky smile.

"S-s-so there are r-r-reasons why, why I am, um, here."

I look into his eyes and can't stop the smile forming on my own face. His eyes are that powerful. They don't make it hurt to smile when I'm around him.

"I w-wanted t-t-t-to ask you… out on a… d-d-d-date?" he states, sounding unsure as he gets to the final word.

A *date*? Me? Why, I am craving to ask, but no, I shouldn't. Jill says I need to act confident, although I might have to fake it.

"A *date*?" The word sounds foreign on my tongue. I mean I have been on dates before… it's just been a while. A long while, and none of them were very good. I never even made it to a third date before. By the second date, they all found me too weird or messed up to want to see again. My life leading up to the hospital stay was a continual *dark day*.

"Y-yeah… I h-h-hope that is, is okay?" The smile falls from his face, and a blush rises to his cheeks. He looks down toward the ground. "If it isn't, you c-c-can let me know."

"Sure, yeah. That'd be nice," I finally answer. The moment I answer, I somewhat regret it. Should I really be going on a date? Should I throw myself into someone's life? No one should have to deal with my baggage. It's my baggage to deal with on my own.

His smile grows wide, and I am almost sure he'd float away if it weren't for the grand thing known as gravity. "That is s-s-swell."

Swell. I like that. It's not a word you hear often anymore, but it suits him. I like that he says swell. It just adds to his allure.

"Exquisite," I respond back, using my favorite word.

"S-s-see you to-tomorrow."

"Tomorrow?" I ask. Shouldn't we plan on a date first, before he tells me a day?

"Therapy?"

Right. That's tomorrow night. It's been a little under two weeks since we first met, but it oddly feels much longer, in a good way. Getting to talk to him has just been wonderful. It feels right to have in him in my life, like he belongs in my life.

Now the only question is, can I handle having someone in my life?

CHAPTER SIX

WHILE LYING in bed, my thoughts turn toward Adam. I'm happy he asked me out, but I can't lie and say I'm not apprehensive about this. The last time someone asked me out on a date, it was a long time ago—I hardly remember how long it has been—and it ended up being a prank. Afterward he made fun of me with all of his friends about how he went on a date with the crazy guy in town. Oh yeah, even before my stay in the hospital, people already thought I was crazy. I sometimes had a habit of lashing out at others. Nothing too bad, but I would get paranoid, and I guess I yelled at a few people? I don't really remember much. I had an emotional breakdown, and I'm still reeling from all the side effects. I remember punching a hole through a wall when I was home, and I remember how it completely freaked my mom out. She called my dad up crying, saying they needed to get me help. That was the first time she really noticed how messed up I was.

That was also the week I slashed my wrists open.

My phone vibrates, and I grab it off the nightstand. It's Alex.

"Hey. What's up?"

"Hey, Jess. Do you want to do something tonight? Tommy is already drunk, and you know how he is. I brought him home, but do you want to hang out?" His voice sounds hoarse over the phone, almost as if he has been crying.

"Yeah, sure."

"Cool, I'll pick you up in five minutes."

The dial tone buzzes, and I pocket my cell phone. I lie back on the bed, wondering what's wrong. Alex is much more open with his feelings than Tommy, but I don't remember the last time he cried. Probably when Nikki broke his heart in two. She didn't just break it. She ripped it out of his chest and crushed it until it was dirt on the ground.

I hear a car pull up to my house, and I am out the door, telling my parents I'll be home later tonight. I jump into the passenger seat of the car. Alex looks at me and gives me a small smile.

"Where to?" he asks.

I shrug. "Surprise me."

He hits the pedal, and we're off. He is a much more cautious driver than Tommy. He actually pays attention to all the road signs and speed limits. I feel much safer being in his car. When I'm with Tommy, I fear for my life. It's funny how I'm afraid to die with *him*, but not too long ago, I was willing to take my own life.

Alex comes to a halt outside the abandoned warehouse, our usual hangout spot. I guess he couldn't think of anything new. Now I'm really wishing I didn't say to surprise me. A person can only have so much of a crappy old warehouse, especially when it's falling apart.

We get out of the car and sit on the stolen old couches.

"You look good, Jess."

"Thanks," I say, before we are bathed in silence once again.

We just sit there, my eyes on the ground. My fingers tap along my leg with a slow rhythm. I don't know what to say. I just don't know how to interact with people anymore because I'm afraid of what's inside me, and I don't want it to get out.

"Jess...," he whispers.

I turn toward him. He looks up and stares right into my eyes.

"I really did miss you while you were away...."

"You mean, while I was locked up basically."

"You say it like you're a head case."

"Well, aren't I?"

"No. Not even close. If you were a head case, you'd be like murdering people in one of those slasher films you love so much."

"Well, maybe I have a machete hidden away with my hockey mask somewhere," I joke.

He laughs.

"When I'm a teacher, please don't come near my children."

I laugh with him. For as long as I've known Alex, he has always loved children, and he is attending community college to study education. He wants to teach elementary school. One of his goals in life is to be one of those inspirational teachers they always make bad movies about.

"Jess?"

"Yeah?"

"I, um...."

What is he so nervous about? I look away to stare at the dirt on the ground. I kick at it with my dirty old Converse. When I look back up, Alex is still staring at me. He looks at me with an intense hazel gaze, his dark brown hair falling into his face. Even I can admit he's an attractive man, with his big eyes and youthful face.

"What?" I ask.

His eyes are intense as he continues to stare at me. I'm starting to feel awkward under his scrutiny, as if I'm nothing but a germ underneath a microscope.

"Alex?"

In an instant his hands are on the side of my face, and his lips are on my mouth. His eyes are closed, but mine widen in shock. My hands ball into fists as they just hang out in the air. I don't push him away, nor do I pull him more into the kiss. I don't know what to do right now.

He backs away, his cheeks a bright red.

"I'm so sorry. I'm such a shit friend. I didn't mean for that to happen… I'm just…."

"You're just what?"

"I ran into Nikki before, and she already has a new boyfriend. She moved on that fast. She only broke up with me a few weeks ago, and she already found a new man. I really thought she and I had something special, but apparently not."

I really hope he doesn't cry. I can never handle when people cry. I feel bad, but then I don't know how to respond. I usually end up rubbing their back like I would to a dog.

"I'm being really selfish, Jess. I'm so sorry. You don't need to hear any of this. I can't believe I just kissed you. I'm so sorry."

"It's okay. You're fine. Honest." I look away from his eyes, not knowing if there is anything else I can say. I know Alex is bisexual, but there was never anything between us. He's just confused with seeing Nikki. I know he isn't attracted to me, but what the hell do I say after that?

To answer that: silence.

Neither one of us will look at the other. I know Alex, and I know in his mind he is sitting there thinking we need to talk about this. He's always been one for sharing his feelings and talking—although sometimes he shares his feelings too much. I mean, it's fine to talk about, but when the discussion of feelings comes around, then I start to get antsy in my seat. I just don't want to feel like I'm being poked and prodded all the time like a circus animal, and when people want to discuss my emotions, that's what it feels like for me.

"Maybe we should go," I finally say.

"Yeah," he responds.

The car ride is spent in more silence, and as I open my car door, he apologizes once more, and I just nod. His kiss still lingers on my lips, but it isn't how I pictured kissing a guy would go. Alex is an attractive guy, and he's my friend, but that is all he has ever been to me. Nikki must have really screwed him up bad....

I TAKE an extra pill to fall asleep because my mind just won't allow me to. My brain has this annoying habit of making me relive moments while I lie in bed, *trying* to get some sleep. I'm already at a pretty high dosage of Trazodone but ignore it when I swallow the extra 100 mg. I might regret it in the morning when I'm feeling sick to my stomach. Trazodone is good for sleep, but in the morning it's impossible to wake up.

WAKING UP the next morning is quite painful. I feel like I'm going to throw up, but I know it won't happen. It's like something is battling its way out of my stomach, but it's being held back. It just keeps fighting and making me feel sicker.

Memories of yesterday seep into my mind, and I smile at the thought of Adam in his bow tie asking me out on the date, but then those are followed by the encounter with Alex.

I look at my phone, and I see I have four text messages: one from Tommy, one from Adam, and two from Alex.

Tommy: *yo we need to talk ASAP*

Adam: *Good morning. :)*

And finally Alex: *I'm so sorry for last night. We should talk.—Alex*

And then, again from Alex: *Please don't hate me.—Alex*

I respond back to Tommy and Adam, but to Alex, I don't know what to say, so I simply tell him I don't hate him. I know it's not a big deal, but it feels like it is. I just don't want anything to ruin our friendship, and we've already gone through an awkward stage I would rather not repeat in life.

When we were seniors in high school, Alex and I had this really weird stage where he told me he had feelings for me; at least he thought he did. That was the only time in my life where I had to turn someone down, and I felt terrible about it. There was no spark for me. When you like someone, it should feel like there is a flame within you, and every time you touch or even anytime you just hear his name or think of him, it's like the flame erupts and grows, setting your entire body on fire. When I see a text from Adam, it's like my heart beats a thousand times faster, and it's like my body is made out of bubbles, and I'm just floating through life.

That just never happened with Alex. He's nice, and he's not bad-looking, but he's also one of my good friends—one of my only friends. I know I should talk to him again, but I just can't bring myself to.

I feel the vibration of my phone, and when I see Adam's name once again, I feel the flame inside my body.

THE DAY goes by in a blur as I work in the bookshop and then head to therapy. Dad just drops me off and says he'll pick me up later. In the waiting room I see Adam, and as we wait for Dr. Wheeler to call me into her office, we share sly smiles and cute glances. The session itself is boring, and I hardly speak, I think to the annoyance of my doctor. I just don't know what to say. I started seeing Dr. Wheeler about a month ago, and this is still weird to me. In the hospital I had to talk to a few doctors, and I'm not good at sharing my feelings, even the good ones, so I feel bad for her. I really do. She tells me she wants to help me, but she also tells me I have to want to be helped.

The session comes to an end, and as I reach for the door, she says my name, and I look back at her. "I can't save someone who doesn't want to be saved." I simply nod, and I walk out.

Adam gives me a smile, and I manage to muster up one back. I think he sees how painful my smile is, because right now it hurts. It hurts pretty bad. My doctor is right. I really want to get better... but am I getting better? Maybe I'm not doing the right thing by accepting his date? He should be with a guy who can actually be happy and who can treat him well. Someone who can just fucking smile without it hurting. I basically run out of the building, without a word to Adam.

Dad is outside, waiting in his car, and he asks how the session went, so I say my usual answer: "It went fine."

At home we eat dinner, and I don't really eat much, and Mom looks at me sadly. Dad just seems disappointed as usual. I feel my phone go off, and I leave the room to answer it.

"Yo."

"Hey, Tommy."

"I'm outside."

Yeah, he has a habit of just showing up and not actually asking to hang out. I've just grown accustomed to it. It seems like he always knows when I'm home. I guess it's because I don't leave much.

TOMMY AND I drive to the warehouse. I've had enough of this place in the past couple of days. Why can't we find a new place to hang out and relax, like the twenty-four-hour diner or something? I think that is what the people here do for fun.

We sit down on our usual couches, and memories resurface from last night. I feel Alex's lips once again, and my heart seems to claw at my chest, wanting to escape.

"Alex told me what happened."

I nod. Alex is the opposite of me. He doesn't let anything stew within him until everything comes to a boiling point and he explodes. No, he's normal and rational and actually talks his feelings out with people. Many are shocked to learn this, but *sometimes* Tommy is a good guy to talk to.

"I knew he would. That's Alex for you."

"Is there anything you want to talk about?"

I shrug. "I don't really know."

"I just feel like there's nothing I can do sometimes, and it sucks to watch your friend disappear. You *never* talk to me. I know I'm not that great at talking either, but it's like sometimes you don't even exist."

I look away, feeling the guilt. He's right. "I'm sorry."

Tommy lets out a deep sigh and then a small laugh. "When we first met Alex, I actually thought you two would get together. I was kind of hoping it would happen."

"Why?" I ask.

"I know how he used to have a crush on you, and because he's a good guy, and you deserve a good guy. No matter what you think, you do deserve to have someone in your life, Jess. I just worry that you're lonely sometimes. You never talk."

I shrug.

"Why aren't you with Alex?" Tommy asks, in a rare moment of compassion. He spends so much of his life hiding it away and pretending to be so tough. I like when he just shows his true feelings.

"I just don't feel that way about him."

"Are you lonely?"

"Yeah," I answer truthfully. No point in lying. It's not like I ever really hid the fact that I'm lonely. It is written all over my face.

"So why not Alex?"

"Yeah, it sucks to be so lonely all the time, but I guess it's better to be lonely than to live a lie."

Tommy just nods as if he understands. I've always been lonely, and I may always be lonely. But I'm never going to be with a guy just because I want to be with a guy. I'm going to be with a guy when I like him and I want to be with him, and when I know he won't hurt me. Tommy tends to look for a girl to last the night, but he never wants to get to know any of them. I'm just not like that. I want something that lasts forever. I want someone like Adam.

I'm shocked when Tommy pulls me into a hug. At first, my arms hang flaccid at my sides, but then I reach up and wrap them awkwardly around him too. He does that manly thing guys do when they hug.

He lets me go and says, "Jess, no matter what, I'm here for you. I know I'm not good with all this emotional bullshit, but I really did worry about you back when you were in the hospital. I don't want you to think I didn't, okay?"

I nod, unable to find my words at Tommy's emotional confession.

"Good. Now I want you to be happy. I really do. I know you're going to be fine. You're stronger than you think you are."

There we go, another person telling me how strong I am. What does everyone see in me? Because I'm not seeing any of this courage or strength in me. I just see darkness and weakness.

"Thank you, Tommy," I finally respond after my awkward attempt at a hug. We sit there in silence for what seems like another hour before he drives me home. As he pulls outside of my house, I start to open the door.

"Wait."

I turn around, and I look into his jade-green eyes.

"I just don't want you to go to that dark place again. Promise me, you won't go back there."

There is so much agony in his eyes as he pleads for me to stay. I nod and tell him that I'm trying. And I am, I really am trying. It's just incredibly difficult, when the darkness is so strong and it's pulling you away.

I watch Tommy drive away, taking in what happened tonight. Tommy opened up; he really opened up to me. I know that's not an easy thing for him. I think his father taught him that emotion is weak, but I guess I kind of think the same way. Why else do I bottle up everything inside? Tommy's father started drinking not long after Tommy's mother died, and it all went downhill. Tommy never brings up his mom, and if you even mention her, he'll change the subject. I have a theory that he is angry with her because he blames her for what his father does to him. He's tried moving out, but he just doesn't have the money, and the car garage he works at doesn't pay enough for him to live on his own. If there is a God, he's one fucked-up God. We must just be a giant game to him, kind of like *The Sims*, where he can just play around with us and make us do whatever he wants. He can kill whomever and hurt whomever he chooses, and I bet he gets sick satisfaction out of it. And people ask why I don't believe in God.

The moment I'm inside my home, I send Adam an apology text, and he texts back instantly. I did run out of that office rather quick. I have a feeling he is one of those people who always has his phone on him and never leaves without it by his side.

For a while there, I thought I freaked you out when I asked you on a date.

Well, he did, but that he doesn't need to know. He also doesn't need to know I'm still freaking out.

No, you're good, no freaking out from me. I lie.

Good, so is everything okay?

Yeah.

And I guess I'm okay. I'm better, thanks to Tommy at least. Tommy is just trying to make sure I'm okay. I know he is, but this is all just so new to me. I've only been out of the hospital for a month now. I guess I need to talk to Alex sometime as well.

So I was thinking, are you free Friday night, if that isn't too short notice?

Here's where everything comes down to it: do I give into my feelings and say yes? Or do I turn to my fear and say no? Right now both options sound lovely. But I think of his soft lips and his effervescent personality, and I know what direction my heart leans toward. Just the thought of him allows my heart to skip a beat.

I am. I'm done with work at 6pm.

I really hope I don't regret this. Please, please don't let me get attached.

Swell :) I'll pick you up at 8pm! I remember your address.

I laugh as he sends a second text very quickly afterward, which states: *That wasn't supposed to sound so stalkerish, I swear.*

Sure. You're stalking me, aren't you?

Maybe a little bit.

I laugh at the memory of how not too long ago I was kind of stalking him at the bookshop. I let out a yawn. I guess everything these past couple of days just took a lot out of me.

Good night, Adam. I need to sleep.

Sweet dreams. I can't wait for Friday :)

A part of me can't either.

CHAPTER SEVEN

FRIDAY ARRIVES, and I can't put into words how nervous I am. People overuse the expression that they have butterflies in their stomach. No, I don't have butterflies twittering about in my stomach. I have huge condors flapping their huge fucking wings around in my stomach. If I throw up, would that be considered bad date etiquette? Probably, I assume. Who created the etiquette of a date? It's stupid! Who's to say that throwing up is bad? Maybe it's a good thing. It could be a sign you like the guy.

Or, I'm just an idiot.

I look at my black leather watch, which I always wear on my left wrist—never my right—to see that it is nearly 6:00 p.m. Laurie looks up from behind the counter.

"You keep looking at your watch. Are you late for something?" she asks in a hushed voice.

I think she forgets sometimes this isn't a library. She always talks so low in The Book Revue.

"No. It's nothing," I state.

Is it nothing? Or is it something? Which do I want it to be? Why must I be so confused by something that should be so simple? What am I going to ask myself next… the meaning of life? Geez. Even I'm getting on my own nerves.

Then 6:00 p.m. rolls around and I'm walking home, with my black peacoat closed and my messenger bag slung over my shoulder. What if I say something wrong tonight? What if I insult him? Accidentally, of course. I wouldn't insult him on purpose, unless he deserved it. I feel my breathing quicken in pace with the beating of my heart. Is this normal?

Get ahold of yourself. Breathe, Jess, breathe.

I try to take my own advice, and I take a deep breath. Inhale. Exhale. Inhale. Exhale. I try to calm my mind by listing some of my favorite words. Exquisite. Swell is a new favorite of mine. Effervescent.

Bewitching. Lithe. Epiphany is another good one. My breathing is calm, and my mind is like a tranquil ocean. I try to ignore the fact that an ocean can become turbulent in an instant with one storm, even though a part of my brain tries to remind me.

I arrive at my house and quickly run to my room. I only have two hours to get ready. I shower and brush my teeth, and now comes the hardest part: what the hell do I wear? I already know Adam will be wearing some impeccable outfit, so I know I won't live up to him, but halfway decent will be fine by me.

I end up wearing a nice blue button-up, which I hear brings out my eyes, along with a pair of my tightest faded, light blue skinny jeans. My battered low-top Chucks come on next, and for once in my life I wish I had a nicer pair of shoes. I even wear these sneakers in the coldest winters and through the highest snow. These shoes have seen many blizzards in their days. I could duct tape them, but that might make a worse impression. I think I should rewrite the book on date etiquette.

1. Throwing up is a sign of attraction.

2. Beaten-up and duct-taped shoes are great attire for a date.

I'm already on a roll. My new rules will change the world of dating and take it by storm. It'll be like when people were first introduced to color films and television. At least that is what I imagine in my head. Images of lonely nerds, like me, with their thick glasses and taped-up shoes come to my mind. A nice ideal.

I clean my glasses on my shirt before grabbing a royal blue cardigan. When I enter the bathroom, I look into the mirror. Well, this isn't too bad. I run a hand through my messy mop of dark brown, almost-black hair, and I just let it spill all over the place, each section standing in a different direction, a lot falling into my sapphire-blue eyes. I brush my teeth again, just to play safe, and when I check my watch I see that I still have an hour left.

I guess I didn't have to rush after all. I exit the bathroom, and almost walk right into Clara. She's so quiet that sometimes I actually forget she's home for the weekend.

"You're looking quite dapper tonight. Where are you going?" she asks with a coy little smirk. I know she is hankering to know where I'm going tonight.

"Nowhere in particular."

"Is this nowhere with a certain guy?"

I stop in my tracks, keeping my eyes on the ground. I can't look up into her eyes because then I won't be able to stop the guilt for not telling her.

"Maybe," I answer with a shrug. Part of the reason I don't want to talk about it is so it doesn't become a big ordeal.

"What's his name?" I can hear the exuberant cheerfulness in her voice as she asks. I already know what she is thinking: *My brother has a boyfriend. He must be happy.* And that is a no. I'm neither in a relationship nor am I happy. Both would be nice ideals to reach, but so would living on my own private island where no one can bother me.

"Adam," I respond, satisfying her inquiry.

"I like that name." Gosh, sometimes she is just like Mom.

I nod and give her a small smile.

"Where are you two going?"

"Geez, is this an interview?" I spit out, with a little more anger than I meant to. I just really don't want to talk about this.

She looks away, and I know that I stung her with my words.

"Sorry, Clara. I didn't mean to get mad. I'm just… getting overwhelmed." I tell her the truth. I should probably start doing that instead of saying everything is fine. At least sometimes.

"It's okay. I hope you have fun. I have one last question." I try to hold back my groan. "Is he a gentleman?"

"A perfect gentleman," I respond, and the smile reappears on her face.

"Good. Have fun. I want to hear about it when you get home."

She embraces me and kisses my cheek, and then I get her back with one of my infamous awkward hugs.

After she leaves my side, I try to keep busy walking around the house. I fix some of my books, noticing some are out of alphabetical order. I like to have my books organized by each author's last name, and then within the authors, I organize the novels by title. I may or may not be a bit OCD.

After I brush my teeth a fourth time that night, I hear the doorbell reverberate throughout the house. I grab my jacket and my bag, and I see my sister waiting downstairs in the kitchen.

Love you, she mouths to me.

"You too," I respond.

As I open the door, I find Adam standing outside, his hair nicely styled like it usually is, and he wears a bright green bow tie, which matches the green-and-white plaid button-up he wears. It's tucked into a pair of tight black skinny jeans, and he wears a black peacoat over everything, which sits open. Yeah, he put me to shame, as I look down at my own outfit of choice. Even his black leather shoes are nicely polished.

"I g-g-got this for, for y-you," he anxiously states, holding a single lily flower in his hand.

I can't stop the smile from blooming as I take the flower.

"Thank you."

I look back to see my dad's confused face and my mom's beaming smile looking on.

"H-h-hello, I am A-Adam." He tries to act confident, but I see the deep red blush covering his cheeks as he stutters.

"Nice to meet you, Adam," my mom greets him, thankfully ignoring the stutter.

"You look familiar." Very nice, Dad.

"We m-met a-a-a-at the th-therapist's office...."

"Right. Have fun, kiddo."

"I'll be home later."

As I close the door, I hear my father shout "Not too late." Well, that was only sufficiently awkward.

"They s-s-s-s-s-seem nice."

I guess it was only awkward for me, then. What else is new? My whole life is one *long* awkward moment.

"They're cool," I state, trying to pretend that I'm being cool and confident, even though I'm closer to being a nervous wreck. "So where are we going tonight?" I ask.

We walk up to a small white car, and he opens the passenger door, like the perfect gentleman he is. He gets into the driver's side and turns the car on.

"Ah, i-it's a s-s-s-s-s-surprise," he finally responds. I'm noticing he has a lot issues with the letter *s*, well more so than any other letter.

"A surprise?"

"Yep." Why does he sound so chipper?

"Okay... that's cool."

It'll probably be great… yet why is there a gnawing feeling inside my stomach. I close my eyes and take a deep breath. It'll be fine.

"Ar-are you ok-k-k-kay?" He looks over at me concerned.

I open my eyes to see that he has pulled the car over to the side of the road, and I nod and I smile. "Yes, I am. Let's go. Onwards."

He continues driving after giving me a reassuring smile, and I can't help but watch him as he drives. I bring the lily, which sits in my lap, to my nose, and I breathe in the aroma. The scent is enthralling. He has good taste in flowers. I never knew I was a fan of flowers until now. We come to a stop in front of a small, quaint restaurant, and he tells me to wait in the car. He quickly runs around and opens my door and helps me out. I leave the flower on the passenger seat.

He opens the door for me once again. And people say chivalry is dead. It's a homely small restaurant, called Angelo's, which has pretty good Italian food. Adam hardly knows me, and he already knows my favorite kind of food. He's good. I come here every year on my birthday with my family.

A hostess leads us to a small table in the back, and Adam and I take our seats. I take in the small wooden tables and the beautiful paintings of Italy that hang around the restaurant. The walls are painted yellow and have murals of vines and of sunsets and villas. I know this is probably just the fantastical idea of Italy, but I still love this place and all the images it provides me with of relaxing in a small Italian villa with a cup of tea at my side.

"So have you come here before?" I ask him.

"N-n-no, I haven't. H-h-have you?"

"Every year on my birthday. It's my favorite restaurant. I haven't been here in a quite a few months, though."

Almost nine months, now that I think of it. It was right before my mental breakdown, and right on my nineteenth birthday. A couple of days after that was my breakdown, and then everything just went to hell.

"S-s-so I, I did g-good?" He has a small smile, begging to know the answer. He brings another smile out of me, and once again I wonder how he makes me feel like this. He makes me feel somewhat… good. No guy has ever made me feel good like he does. He makes me feel like… I matter.

"Yes, you did *very* good."

He pounds his fist in the air, and I can't control the laugh that erupts from my body. It is loud and vivacious, a word that hasn't been used to describe me ever. A couple of people turn around to see where the sound of the loud chortle originated. Well, everyone, it came from my skinny, short, pale body.

I look away embarrassed and stare down at the table.

"Y-you're a-a-a-adorable."

I look up, shocked. He smiles at me, and as the waitress comes, I don't listen to her name. I think she says it is Jane? Or Janet? I don't care. I just want to be left in my own little world with Adam, and I want everyone and everything else to drop away.

We order our food, and we get right back to sitting in silence.

"So, Adam, why are you in therapy? You seem rather sane."

"Dr. Wheeler is, is h-helping m-me with m-m-my s-s-s-s-s-s-stutter."

"Have you always had it?"

"Sadly y-yes. Through, throughout school, including c-c-college, e-e-e-everyone has made f-f-f-f-fun of my s-s-s-s-s-stutter, and I-I am, am just s-s-sick of it."

I look up to see the sadness in his eyes. Why would anyone make fun of someone so sweet? There aren't a lot of truly good people left in the world, and here I am on a date with one. I almost want to go and punch all those people who hurt him in this way.

"I'm sorry, Adam. I really am. People suck."

"Y-yes. But I s-s-survived."

So he is already much stronger than me. What is my problem? I'm sad. I'm just always damn sad. So many people are hurting out there, and then there is me, who doesn't really have a problem. I wish I knew what was wrong with me, other than being mentally insane.

"So you graduated from college?" I ask him.

"Y-yes. I-I studied e-e-e-education."

"Oh, my friend Alex is studying to be a teacher. He wants to teach elementary school because he loves children. He even babysits all the time for money."

"I-I want to t-t-teach ch-children too," he begins. "I'm applying to g-g-g-grad schools n-now. That, that is why I w-w-want to help my s-s-s-s-s-stutter, s-s-s-s-so I can be a b-b-better teacher."

I nod in understanding.

"Why ar-aren't you in s-s-school anymore?"

I shrug. I should answer, but I really don't want to. Do I really want him to know about the kind of person I am underneath? I don't want to scare him away before it even begins… if it begins. Do I want it to begin?

"I dropped out," I finally state.

"W-why?"

"Because eight months ago I had a mental breakdown and tried to kill myself. I proceeded to spend the next seven months locked away in a mental asylum. I'm heavily medicated on antidepressants, and Dr. Wheeler is my doctor helping me. That's the truth."

I bring my hands to my mouth, and I look away. Why did I state all of that? I didn't mean for any of that to come out. It seemed to just roll right out of my mouth, falling off my tongue. I'm pretty sure that's a big no-no for a first date: telling them you were in a mental asylum. I'm remembering now why I never dated often. I suck at it. I can't look at him, afraid to meet Adam's eyes. What must he think of me? But I feel the soft touch of his hands on mine, and I look up to see his warm blue eyes, and they just look so inviting.

"I'm s-s-s-s-s-so s-s-sorry, Jess. Wh-wh-what happened? I'm s-s-s-s-sorry if, if that is, um too m-m-much information…."

I shrug once again. Why not get everything out already?

"I'm going to tell you now, Adam: I'm an incredibly sad man. I always have been, and I just sometimes don't know how to control my sadness. I used to be in a really dark place, but I'm trying to get through it. The medication is helping a lot, and so is the therapy. I know you must be thinking why you asked me out now?"

I awkwardly chuckle, and Adam grips my hand. I like the feeling of his hand in mine. It feels nice. It feels right.

"N-n-not at all. I, I am g-g-g-glad I am h-here. With y-you."

I can't stop my smile, nor can I stop the blush that rises to my cheeks. How is it humanly possible for someone to make someone else feel this good?

The waitress brings the food to our table, and we eat and keep on talking. As we continue to converse, it's like the world is a canvas, and everything bleeds away except for just the two of us. The canvas is blank, and we only focus on one another.

AFTER DINNER, which Adam pays for, we get back in to his car, and he drives away. He holds my hand, while keeping one hand on the steering wheel. His smile is so big; it's like a child's grin.

"Is th-this o-okay?" he questions, sounding worried.

"What is?" I hope he isn't getting second thoughts already.

"M-me holding your, your h-h-hand?"

I smile. "Definitely. It's more than okay."

"Good. Do you w-w-want to s-s-s-s-see my apartment?"

The smile fades from my face. Is this why he wanted to see me? He wanted to get some action. I should've known. He had an ulterior motive.

"I'm not having sex with you," I broadly state.

The car comes to a screeching stop, almost like a hiccup, and then Adam drives again. His cheeks turn bright red, and he opens his mouth, but I think I made him too flustered to say anything. Every time he opens his mouth, nothing comes out.

"I, I, I didn't m-m-m-m-mean it, it, um, like th-that…."

"Oh… sorry."

Fuck. Shit. Fuck. Well, I just ruined a good moment, once again. I'm really rewriting *all* the rules of first-date etiquette tonight, aren't I?

"I l-like you, J-Jess and I, I w-w-w-want to g-get to know you b-b-better. That is, is my o-only motive. I s-s-s-s-swear."

He sounds so sure, and when I look up at his face, I know to believe him. There is something in his eyes. Honesty.

"I believe you. I'm just awkward and weird. I'm sorry."

"It's okay," he mutters.

He drives the two of us to a small building, and he leads me inside. I follow him up a staircase, and we stop outside a white door on the second floor. He pulls out a key, and he leads me into a small but quaint apartment. Family photos line the walls, and I see posters of musicians. There's a bookshelf full of books and a small television, with a large mess of DVDs piling high.

"W-welcome to my h-h-home."

"You said your uncle helped you get this place?"

"Y-yeah. I was living in New-New York, but my r-r-r-roommates screwed m-me over, and they, they both l-left. I was forced to m-move out, s-s-s-s-since I couldn't pay the, um, rent by my-myself. My uncle off-offered to help me, and h-here I am."

"Geez, I'm sorry," I tell him. "That really sucks. Why didn't your parents help you?"

He looks away, and I instantly realize I shouldn't have asked that. I'm really on a roll tonight....

"They died," he chokes out.

"I'm so sorry." I don't know what else to say. What do I do? Should I hug him, or should I just leave him alone?

"It's o-o-okay. I, I was young. My un-uncle r-r-raised me. He m-m-moved to Wilshire a c-c-c-couple years ago w-when I w-w-w-was still away at c-c-college, and w-w-w-would always t-t-tell me how, how much he l-loved it here."

I don't know what causes me to do it, but I instantly pull him into a hug, wrapping my arms around his neck. I have to stand on my tiptoes to even somewhat reach, but it's worth the strain on my toes when he wraps his strong arms around my waist. He pulls me close, and he looks down into my eyes. He closes his eyes, and I follow suit. His lips are everything I imagined they would be. When they meet mine, they're soft and perfect. They taste like heaven. The kiss is short but sweet. As he pulls away, I want his lips back on mine again, but his smile makes it worth it. His eyes seem to sparkle, and I know at that moment, I might be in deep. I might be in *very* deep. Shit.

We sit on his couch, and as he wraps his arm around my shoulders, I cuddle up. My body seems to fit perfectly with his. I close my eyes and rest my head against his chest. I must let out a sigh, because Adam tells me this feels good too.

I open my eyes and look at the bookshelf.

"What books do you have?" I leave Adam's side, the magnetism of books drawing me toward them.

"They're all m-m-music."

He isn't kidding. Each book is about a different musician or composer, and many of them are music composition books.

"Are you a musician?"

"Y-yeah. I p-play the violin. M-music is my l-life. I want to t-t-teach m-music. I g-g-g-give v-v-violin l-lessons to g-g-get s-s-s-s-s-some extra money."

"Are you good?"

"Quite," he responds with a proud smile on his face.

I return to the couch, and he pulls me back to him.

"One day, you should play for me."

"D-deal."

He kisses the top of my head, and I just want this moment to last forever. I want to freeze time, so neither of us can leave this moment. A never-ending perfect moment. It's like I'm forgetting about the darkness within me.

"S-s-s-s-so what is your f-f-f-favorite s-s-s-s-song?" he asks me.

"'Mad World,' by Tears for Fears. Yours?"

"I-I Want t-to Hold Your H-Hand, by the B-B-Beatles."

And there he goes picking something beautiful and somewhat happy, depending on how you look at the song. The song is about simplicity. That is what makes it so beautiful. It takes raw human emotion and narrows it down to just wanting to hold someone's hand. It is also quite complex, because holding a person's hand can be the most important thing in the world. It can be scary, but it can be life-changing. What makes the song even more brilliant is that while someone is singing about wanting to hold someone's hand, you don't know if they are with the person right now or not. It could be unrequited. For all we know, the person is sad and lonely and just wants to hold the other's hand. There are so many songs about love and sex, but the simple act of holding one's hand is like taking a dive into love. There is something so intimate yet sweet about holding hands.

I take hold of Adam's hand.

CHAPTER EIGHT

I WAKE up the next morning, in *my own* bed, with an actual smile on my face. Memories from the night before flood right back, and I want to go back and relive all those moments. After Adam and I spoke for hours on end in his apartment, he drove me back home, and he kissed me good night. I learned so much about him. He loves Chinese food, and he loves children. He is a huge science-fiction nerd. I also learned that he really is as genuinely nice as he seems. Neither one of us were ready to say good-bye as we stood on my doorstep. I wanted to just stay with him for as long as I could. The kiss lasted a bit longer, and as I entered the house, I was met by my mom *and* Clara sitting in the kitchen. They each had a huge grin on their face, and they barraged me with questions. Was he nice? Did you have fun? Where did you go? Do you like him? Are you going to see him again? I answered each and every one of their questions in my own standoffish way— with as little words as possible. After about an hour, they finally let me go to bed, where I could lie there and just think about everything that happened.

I am so happy to not have work today because more than anything I don't want to get up and work. I love the bookshop, but I just want to bask in last night's glory. It's not often that I am happy, and last night I was truly happy. I want to savor that happiness, because if it disappears again, I want to make this last as long as I can. Maybe it'll give me something to remember, something to pull me back. It'll be my lifeboat in the sea of darkness.

As I lie here in bed, enveloped by my thick quilt, I think of one notion: dancing. I don't know why the thought of dancing comes to my mind, but I have the image of Adam and me dancing together. No one has ever asked me to dance before. I wonder what it must be like to be swept away by the music and to move your body to the rhythm. To move your body with another in perfect synchronization. Is there anything more powerful than that? Or anything more heartfelt than that? It's two bodies coming together, connecting and moving in perfect harmony. It's true beauty.

As I fall back to sleep with the sun peeking through my window, I welcome the dreams about dancing. My dream is like my own personal ballet. Adam and I dance together, but it's not just Adam and I. Tommy dances, and so does Alex. My family and Clara are there. Everyone has their own dance, with each dance telling a different and unique story. Everyone is happy in my dream, even I.

When I wake up for the second time, I wish to fall right back to sleep to be back in my dream world. I desire to return to that fictional life where everyone is happy, and I'm smiling and it doesn't even hurt. Nothing hurts in the dream.

I check my phone to see a text from Alex. If I ignore it, does that make me a bad friend? I just so badly want a text from Adam. I instantly feel guilt over the slight annoyance of seeing a text from Alex instead.

Hey Jess.

That's all it says.

Hey, I respond back with a sigh.

Can we hang out? I already texted Tommy. He's not working at the garage today. He's picking us up in a half hour.

Why did he even ask, if Tommy is picking us up? I never seem to have a choice in the matter anyway. Why is this all so damn awkward? Yeah he kissed me… but he didn't mean it. He saw his ex-girlfriend, and he needed a companion. He was lonely and sad.

Sure.

I quickly dress into a tight T-shirt and a hoodie, zipping it up. By the time I'm done, I hear the sound of Tommy's horn blaring. I jump into the passenger seat.

"Hey, man."

"Hey, Tommy."

"So this is okay for you?"

"Yeah, I have to see him sooner or later. I can't avoid Alex, although with the way he is acting, I kind of want to. I can't just ditch him. That'd make me a bad friend, I guess."

"Yeah, that would make you an asshole. A major one at that. This is the smart, mature thing to do."

If I am doing the "smart, mature thing," then why does it feel like my heart is about to give out any moment from the speed it's pumping blood? I simply nod and ask Tommy what we're doing. He tells me we're going to pick up Alex and then we're just going to hang out at his place. His dad isn't home. He's at work. I'm honestly just happy we're not going to the damn warehouse.

Tommy pulls up to Alex's house, and he's already waiting outside, with his button-up shirt buttoned all the way to his neck and tucked into his jeans. He always looks like he is ready to go for a job interview. He quickly walks to the car and gives us that small scrunched-up smile of his and he gets into the backseat.

"Hey, man," Tommy greets him in his normal welcoming manner.

"Hey, guys. How are you both?"

"Awesome," Tommy responds.

"Fine," I lie.

The rest of the car ride is spent in silence until we get to Tommy's house. We come up to a small one-story house. It looks nice on the outside. The lawn is freshly cut, and the outside is nice enough with the clean windows and white door. Inside, though, the house is a mess. Clothes are everywhere. Dishes pile up, close to reaching the ceiling. Mold is crusted into the corners of the walls. I'm pretty sure I saw a family of mice living here once too.

Tommy kicks the clothes off the couch, and we sit down. Tommy disappears off to the kitchen, and Alex doesn't waste time apologizing.

"I'm so sorry, Jess. I didn't mean to kiss you. It was stupid, and I was lonely. The kiss was stupid. You're my best friend, and I just don't know what came over me. I hate that you're mad at me… please make me stop rambling."

"Alex, it's okay. Really. I'm not mad at you. It's just all a bit weird for me."

He lets out a sigh. "Really?" He still wears a frown on his face.

We go back to sitting in awkward silence. Wonderful. I'm a master at the art of awkward silence.

"I hope neither of you are doing anything today."

Alex and I both look up at Tommy with confused glances. What does he have planned for us? I'm afraid.

"I invited some friends over, and I know it's daytime, but we are going to party before my dad gets home tonight. I invited Alisha and Tammy."

"Aren't those the girls you hooked up with?" I ask.

"Both of them," Alex states incredulously. It's amazing, how after being friends with us for so long he still is shocked over the stuff we do. Every time Tommy or I do something, it's like his eyes are opened up once again. Innocent, little Alex with his big green eyes.

"Yes. Not at the same time, sadly. Maybe tonight I can try again," he says with a wink.

"You're gross," I state.

"I'm a man. I have needs. And hopefully one of those girls won't mind helping tonight."

"Why exactly are we here?" I ask him. Seriously, if this is just an elaborate ruse to get laid, why are Alex and I here?

"Because I wanted you two to have fun. Alex, you have been working way too hard lately, and you, Jess, need some fun."

He does have a point. For seven months my life was nothing but pills, doctors, and white walls. There wasn't really a chance of having fun there. While I've been out of the hospital, I really haven't been doing much. My parents were happy that I was out before Thanksgiving. My mom really loves holidays, and even though we don't have a big family, she still loves the idea of everyone being together and having a nice big meal. We all sit around the table, the scent of turkey wafting through the air.

The doorbell rings.

"The girls are here."

Tommy is the *only* guy I know who would throw a party in the early afternoon and get drunk. A pair of *beautiful* women walk into the living room. Well, they are beautiful by magazine standards. They are too skinny with fake blonde hair and orange skin. I'd much rather have an average-looking woman—if I was into women.

Tommy breaks out the alcohol, and he is drunk within an hour. The girls drink, and they apparently both lack personality. Tommy is trying so hard to get with both of them that I honestly believe he thinks he has a chance of having a threesome. Although they might be trashy enough to go through with it. Their skirts are so short I can almost see their uteruses.

The day goes on, and the alcohol is going fast. I ask Tommy what about his father noticing, and Tommy just says to "fuck it." I don't ask again. I take my seat on the couch and watch everyone have their fun. Even Alex seems to loosen up. One of the girls, I think it's Tammy, seems to take a liking to him, and Alex seems to enjoy the attention. The last girl he dated was Nikki. He loved her. I couldn't stand her. I liked the girlfriend before her, Annabel. She was this cute, spunky tomboy with a dark brown pixie cut. There was no bad blood in the end, though. It was a mutual breakup as neither of them felt it was working. It's not like Alex broke up with her for Nikki. Annabel and him still talk from time to time. She didn't like Nikki either. She and I both agreed there was something fake about her. Before Annabel, Alex dated Mitchell. Mitchell was a nice guy, and oddly enough he and Annabel hit it off really well and became friends.

When I look back on Alex's relationship with Nikki, I wonder if it could be that he was just fooled by the lust of liking someone. Some people are so desperate to be liked or to like someone else that I wonder if that clouds people's judgment.

I look around at the small, inebriated crowd, and I feel irrevocably alone. Even when one of them tries to talk to me or tries to include me in their reindeer games, I just feel alone. I feel like a person in the movie theater watching what is going on before him. I watch, but I don't participate. I don't know what is worse: actually being alone, or being alone in a crowd. When you're alone, you're just alone. There is no one to ignore you and no one to disappoint you. But when you're with others and you feel alone, it is like a part of you is screaming and crying out for help, but no one notices... or cares.

"I'm going to go," I tell Alex.

"You okay?" Alex asks.

"Fine," I say, and I'm out the door. Please don't let this be the beginning of the darkness coming back. I really don't want to deal with it. Everything was so perfect last night, and now I'm feeling completely alone.

I walk into my house and am met by Clara, who is making coffee at the stove.

"Hey, where have you been today? I tried texting you earlier."

I run my hands over my pockets, realizing my phone is still plugged in upstairs on my nightstand.

"Sorry, I was with Tommy and Alex."

"Oh…." I see the look on her face. She knows that something is going on inside of my head.

"Are you having a…," she begins, but she obviously doesn't want to finish. She's scared. I can see it on her face. "Dark day?"

"No, I'm just feeling… weird. I don't know."

"Just please, don't leave me okay?"

I nod. She is afraid I'm going to try to kill myself again. It's not that I always want to die, but some days I just don't want to live.

"I'm going to lay down," I notify her in a monotone voice, and I find myself upstairs in my bed. I close my eyes and just take in the warmth of my blanket. No one realizes how much it sucks to be lonely.

I need to get out. I need to walk around or something. I grab my bag and jacket and tell Clara I'll be back later. I also make sure to grab my phone, with a text showing from Adam.

Hey, Sweetie. How are you?

His text brings a small smile to my face. *Sweetie.* No guy has ever called me that before, and it feels nice, but I don't want to subject him to the way I am now. It wouldn't be fair. He is such a good guy, and he already probably knows too much about the way I am. I pocket my phone, deciding to text him back later. I just want to be alone for now. I button up my peacoat and walk along the sidewalks. I keep my eyes focused on the ground, so I can ignore the stares. I just want to be in my own world and pretend not a soul lives here.

"Oh, Jesse Holbrooke."

Well, there goes that plan. I look up to see Mr. Samuels with a large smile on his face. I never see him without a smile. I have a theory he might be a robot, because no one in the world can be that happy, except for maybe a game-show host. The world is a messed-up place, so where does he find all this good? I want to know his secret for being so happy all the time.

"Hey, Mr. Samuels."

"How are you today?"

"I'm fine. And you?"

"I'm doing well. Would you like to come over for tea? I also have scones."

"Um, I don't know. I might have to...."

I stop as I see his huge smile. Well, I guess one cup of tea won't hurt.

"Sure," I answer.

"Oh lovely. I have really good tea and scones."

He rambles on, but I don't catch most of it. His senile babble tends to go over my head a lot of the times, so I just follow him until we're outside his house, which is small and somehow perfect for him. It almost looks like a storybook cottage, with the brightly painted yellow outside and bright blue shutters.

Inside the house is very neat, maybe a bit too neat. It's almost disconcerting. He sets up a kettle on the stove, and he tells me to sit at the kitchen table. I see pictures of a woman all over the kitchen. She also seems to be in every room. Some of them are of a beautiful young woman with bright red hair, while others are of an older woman with curly gray hair.

Mr. Samuels bring the tea to the table and pours it into a pair of teacups.

"Thank you."

He sits down, and I close my eyes as I take a sip from my tea. It's burning hot, but it feels good. Mr. Samuels starts to talk about his day and how he was looking for the birds because he loves the birds. For as long as I've known him he's been obsessed with birds. As a kid I used to find him bird watching on his front lawn. He had a large pair of binoculars around his neck and would wear these brightly colored shirts. He became a town joke.

"So how is Claire?" he asks. I don't correct him.

"She's good. She's enjoying being home from school."

I sip my tea.

"She's a good girl."

"So who is the woman in the photos?" I ask him.

The smile slowly disappears, but it comes back after a moment. "That is my wife, Claire."

"I didn't know you were married?"

"Oh yes, very happily so. But she died over twenty years ago."

He's been alone all this time? But why?

"She was the love of my life. She still is. Claire is the most beautiful person I know. Your sister reminds me so much of her. So pretty and smart and sweet. Claire used to help out at the homeless shelter, and she made the best tea. She put up with my mind, and she gave me nothing but love. She died in a car accident sadly."

I almost drop my tea. I never knew any of this. My eyes widen, and I can't find the words to say, except for "I'm sorry." I look away, not wanting to face his eyes.

"It was so long ago, but she's still here. She's here all the time. She's here when I look for the birds. She used to love the birds, my Claire. She wanted a pet bird so badly."

He looks at his watch, "Oh God. I have to get going. I have to go to the park. There is a bird I'm hoping to find. I know it's out there. I just want a photograph of it, to show my Claire. I'll make you a scone next time."

I nod, and as I walk out of the door, I turn around to see Mr. Samuels looking at a photograph of Claire.

"Please don't think of me as a senile man, Jess."

"I won't, Mr. Samuels," I promise him. He's not senile; he's heartbroken. But why does he smile so much?

"Please call me Richard. Will you come around again… soon? I'm so lonely in this house."

"Yes."

His smile brightens a bit, but all I feel is guilt as I lie to him. I won't be coming around anytime soon. I don't plan to come around at all.

CHAPTER NINE

I DON'T see Adam for a couple days, but those hours without him are filled with countless texts and lots of smiling from my end. I'm on my way now to the coffee shop where he works. Through the window sits Adam at the table. He's wearing a black apron over a tight polo shirt, which shows off his muscular arms.

I enter the shop, and Adam smiles at the sight of me walking into his place of work. Adam stands up and meets me at the register. He orders a coffee for him and a tea for me, using his discount.

"Coffee today?"

He happily nods. "Y-yeah. I p-p-prefer coffee."

"I'm not a fan."

He almost drops the coffee mug. His jaw falls open.

"What? I, I c-c-cannot believe y-you don't l-like coffee. It's h-heaven in a c-c-cup."

I laugh. "No, sorry, but that is tea. Coffee is okay, but it tastes weird to me. Tea tastes wonderful, and it's also healthier too," I respond.

"T-tea reminds me of s-s-s-something B-British."

"Fun fact: I started drinking tea when I was little because I secretly wanted to be British. I was the biggest anglophile. I think a part of me still desires to be British. I even used to fake a British accent. It was so awful, but my family never stopped me. They enjoyed my fake Britishness," I admit, feeling the fire rising up to my cheeks.

"Tha-that is s-s-s-s-so adorable," he says with a big goofy grin.

"It's dumb," I respond.

"No. It's a-a-a-adorable. I'm r-right." Adam brings the mug of coffee to his lips, and he jumps as it touches his tongue. One would think he was just bitten by a snake, from the way he jumps out of his seat.

"That is fucking hot."

I giggle at the sight of him holding his mouth in pain, staring daggers at the coffee. I have never heard him curse before, and it sounds so weird coming out of his mouth. I feel he shouldn't speak like that. His mind should be all unicorns and rainbows or something.

"S-s-seriously, that was like l-lava."

I continue to laugh at his childish antics. Every time I have doubts, he just makes me smile. He reaches his hand over the table and takes mine in his. His soft hand feels just as good in mine as it did before. I am overcome by a sense of warmth, like I'm being wrapped in a thick quilt. The warmth reaches every area of my body and even seems to blanket the darkness, so it can't be seen.

"*D-D-Doctor Who* is B-B-British."

Ever since the last date he has sent me so many texts about the show, trying to get me to watch it. Science fiction isn't really my thing. When it comes to movies, horror is more what I lean toward. Science fiction just gets a bit too confusing, and a lot of it goes over my head. It honestly makes me feel quite dumb a lot of the time. I don't want Adam to see me as dumb, so I've been putting off watching *Doctor Who* with him. I know it's silly, but sometimes I don't know how my mind works.

"I'll watch it with you soon."

"Maybe W-W-Wednesday night, after th-th-therapy? I, I, I can pick you u-up and d-d-drive you, um, back to my p-place?"

Tempting. So tempting.

"Maybe. I don't know. I'm always so exhausted after my sessions."

"P-please. For m-me?" He looks at me with those big gray-blue eyes that make me melt, and his smile is so big. I love that lopsided smile of his.

"Fine, yes. It's a date."

"Oh y-yes, a, a d-d-date," he says, dancing around in his seat. He just happens to get cuter and cuter every time I see him.

I laugh and grip his hand a bit tighter. I look at my... what is he exactly? Is he my boyfriend? Or are we not there yet? Are we just dating?

Why must dating be so complicated? Is it bad etiquette to just ask?

"Adam," I mumble.

"Yes?"

"Are... are we, um, boyfriends?" Why must I sound so dumb asking that? I sound like a damn child.

"I, I don't know. W-would you like, like th-that?"

Would I? Yes. I would. I know I would. But should I subject him to my life and my mind? He's so good and sweet, and there's me. Fucked-up Jess Holbrooke. He's never seen me on one of my dark days. What would he do when he sees how I really am? Would he sit there and help, or would he run away?

I take a deep breath and close my eyes. It's time for me to be brave.

"Yes. I would a lot."

I open them to see his big smile, and I smile right back.

"Me t-too. S-s-s-s-s-so let's m-make it official. J-Jess, w-w-w-will you b-b-be my b-boyfriend?"

"Ummm… sure, why not?" He pouts as I laugh. "Of course, yes."

Adam Foster. My boyfriend. I smile at the thought, feeling the hope swell up inside. Hope, that's a new feeling and one I like.

We go on to talk about his love of children and how someday he'd love to have a family. He wants to have two children, with plans to adopt them. He wants lots of dogs, and he wants a nice house big enough for everyone, and a backyard is necessary. He also tells me how he is still waiting to hear back from grad schools. He has a degree in elementary education, and he wants to put it to good use. I tell him how I studied English at the college in town, but I didn't actually know what I wanted to do with my degree. I still don't really know what I want to do with my life. Right now I'm working on getting it back on track.

He looks at his watch, and with a frown, he tells me, "B-b-back t-to work I g-g-g-go."

He gets up, and we walk outside the shop, standing by the door. I look up at his towering body, and I watch as he shivers in the winter air in his short sleeves.

"Good n-n-night, b-boyfriend."

I smile up at him, "Good night, boyfriend. Thank you for making time for me during your work schedule."

He pulls me into a kiss, this one longer than our first one, and as I back away, I almost feel like my knees are about to give out. I hold on to the doorknob to keep me steady. So that is what a kiss feels like. I mean, a real kiss. Wow. I've had kisses before, but never any like the ones from Adam. His kisses make me feel lightheaded.

He smiles at me once more, and I miss the feeling of his body against mine as I watch him enter the coffee shop. I lightly touch my lips and smile to myself. I walk home to hear my parents watching a movie in the living room with my sister.

It's some bad romantic comedy that I would usually have no interest in.

"Do you want to join us?" my mom asks.

"Sure."

I like that she smiles as I sit down on the couch next to her and Dad, and she lightly hugs me.

"Love you."

"You too," I respond.

The movie is quite bad. The lead actress, who can't act, ends up with the once-douchebag actor but is now magically nice. It's predictable, but I guess it's fun. It fools people into believing that true love exists and that there is redemption for everyone. Maybe that is why so many people love these kinds of movies. Either way, it was nice spending an hour and a half with my family. I also liked that I made my mom happy. Clara's face was glowing and I think I even saw a hint of a smile on my father's face.

When I go up to shower, it feels like I'm floating on a cloud. It's as if I am just gliding up the stairs. I feel as if the darkness could never reach me here. I've escaped the dungeon, and now I'm running off toward something better, something brighter. I'm running toward Adam. I sound like I'm in some terribly clichéd romance novel. Well, if my life turns into one, I'd be okay with that. Don't those characters always have happy endings and find contentment in life? I could use a content life.

I wonder what that would feel like—to be completely and utterly happy and content with everything. I would imagine that it feels like there is no darkness inside. It's just lightness, and everything feels good. It won't hurt to smile. It won't hurt to live.

I shower and head to bed, only for my night to be full of dreams about Adam and his magnificent lips and that bewitching gaze. I've only one thought when I wake up, that I'd love to drown in his eyes, and in my dream I did. Those eyes took over my sleeping mind, and as I wake, they're all I can see even now. I'm drowning in a sea of blue, but it's the kind of drowning that a man could get used to. Instead of death I'm finding life in his eyes. There is a small spark of something. Is it hope? Is it the will to live? I think for the first time in my life, I want to live. I want to see what happens next in my life.

For the first time I feel something close to happiness.

I get up and dress, and as I enter the kitchen, my father and Clara are sitting at the kitchen table. Mom is at the stove, and I smell eggs and bacon. Everyone stops and turns toward me. I'm met by surprised eyes and immense (my word of the day) smiles.

Immense; adj.

Huge, vast, massive, enormous, gigantic, colossal, great, very large/big, monumental, towering, tremendous; giant, elephantine, monstrous, mammoth, titanic, king-size(d), economy-size(d), whopping, humongous, jumbo, astronomical, cosmic, Brobdingnagian.

My mom's smile especially shines bright.

"Good morning, love." As a young boy, before the depression got really bad, I used to love when she called me "love."

"Hey, Mom."

It's then I realize why everyone is shocked to see me this morning. I catch my reflection in the window, and there is something different about me. Something people don't see as often. I am shocked to see that I have a smile on my face.

I sit down to breakfast and eat with my family, and I watch as everyone laughs. Everyone looks so happy. Clara talks about her friends at school and tells us how she wants to start running in the morning again—she used to but stopped when school just got too busy. Dad talks about his office job and how his boss is an asshole and is "up his ass" (his words) all the time. When he starts talking about insurance it goes right over my head. He deals with computers on a daily basis. I just don't trust any of it. I think books are going out, and it's a shame because they are so much more reliable than computers ever will be. Computers can crash and you can lose everything. Books never change. They don't crash, nor do you need to go searching for a website. You don't need to save any of the information, because it's never leaving those books. People don't realize it nowadays, but there *was* a time when people used books and not computers for school or work. I know, crazy, right?

Meanwhile throughout breakfast, Mom just watches and smiles. She's always been more of an observer. She's like a silent angel—

always watching and listening. When I was in the hospital, Mom would make sure to come every week, sometimes even more than once. We didn't talk much. Or at least I didn't talk much. She would tell me how everyone was doing, as if a lot changed in a week, and then we would just sit there. She'd stroke my hair and tell me she loved me and how much she missed me. My mom has always been there for Clara and me. She's dealt with all my craziness, and now I just wish I could make it up to her. I wish I could do something for her to thank her for never giving up on me.

I check my phone to see that I have a text from Adam.

Good morning, boyfriend :)

Boyfriend. I have to get used to that. I've been on dates before, but I've never had a boyfriend before. It's a new feeling, one I like. One I can *definitely* get used to.

"I'll be back," I tell my family.

Before they answer, I'm up and I'm texting back. I walk up the stairs and fall right back onto my bed. My blanket is curled into a ball at the edge of my bed, so I just stick my bare feet underneath to keep them warm.

Hello! How are you?

I'm BEYOND swell thanks to you

Thanks to me, he says. I'm making him *beyond swell*. As happiness fills my heart, it is as if a pit is opening in my stomach and swallowing everything. I don't feel empty, though; I feel limitless. The pit seems to swallow the darkness, and right now I'm only with the light. Right now I feel like I could take on the world. I feel like I'm Ash, but *Evil Dead II* Ash, when he has the chainsaw for a hand, and he doesn't let anything stop him. That's how I feel right now, minus the chainsaw of course.

I'm glad to hear that! I'm feeling pretty good, thanks to you, I finally respond back.

We go on texting for a while, and with each text that comes, my smile seems to grow wider, and my heart continues to beat faster and faster. If he continues to make me feel this way, there's a chance I might have a heart attack before I turn twenty. At least I'd die happy, unlike the last time I tried to die.

But today I'm feeling good, and I don't want to think about what I tried to do almost nine months ago.

My day goes by in a bit of a blur, but it also goes by rather smoothly. Work isn't as slow as usual, and Peter spends it in a drunken stupor. I do wonder how he manages to keep this shop going, though. I have a feeling it will get closed down soon, if he continues to act this way. Peter hasn't always been like this. There was a time when he cared about this shop and about his business. I don't know what happened. That was before I started working here.

Today I work with Laurie, and she mostly carts around the books to keep the store in order, and I work the cash register. Honestly, I prefer to do the other job. I like to walk around and make sure all my precious books are where they are supposed to be and in good shape. I mean, when I do the cash register, I can read my book or look through my thesaurus, but when I'm on the sales floor, I feel like I'm with my books. I must seem crazy, talking about books as if they are people, but in a way they are. Each novel has a personality, one quite different from the other. Each one has a story to tell, and the only way is to get to know the novel in a way. So yes, novels are similar to people... or maybe I'm just crazy.

We have a nice steady line of customers today; just enough to keep me busy but not so many where I become overwhelmed. These are the days I like best. It gives me a purpose, but I can also take it easy. You can't do that at Barnes & Noble.

When I get home, the first thing I do is text Adam. It's like that is always the first thing I want to do these days is talk to him. He's the first and last person I want to speak to every day, but I'm still getting to know him. I feel that this is too early for me to feel all of these emotions. Shouldn't that happen weeks or even *months* after dating a person? Maybe I'm just thinking I like him this much because he's the first person to ever really seem to want to be with me. Could I actually be fooling myself into thinking I like him? Is this my mind tricking me? What if none of this is real?

No. I refuse to think like that now. I demand for these thoughts to stop. Why can't my mind just let me be happy for a change? When something good begins to happen, my mind must add doubt to the equation, and doubt is always only the beginning. Once doubt is added to any situation it's like a disease. It starts slowly, and then it makes its way through your body, never ebbing away. But it takes its time, making sure to plant its roots in so deep you can't pull them out. It poisons your entire blood and soul until you think everything to be false. I will not allow my doubt to win. Not this time. I want to be happy. I *deserve* to be happy.

At least I hope I deserve to be happy. Why don't I? Maybe I've done something in my life and that is why I can't be happy. This is all punishment.

Why am I thinking like this? I have never in my life believed in karma or any of this religious crap, so why am I starting to doubt it all now? There it is again, that merciless, abhorrent word once again. Even as a child I didn't believe in Santa Claus. A fat man in a red suit fitting down a chimney never made sense to me, and in fact it creeped me out. He's an old man leaving presents for young children. That screams pedophile more than martyr to me. I would wake up crying on Christmas Eve saying how I didn't want Santa to come, thinking of him as a story from a nightmare instead of childish fun.

My phone once again pulls me away from my thoughts. I see Adam's name on the screen, and for a second there I forgot I texted him.

I can't wait for our next date, his text reads.

See, I shouldn't allow doubt to take over. I think he truly likes me, and the way he makes my heart feel, I must like him. No way could my mind trick my heart into believing a lie as well. Why not just allow myself to be happy? Why must I always crush it? I always talk about my mind as if it's some other entity, but it's a part of me. So it's me who ruins all my happiness, and I don't even know why. I'm the way I am, and I have no control over it, I feel sometimes.

I try to shake away the doubt creeping in, and I text Adam how I feel: *Me too. I like you, Adam.*

There, I said it. I'm still alive, and the world isn't crashing down around me. Adam texts back almost instantly.

I like you too, Jess.

In fact the opposite happens. It's as if my world is coming together for the first time. I read over our past texts, and I'm coming to realize that Adam is so much more carefree in text. When we talk in person, it's as if he holds back somewhat, but in text he lets everything go, and that somewhat immature-cute personality really shines through his words.

You're so much more personable in text.

Maybe I shouldn't tell him that. That might be considered rude. Why am I the most awkward person alive?

Yeah... I've heard that before.

Why is that? I ask him.

It's pathetic.

Try me.

It's my stutter. I'm embarrassed by it.

Don't be, I reassure him. I like his stutter. It makes Adam, Adam.

I can't help it. I've always been judged by it, and I hate listening to myself talk. When I speak, I just want to yell at myself to speak like a normal person. Go ahead and judge away.

But I don't judge. Instead I find understanding. Adam is a person who's battled his own demons. His are different than mine, but they are still there haunting his life. He's not perfect. He's human, after all. I further find myself a kindred spirit.

You shouldn't be embarrassed. It's honestly nothing.

Yeah, try saying that when we go out. You should look at how the waiter or the people around us stare next time. It makes me want to claw my eyes out and rip my hair out.

Don't! I text, *I love your eyes too much :-P*

LOL Thank you, Jess. I love your eyes too. :)

This goes on until the late hours of the night, just harmless flirting. After reading Adam's confession, I know that there is more than just a happy, dapper young man there.

We wish each other sweet dreams, and I know mine will be sweet because I guarantee he'll be in them. He's been in many of my dreams the past week or so, and most of them have been so amazing. I feel like Wendy finding Peter Pan. In my dreams I just want to stay there and never grow up. I want time to freeze so Adam and I can dream and be happy. When I wake up, I just want to return to my own private Neverland.

I pop some pills, 300 mg worth, into my system, but before I even get into bed, I hear a soft rap against my window. Who could be there? I live on the second floor. I ignore the sound, blaming it on the trees. They always seem to scratch up against my window at night. Outside my house is this tree that reminds me of the creepy tree in

Poltergeist. As a child it used to frighten me, and I honestly thought it would crash through my window and take me away or swallow me whole. Is there anything worse than being swallowed whole? You'd have to go through an *entire* digestive system, completely conscious. It's pretty revolting. I'd much rather be chewed up first if I'm going to be eaten. Tell that to any of the cannibals, planning their dinner.

The sound is at my window again, and as I look over, I notice a small pebble hitting my window. I walk over to see Tommy on the grass. Blood is streaming down the side of his face. I quickly open the window.

"Can I come in?" he pathetically asks. It sounds as if he is holding back tears.

"Yeah. I'll be right there."

I quickly dress and race downstairs, not even bothering to be quiet. My parents will live. Tommy is standing at the front door when I tear it open. Before I can even breathe, his arms are around me, and he starts to cry against my neck. I don't even mind that he is bleeding on my shirt. It's old anyway.

"What happened, Tommy?" I ask him in a soothing voice.

He doesn't answer.

"Tommy, what's going on?" I begin to plead, worry taking over.

"My dad got drunk and decided he needed a punching bag. I hit him back… and well, that's a huge no-no in his household. That fucking bastard did this to me."

His sobs echo throughout the house, and I hear a door creak open. Shit. This will be hard to explain to Mom and Dad.

"Jess, what is going on?"

I look over to see Clara standing on the staircase. She wears her fuzzy pink bathrobe, and her hair is in a wavy mess.

"It's nothing. Go back to bed, Clara," I demand of her, as I watch Tommy hide his face away in shame.

She doesn't listen and makes her way toward Tommy.

"Oh my God," she gasps. "What happened?"

I hear the worry in her voice, and I let Tommy know he can trust my sister. He tells her the story, and I watch as her face contorts with a look of disgust. She says she'll be right back, and the way Tommy stares at her is similar to how a puppy stares at his owner when they leave, thinking they'll never come back.

Clara comes back with a first aid kit and a wet towel. She sits on the other side of my friend on the couch. She brings the towel to his head, and she cleans up his blood. Tommy tries to hide his tears, but I see how much he struggles.

"It's okay. You can cry. I'm not going to judge you," she says in her soft, conciliating voice.

Tommy simply nods, but he still tries to stop his crying anyway. Clara gets him all cleaned up, putting a bandage on the right side of his head. She tells me to sneak him upstairs to my room to sleep. As I help Tommy up the stairs, he stops and turns toward Clara, who still sits on the couch.

In a soft, thankful voice he says, "Thank you."

"Of course," she responds.

Tommy turns around and walks up to my room. He strips down to his boxers, and he gets onto one side of my bed. I keep my T-shirt and lounge pants on, embarrassed of my scarred body, and lie on the opposite side. Before I know it I hear the soft sounds of his breathing. The side effects of the pills cause my eyes to become heavy to the point where I can't keep them open, and soon I join Tommy in the world of unconsciousness.

CHAPTER TEN

I WAKE up confused when I feel the warmth of another's person's body next to mine, but then the memories of last night come flooding back into my mind. Tommy's red hair plastered to his pale face with blood and sweat. Tears were running down his face, and he was badly bruised. I look over to see that he is still fast asleep. I sit up against my headboard, moving my pillow to make it more comfortable. I move as quietly as I can so as not to wake up Tommy. He needs the sleep. I grab my book off the nightstand, and I open it up toward the end. I'm so close to being finished. Just a couple more chapters.

As the novel comes to a close, I wipe a tear from my eye. I don't think there are too many things worse than finishing a good book. It's like telling a friend good-bye. You can always visit them, and each time it is wonderful. There is no better expedition than that of reading a novel. When I open a book, I'm not just reading words on a page, but I'm transported into another world, and I feel as if I'm a different person going on this fantastic journey. Books are the closest we'll ever get to magic in our world.

The silence of my bedroom is broken by the mumbles of a sleeping Tommy. I look over to see him moving around, mumbling nonsense under his breath. Fear is drawn across his face, and his mumbles turn into gasps. I place the book on my nightstand, and I lightly touch Tommy.

"Come on, wake up. You're okay," I lightly soothe as he comes to.

Tears run down his face, and he wraps his arms around my waist. I let him cry against my chest.

"It's okay," I tell him once again, rubbing his freezing cold bare back with my pale hands.

We stay like that for a while, the usually tough Tommy holding on to me while I continue to rub his back in small circles. We don't speak, even after his sobs die away. All that is left is our simultaneous breathing meshing into one. We aren't just men or friends. In this moment we are so much more. We're brothers.

Tommy slowly unwraps his arms and looks up to give me an awkward smile. He's acting shy, as if he is a small, embarrassed child. He looks away in shame.

"You don't have to feel humiliated. It's okay, Tommy. It's okay."

He wipes away all the tears. "Thank you." He speaks in a quiet but shaky voice.

"It's okay. I'm here for you. You're safe here."

He slowly nods, and he maneuvers his pillow so he can sit up like I am. We sit there in silence.

"Thank you, Jess," he says once more.

I look over at him, and he stares at me with his big green eyes.

"I really mean it. Thank you."

I nod because I can't find the words to say. His eyes are so serious and full of pain. It's like every wall he has ever built has come crumbling down in one moment. I don't feel pity for him; I only feel sympathy. I want to hug him and make sure he knows everything is okay now. But will it be okay in the future? He will have to leave soon, and he will have to return to his home. When that happens, what will his father do?

There's a knock at my door, and I look over to Tommy, who gives a slight nod.

"Come in."

The door slightly opens, and Clara walks in, a blush rushing to her cheeks at the sight of Tommy shirtless.

"Sorry...."

"It's okay," he says.

Clara has always been one to get embarrassed easily.

"How are you feeling today?"

He shrugs. "Yeah, never fucking better."

There's the Tommy Riley I know and love. Clara's smile doesn't disappear. She just looks on at him with sympathy.

"Sorry. I didn't mean to say that. You were great last night, Clara. Thanks for cleaning me up."

"It's okay."

She closes the door and walks over to the bed, sitting on the edge. She grabs Tommy's hand, catching him by surprise, and she rubs it between her fingers.

"Tommy, I may be just the older sister of your friend, but I am here for you too, okay? We need to do something. You can't stay with your father."

"Yeah, what am I supposed to do? I'm nineteen. It's not like I can go into foster care. I don't have the money to move out and get my own place. Dad doesn't always beat me. Just when he drinks too much or not enough. If he's not passed out drunk, he's angry.

"Thank you for the help, really, but I'm fucked. I'm completely fucked in life. I'm just a fucking deadbeat who can't live on his own."

Tommy has tears welling up in his eyes, but this time he refuses to let them spill. I watch as he bites his lip hard. He turns to anger instead, allowing his voice to rise. Clara and I just sit there patiently, wanting him to get his feelings out. When he stops, Tommy apologizes once again and says he must go.

"No!" I shout. "You can't go back to your house."

"I have no fucking place to go."

"Just stay here, maybe we can figure something out."

He lets out a laugh.

"Please," he jokes, as if I said the most ridiculous thing in the world. He pushes the blanket off him and grabs his baggy jeans, pulling them over his boxer briefs. He searches for his T-shirt and pulls it over his head.

"I really should go now. My dad should be at work, so it'll give me enough time to shower and change out of these clothes."

He looks down at his shirt and grimaces. "Fuck. I really liked this shirt too." He tries to laugh again, but it just comes out incredibly awkward and forced. It sounds like he's in pain, which I'm sure he is.

"At least stay for breakfast," Clara offers in a soothing voice.

When you have a problem, Clara is the person you always want with you. The way she talks and acts, it is as if just with her voice alone, she can make you feel like everything will be okay.

"I don't know. How will your parents react when they see my face?"

"They'll live," I respond.

He nods. "Fine. Let's see how awkward I can make your parents this morning."

Clara lets out a small giggle. "I'll meet you two downstairs."

She lightly closes the door behind her. I look at Tommy and tell him I'll be right back. I grab some clothes and bring them into the bathroom to change. As I undress, I turn around and look in the mirror. The fluorescent light allows my pale skin to almost illuminate. I close my eyes in disgust because the lights also show off every single one of my scars. Many long, thin scars run up my sides. They're faded, but can still be seen. They go up in rows, some crisscrossing and others looking like X's. I look like fucking Frankenstein's monster. I look down at my arms, the finishing touches to my skin, as a deep scar lies on each wrist. I lightly run my fingers over my left arm, feeling the raised skin. I open my eyes and look down, and shame washes over me. Why did I do this to myself? How could I let myself get this bad and not do anything to stop myself?

I quickly pull my sweater over my head and a pair of skinny jeans up my legs. Tommy still sits on my bed in his bloody T-shirt.

"Do you want to borrow a shirt?" I ask.

"Yeah, why not."

He pulls his shirt over his head, the muscles tensing in his stomach. He might be skinny, but he does have some defined muscles. I grab a plain T-shirt from my closet, and I throw it at him. He pulls it over his head, and it clings to his body, making him look more muscular than he actually is. I would be lying if I said he didn't look good in it.

"Damn, you're one skinny fucker."

He pulls the hem of the shirt, but it shoots right back, like a slingshot, clinging to his toned body.

"Maybe you're just fat," I tease.

"Would you really make fun of your friend in his time of need? That pains me, man. That really fucking pains me." He finally has a wide grin on his face, forgetting about what happened for the moment at least.

"And you have a bad fucking mouth," I spit right back.

We both break out into laughs. "Come on, let's go," I say.

He follows me downstairs, and I lead him into the kitchen. My parents aren't shocked when they see Tommy, so I assume Clara forewarned them. But that's before they notice his face. My mom almost drops the bottle of milk in her hand when her eyes take in Tommy's bloody form. I guess Clara failed to mention the extent of Tommy's injuries.

"Tommy," my mom begins. His name sounds so soft on her tongue, as if she is saying something foreign that she doesn't understand.

"Hey, Mrs. and Mr. Holbrooke... how are you?"

Even my tough-as-nails father, who hates emotion, can't hold back the pity in his eyes. I know people mean well, but pity is so undermining. It makes you feel sad and weak, like you're worthless. My mother's eyes are full of sympathy. Many people don't realize this, but there is a thin line between sympathy and pity. It's like the line between love and hate. Thin, but it's there.

I look over at Tommy as he fiddles with his hands. He seems to scrunch up behind me, a redness rising up his neck and to his cheeks.

"Let's sit down," I whisper.

Tommy nods, and we all sit down at the table. We eat in silence, as my mom tries to bridge the gap with meaningless conversation. She is smart enough not to ask what happened to Tommy in front of everyone else. I know her well enough, though, that if she gets him alone, he will be forced to answer what happened.

"Tommy, why didn't you tell us about your father?"

We all look up to see my dad staring at my friend, with his serious dark brown eyes.

"Um...." Tommy flusters underneath everyone's stares.

"Maybe now isn't the time," Mom whispers to him. Well, she tries to whisper, but we all hear her. Mom has never been good at whispering.

"I should probably go."

Tommy is up, and he nearly runs out of the house before anyone can stop him. I hear the front door slam shut, and I know he's going to head home to a house that isn't safe.

"That poor boy," I hear my mom state. "I wish there was something we could do to help him."

"He's an adult. He can move out if he wants to," my dad says, sounding loving as usual toward Tommy.

I look up at him, and with the most anger I can find, I state, "Dad, he doesn't have the money to leave his house, otherwise he'd be gone already. Don't talk about things you don't know shit about."

"Jess," my mom begins.

"I'm going upstairs." I've had enough.

I hear my dad call for me, but I ignore his voice, and I lock my bedroom door behind me. Anger wells up inside my body. I feel it in every part of myself. I feel as if I'm boiling, and I need to explode. I need to get out my anger, or I might just erupt. Why is this happening to Tommy? He's a good guy. Why would the world do this to him? And Adam? All the pain he has in his life. Not only was he given the stutter, but he also had to have his parents ripped away from him at such a young age. How can the world allow any of this to happen? This is the reason I don't believe in a God. If there were one, he wouldn't allow so much pain to go on in the world. He wouldn't have made me the way I am.

I grab my phone, and I text the only person I want to talk to.

Hey, Adam. Can I see you today?

He texts back immediately, up early as usual.

Of course :) What time!

I can feel his excitement even through the words he sends on my phone. It's like he has an energy about him that is so infectious.

Now good? I can walk over to your place.

Yeah, is everything okay?

Not really, I want to send.

I just need someone to talk to is what I send instead.

Okay, you can come over here now *huggles*

Huggles, that's cute. I like that word. It sounds like something he would say.

I'll be over soon.

I grab my bag and coat and tell my family I'm going out. The wind is bitter when I walk outside, and I almost wish I had a ski mask to protect my face. As I walk against the wind, I feel the coldness in my teeth. They're so cold it almost hurts.

When I see the sight of Adam's apartment building, I almost want to dance, and I don't dance. Ever. Well, unless it's by myself in my bedroom. I don't care who watches as I break out into a run, and I sprint into the building, race up the stairs, and knock on Adam's door. I hear his footsteps inside walking toward the door. He answers in a pair of light gray lounge pants and a white T-shirt that clings to his muscles and his body in the right way.

"C-c-come in."

I enter his apartment, and he takes my coat, laying it on his couch. We sit down, and I cuddle up to him as he wraps his muscular arms around me. I close my eyes, and I enjoy being in his arms. I feel safe with them wrapped around me, like nothing could touch me, even the darkness inside me.

"S-s-s-s-s-so tell me, what, what ha-ha-happened."

I lay my head on his shoulder, and I just tell him everything about Tommy and how I don't know what to do. Adam never once interrupts me. He just allows me to talk, and he just lets me get all my feelings out. Even my anger seems to disappear with every word I speak. And all because he listens to me. No one has ever really listened to me, with the exception of my therapist. It's a nice feeling to know that someone is there. It's nice to know that someone *wants* to be there.

As I come to a stop, I take a deep breath because it feels like I'm about to run out of air.

After waiting a moment he asks, "Anything e-e-else?"

I shake my head and tell him that's it.

"I'm s-s-s-s-s-orry about your, um, friend. That really i-is a hard thing t-t-t-to do. R-r-r-right now, s-s-s-since h-he's an a-adult, all you can d-d-do is b-b-b-b-be there for him a-and help, um help him out."

"I know. I just wish I could help him more than just by being there for him. I'm afraid for him while he lives with his father."

"I-I unders-s-stand."

"Would it be bad if I just murdered his father and made it look like an accident?" I ask.

"Probably. Unless y-y-y-you d-d-d-don't get c-c-caught." He gives me a little smirk.

I know he can't really change the situation, but I just wish there was a way he could help me figure out how to get Tommy away from his father. I would love to honestly murder his father, but murder is frowned upon in our society.

"There is just so much pain and hurt in this world. Everywhere I turn all I see is the sorrow and melancholy of tragedy."

"Nicely s-s-said."

"Thanks, but seriously. This world is so messed up. It's times like these where I wonder how anyone can believe there is a higher power out there."

"You d-d-don't believe in, in anything?"

"No. Why, do you?"

"I, I don't know. M-maybe? I've s-s-s-spent a lot of my life w-wondering and hoping, but, but the truth is w-w-we'll never know. You s-s-s-s-see all the pain, b-but I also s-s-s-s-see a lot of beauty in the, um, world, Jess. Y-yes there is, is a-a lot of pain and s-s-s-s-s-sorrow, but the truth is, is, is if there were n-n-none, then you never w-would be able to t-t-truly appreciate the beauty in the world. It might be ea-ea-easy to, to miss, but t-trust me. It's out there. You j-j-just have t-to look f-f-for it."

"It's just hard," I respond.

"I-I'll help," he says with that large goofy grin of his. "But you, you need t-to wait in h-h-here and clo-close your eyes."

"Okay?" I confusedly respond.

I close my eyes and wait in the small living room. I hear him running around in his bedroom, leaving me to wonder what the hell he is doing. I don't know whether I should be scared or not.

His footsteps softly tap across his carpet toward me.

"D-don't open y-your eyes yet."

He grabs my hand and leads me in the direction toward his bedroom. Is this going where I think it's going? It might be a bit too fast for that, in my humble opinion. He stops me at the frame of his door, and he tells me to keep my eyes shut longer.

"Okay, open them."

I open my eyes to a blanket fort. I'm not even joking. Adam built a (badly made) blanket fort using his bed and desk chair as support. I look over to see Adam with the proudest, happiest grin I have ever seen. Seeing that smile makes me smile.

"Really, Adam. Really?"

He nods. "Yep. Wh-what do, do you think?"

"It's… impressive."

"Thank y-you. F-f-follow me in-in-inside."

He bends down and lifts up a sheet flap, and I follow him inside. We sit on top of a fuzzy blue blanket, and his MacBook is set up inside the fort. He opens the computer, and he hits on an app at the bottom of the screen. A virtual fireplace turns on, and the inside of the blanket fort is lit with an orange-red light. If it weren't the morning, one would think it was night right now. I wish it were night, so I could fall asleep right here in Adam's arms in this fort.

I look over at him, and I smile. "You are such a dork," I quip.

He does a little bow. "Don't j-judge. Blanket forts are c-c-cool. I, I even b-built y-you this nice f-f-fire." He gives me a little wink, and I can't help but laugh.

"Again, you are such a dork."

"Yeah, but tha-that is why you, you l-l-l-like me."

He has a point there. It is why I like him. A part of it at least. There are a lot of reasons I like him. I mean yeah he's cute, but that's not the reason I like him. He's so sweet, and genuinely sweet, not that fake sweet most people are in the world. When he asks how you are, he obviously means it, and he wants to know how you are. Then there's that dorky lopsided smile I just can't get enough of. When I see or even think of that smile, I feel overcome with happiness. There is the way he holds me close to him, and I love how I fit into his body perfectly, even though he stands about a foot taller than me.

"L-let me give y-y-you the gr-grand tour."

"Show me the place."

"Well, this is, is the living r-r-room," he says pointing to the fireplace. "And the rest is, is the bedroom. Ou-outside the f-f-fort is the wilderness, but out there you m-m-must be careful b-because wild ferocious b-b-beasts roam out-out there."

I laugh at his silly antics. "Oh no. Wild beasts. It's a good thing we have this fire to keep us warm."

"Yep. It w-was a lot of hard w-work. Blood and s-s-s-s-sweat went into it."

"Well, it paid off," I joke right back.

I lightly place a kiss on his lips, and a blush rises to his cheeks.

"Do you feel better?"

"Another kiss sh-sh-should do it."

I place another one on his lips, but this one lasts longer. He grabs the back of my head, and I open my mouth as he presses his tongue in. I close my eyes, and I just let everything go for once. I forget about all the pain and hurt, and I just allow myself to only feel my emotions for Adam.

The kiss is long and passionate. I roll onto my back, and Adam lies on top
of me. He lifts his head up, and he stares right into my eyes. He lightly
runs his fingers over my cheek, and I close my eyes at his touch.

"You're b-b-beautiful…."

I open my eyes in shock. Beautiful? I must've heard him wrong.
He couldn't be talking about me.

"Please, don't say that," I whisper back.

He looks at me perplexed. "W-why?"

"Because I don't want you to say that. That's why." A little bit
of anger slips through my voice. I see the hurt on his face, and I feel
guilty immediately.

I push him away and sit up, wrapping my arms around my knees.
I can't deal with that. Why would he call me that? Is this a joke? No
one could think that about me. This is a joke. A prank. I know it.

"But, but, Jess, I m-mean it."

"Shut up. Just shut up. I mean… come on, look at me," I shout,
my emotion getting the better of me. I can feel the anger, resentment,
and pain rising in me, throughout every bone of my body. I blink back
the tears, which are threatening to escape any second now.

"Jess, wh-what do you, you mean?" Adam looks down at me
with such warm eyes.

"Adam… *you* are the most wonderful person I have ever met in
my life. You're beautiful, and you're sweet. And I'm… not. I'm ugly
and fucked-up…."

"Do you r-r-really th-think that?"

I can't find the words, because I can already feel the tears sliding
down my cheeks. I'm afraid that if I open my mouth, all that will come
out is a sob. I don't want to embarrass myself any further. I simply nod
and look away. Anywhere but at him. I can't let Adam see me like this.

Pathetic.

His fingers are firm but warm on my chin as he turns my face
back toward his. His eyes look into mine.

"You're a-a-anything b-b-b-but ugly, Jess."

Before I can open my mouth to respond, I feel his lips touch mine.
Surprise and shock run throughout my body. What is happening? Am I
dreaming? I finally close my eyes, and I wrap my arms around his waist.
If this *is* a dream, let me enjoy it now before I finally wake up once again.

CHAPTER ELEVEN

WEDNESDAY COMES around, and for once I'm going to have good news for Dr. Wheeler. I think she'll love to hear that I'm positive about something. The thoughts of my day with Adam still roam my mind. I might not believe that I'm beautiful, but I saw the sincerity in his eyes when he looked at me, and I know he believes it. He honestly believes it. He's either stupid or as fucked-up as I am. He has to have some kind of flaw, I guess.

We didn't do much after that. We just cuddled and lay in that fort in silence. It was just what I needed. We hardly spoke. I kept my eyes closed, and he rubbed my hair with his long thin fingers. It just felt exquisite. There really was no other way to describe it, so it deserved the description of my favorite word.

Exquisite; adj.

Beautiful, lovely, elegant, fine; magnificent, superb, excellent, wonderful, ornate, well crafted, perfect; delicate, fragile, dainty, subtle.

It's weird to have someone be there for me. Or I should say, it is weird to finally allow someone to get close to me. I've never really done that before, but I want to try now. No one has made me feel the way Adam does. He makes me feel good. He makes me want to live.

I'm sitting in the waiting room of the therapist's office. Adam isn't here, so I sit in the room alone. A new novel sits open on my lap. After the darkly depressing novel I just read, I decided to go for a more lighthearted novel, one I have read before and a personal favorite of mine: *Pride and Prejudice*. Many say Austen is overrated, and I say they can go fuck themselves. *P&P* is one novel that has made a huge impact in my life. When I need an escape from the hellish world I live in, I find myself lost in the beautiful words of Austen. I imagine her as some witch, but instead of potions she puts words into her cauldron.

"Jess, you can come in now."

I look up to see Dr. Wheeler standing in the doorway. I put my book in my bag and follow her into her small square office with the light beige walls and orange lighting. I like her office because it isn't bright white and blinding like the hospital was. I sit down in the light beige leather sofa as she sits in her matching chair. Her long, pin-straight black hair is down tonight. It looks soft, almost like black silk as it flows down her back and over her shoulders. She should wear her hair down more often. She looks quite beautiful like that.

"How are you, Jess?"

"I'm well," I answer.

"Well. That's great to hear. Why are you well?"

"It's just been a mostly good week."

"Tell me about your week, Jess. What happened, and what were your thoughts and feelings?" she asks in her soothing tone.

"I started seeing someone."

A smile forms upon her lips. "Oh, that is wonderful. What's he like?"

"Well, you know him," I say with a small laugh.

"I do?"

"It's Adam Foster."

"Oh, yes I do. How did that come about?"

"It's weird. We ran into each other three times in one day, and it just kind of bloomed from there."

"Do you like him?"

"I do. I think I like him a lot actually."

She smiles and says, "That's good. I'm glad to hear that, Jess. So has this effected your moods this week?"

"Yeah. I've been smiling and laughing more than usual. So Adam has been helping me feel good."

"Any negative thoughts?"

"Not as many as usual."

"But they are still there."

"Yes, but I don't think I'll ever be able to get rid of them."

The session continues to go like this, almost like a Ping-Pong match between the two of us. She asks a question, and I immediately answer, then she asks another question, and I answer once more. She honestly seems happy to hear about my developing relationship with Adam.

As I talk about our most recent date and how he told me I was beautiful, I also tell her about my mini freak-out.

"Why do you think you freaked out when he called you beautiful?"

I shrug. "I don't know."

"Think. Why would that upset you? Should that not make you happy?"

"I guess. Just no one has ever said that to me before, and I just don't believe it, so I guess that's why I freaked out. Sometimes I think this is just all too good to be true. Like maybe it's a dream, and I'm just waiting to wake up, or what if his feelings are false. This could end up hurting me worse in the end."

"It could, but isn't it worth the risk if it means you can be happy?"

"I guess."

"Anything else that happened this week?"

Tommy comes to my mind, but I feel weird telling her about his problems. I feel as if I'd betray his trust, so I say no.

"I'm really glad you're doing better, Jess. You even look like you're doing better this week."

"What do you mean?" I inquire.

"You came in with a smile on your face, and you looked like you were happy to be alive."

"Well, I guess at this moment in time, I am happy to be alive."

"That is wonderful. I want this feeling to continue, then. I'll see you next week."

I give her the check, and I enter the waiting room to see that Adam isn't there. I wonder why he's not here for his session. I wish I could ask Dr. Wheeler, but I know she cannot speak of other patients. Instead while I'm in the car riding home with my father, I'm left to thoughts of all the terrible things that could have happened to him. A long laundry list of bad things runs through my mind:

1. He could have been badly injured by a gang of thugs.

2. He could have been kidnapped by a gang of thugs.

3. He could have been *murdered* by a gang of thugs.

Okay, maybe none of those. Wilshire isn't exactly a town known for gang violence, unless you count the ridiculous gang of sixth graders from many years back. But what if Adam isn't okay? What if something is wrong, and I don't even know it? I'm his boyfriend, so should I have known? Or maybe this is too early in the relationship for me to be at that stage where I blame myself. Why must relationships be so difficult? Couldn't someone just write a damn handbook on how these things work?

"Hey, Dad, could you do me a favor?"

"Sure, kiddo. What's up?"

"Could you drop me off at Adam's apartment? He wasn't at therapy tonight."

"I don't know if that's a good idea."

"Dad, I'm nineteen years old. I just want to see if he's okay. I would still walk to his place tonight, but at least if you drive me, you save me one trip. It's freezing out. Do you want me to freeze to death outside? I could die, and it would be on you."

"Well, I certainly like how this boy makes you more talkative lately."

I smile and thank him as he changes direction. I tell him how to get there, and I let him know I'll be home later tonight. I walk up the stairs of the complex. At his door, I knock, but no one answers.

"Adam, are you home?" I ask through the thin wood.

I hear shuffling from inside, so I know someone is in there. The door opens, and I look up to see Adam. He is dressed in only a pair of gray lounge pants, and I can't stop from gaping at his torso and chest. His muscles are quite defined, and I am overcome by the urge to run my hands over his abs. I turn my eyes up to his face; his are sunken in, and he looks paler than usual. He holds a crumpled white tissue in his hand. He honestly looks like death, but he still manages to smile down at me.

"Jess, hi. I d-d-d-didn't kno-know you, you were c-coming to-to-tonight," he greets, his voice sounding stuffy.

"Are you okay?"

"Yeah, I, I just f-f-f-feel like c-crap."

He steps aside to let me in, and as I go to kiss him, he backs away.

"Jess, I'm s-s-s-s-s-s-sick."

"Whatever."

I stand on my tiptoes to wrap my arms around his neck, and I pull his face down to me so I can place my lips on top of his. Even sick, his kiss tastes wonderful. He backs away and gives me a large lopsided smile.

"N-now that i-is good m-m-m-m-m-m-medicine," he says with a laugh.

"Did you go to the doctor?"

He shakes his head. "Just a c-c-cold."

"Do you have any tea?"

He shakes his head and asks, "Wh-what do, do you have p-p-planned?"

"First, I'm gonna get you into bed, and then I'm going to make you tea, and we're going to cuddle." I pull out a couple of tea bags from my jeans pocket and packets of sugar from the other side.

His smile seems to grow, and he closes his eyes.

"That sounds wonderful."

I hear him enter his bedroom, and I stride over to his kitchen, setting the small black kettle on his gas stove. I grab a match and light the burner. I sit at the kitchen table, after pulling two mugs out of the cabinet above me. I wait for the sounding whistle, and when the kettle starts to screech, I jump at the ferocious sound. I pour the water into two mugs and grab two tea bags. I make the teas my way—English breakfast tea with two lumps of sugar, some milk, and a dash of honey—because I'm going to show this coffee drinker some good tea. Some people convert their boyfriends into watching their favorite shows. Not me. I want to convert mine into drinking tea. I think it's a pretty reasonable request.

I bring the mugs into the bedroom and see him cuddled up under the quilt. His head rests on the pillow, but I see his muscular chest poking out from the top. He smiles, and I swear he almost drools at the scent of the drinks when I ask him to take a whiff. Even when he is ill, he still manages to be incredibly adorable.

I kick off my shoes and curl up under the blanket with him, handing him his tea. He takes a sip.

"Well?"

"For t-t-tea, I g-g-g-guess i-it's good."

I'll take that. I'll consider that a win for me. I take a sip of the tea, and I must admit I make some pretty damn good tea.

He places his mug on the nightstand and opens up his arm. I cuddle up into the crook of his arm, and he wraps his bicep around me, and I lay my head on his chest.

"Th-th-thank you for, for c-c-c-coming."

"Of course. What are *boyfriends* for." I must admit; I really love calling him my boyfriend. "I have to say, though, that I'm incredibly stupid."

"Why?"

"When I didn't see you in the waiting room, I instantly thought something awful happened."

"Like wh-what?"

I blush, not wanting to tell him the overdramatic thoughts that rushed through my head earlier this evening.

"Tell m-me. P-p-p-p-please." He looks down at me with a smile, and once I look into his eyes, I cannot turn down his request.

"I thought that you were kidnapped by a gang of thugs or something."

"A, a gang of th-th-th-thugs? Do we, we ha-have that in W-Wilshire?"

Adam breaks out into a crazy giggle, and I can't stop the blush that rises to my cheeks.

"Shut up. Don't make fun of me."

"I'm not. Y-you're s-s-s-s-s-s-so a-a-adorable."

He kisses my forehead, and I tell him that won't work every time he laughs at me. He laughs once more, and I forgive him—this time. Next time, he'll have to work for my forgiveness.

We lie there in silence, my head on his shirtless chest, as he strokes my hair. I close my eyes and just allow myself to be happy.

"I, I r-r-r-really like you, J-J-Jess."

"I like you too, Adam."

"I t-t-told my u-uncle about y-you."

"I hope you lied," I joke.

"I, I told him how aw-aw-awful and m-m-mean you are. I t-t-t-told him you, you, um, beat me and tha-that you take m-m-my money fr-from me."

"Oh, I thought I said to lie."

"N-n-no. I t-t-told him that you're s-s-s-so s-s-s-s-sweet and cute and that I, I really like you. He w-w-wants you to, um, come over for d-dinner. Would that b-be okay?"

"Yeah, it could be fun," I respond, with a slight hostility in my voice.

"Is, is that n-n-not okay?" he asks. I silently curse myself for not hiding my fear any better. It's not that I don't want to, it's just that it is kind of a big step. Meeting the family… he might as well give me the engagement ring now. But then again, I told him I was in a mental asylum on our first date, so what do I know about dating formalities?

"It's fine. I want to meet him."

"Yay. Uncle Martin w-w-will be, be s-s-s-s-s-s-so glad. Uncle M-M-M-Max t-t-too!"

I smile, and I just continue to lie there in silence, happy to know that I made him euphoric, which also happens to be today's magical word.

Euphoric; adj.

Elated, happy, joyful, delighted, gleeful; excited, exhilarated, jubilant, exultant; ecstatic, blissful, rapturous, transported.

I hear him yawn, and gosh, even his yawn is adorable. It sounds like a baby kitten that is ready to fall asleep. His breathing becomes rhythmic, and I feel his chest rise up and down with each small breath he takes. I close my eyes, just wanting to savor this tranquil moment. Peace never seems to last long for me, so I want to soak up every serene moment I can. I just want to fall asleep as his strong arm still curves around my thin waist, holding me close to his body. I bend my neck up so I can place a kiss on his cheek, and I watch his smile grow in his sleep. I want to think that he is dreaming of me. Of us. Of this.

I close my eyes and let out a sigh of contentment. I'm content with being with Adam. With this moment right now. And most of all, I'm happy with my own life at this moment.

I WAKE up to the bright sunlight shining through the window. I let out a yawn, and I grow confused when I realize my pillow is strangely harder than usual. My mind is full of groggy thoughts, like a jigsaw puzzle. The thoughts are there, but they're scattered, and I can't piece any of them together. Finally each piece comes together, and I remember where I am. I jump up with a start to see a still-shirtless Adam sleeping. His mouth is slightly open, and a little bit of drool seems to be running down the side of his cheek. Where's my camera when I need it?

Wait… it's light out. Shit. I wasn't supposed to fall asleep here last night. I grab my phone off the nightstand to see three missed calls and eleven unanswered text messages from my mom. Fuck.

I maneuver out of his arm, and I watch as he clings to a pillow. I already miss my spot in his arms. I grab my phone, and I walk into the living room, slowly closing his door, careful not to wake him up.

I dial my home number, and my mom picks up on the first ring.

"Where are you?" There is a mixture of anger and worry in her voice, making me instantly regret falling asleep last night.

"I'm still where Dad left me, at Adam's."

"Are you okay?"

"Yes. He was sick, so I stayed here. I didn't mean to, but I accidentally fell asleep."

"That's it?"

"Yes, Mom."

"You didn't do *anything* right?"

Most parents, when they ask this, mean: "Are you having sex?" But not mine. My mom means if I cut myself or if I tried to slash my wrists open again. She wants to make sure I really am at Adam's house and I didn't run off to be alone to kill myself.

"No. I'm still alive. I didn't stick my head into an oven or anything. I'm fine. I told you the medication is helping. I've been totally fine since I started my pill-popping ways."

"Don't make fun of me. You know how much I worry about you."

"Sorry, Mom," I say, sounding like a small child in trouble after drawing on the walls.

"It's okay. Will you be home soon?"

"Yeah, I have work this afternoon. I'll be home to shower and change. See you soon."

"I love you, sweetie."

"You too."

And I'm not totally lying. The medication has helped me so much. My mood swings are crazy, but the suicidal thoughts have declined, but it's Adam who has probably helped me the most. He's bringing out something in me that hasn't seen the light of day in years.

I hang up, and I make my way back to Adam's room.

"G-good morning, b-b-beautiful," he says in his groggy sleeplike state. He opens his arms wide, and I pretty much fling myself onto the bed and roll into his arms. I feel like a spy in an action movie.

My name: Jess Holbrooke.

My mission: get into Adam's arms.

Okay, there is really no cool fighting and no villains, but the end goal is still satisfying. Although if there were some ninjas or pirates to fight, that'd be pretty nifty too. And I thought I'd be a terrible boyfriend. How many guys would fight ninjas and pirates to be with their boyfriends? Not many, I'm sure.

"How d-d-d-id you, you s-s-s-s-sleep?" he whispers into my ear.

"Quite well. You're a *very* comfortable pillow."

"Are, are, are you c-calling me fat?"

"That's exactly what I'm saying, Adam."

He grabs a pillow and holds it over my head, and even with the fabric over my face, I can't stop the laughs. His giggles are infectious, and even our laughs seem to blend together to create a perfect orchestra of harmony.

"I-I'm s-s-s-s-s-s-so not f-fat."

I run my fingers lightly over his stomach, tracing the contours of his muscular torso, and I hear his breath stop short at the touch of my cold fingers. He removes the pillow from my face, and I stare right into his eyes. His mouth is slightly agape, and his hair is a mess. I run my other hand through his hair, and I watch as he closes his eyes. The small smile on his face lets me know it feels good.

"Yeah, you're definitely not fat."

He bends down and kisses me. As he pulls away, I'm the one with the dopey smile on my face this time. If it wasn't for work, I could stay like this all day. Or forever even. A lifetime of this wouldn't be bad.

A lifetime of Adam would be quite exquisite indeed.

I hear the grumbling of his stomach, and a redness takes over his cheeks. He rolls over, and I miss the feeling of his body hovering over mine. He laces his fingers through mine.

"I g-guess I'm hun-hungry."

"I can't cook," I tell him, with a small pathetic smile.

He gives me a large triumphant grin, as if he is the winner of some game going on between the two of us. "I c-can."

"You can cook?"

He nods with a cute lopsided smirk on his face. My boyfriend wants to cook me breakfast. Boyfriend. My boyfriend. I still haven't totally gotten used to calling him my boyfriend. Adam Foster is my boyfriend, and I wouldn't have it any other way.

He gets out of bed, and with our fingers still laced, he pulls me along into the kitchen. I won't lie, a part of me is dancing on the inside with the fact that he still hasn't put a shirt on. I never thought I was one of those guys who freaked out over something silly like this, but now I see why so many people do. If it were up to me, he'd always be shirtless... well, with just me. I almost feel as if this is some treasure I have just unearthed, and just like any man's gold, this is one I do not want to share.

"D-d-do you like f-french toast?"

I nod. I actually do. It's my favorite of the breakfast foods out there. Most people will say pancakes, and to that I say whatever. Pancakes are overrated. French toast is where it's at.

"P-perfect."

I sit at the table and watch him cook. When I offer him my help, he says he doesn't want an amateur to ruin a master at his work. It's funny; sometimes he can be quite cocky.

As we eat, the kitchen is full of our chatter and giggles. I can't stop my smile because this morning is honestly perfect. A man could really get used to a life like this. To wake up with Adam every morning would be a dream. Most people say dreams don't come true, and I have always been one of them, but this is a dream I'm hoping does come true.

Adam is my new dream.

CHAPTER TWELVE

"WHY HAVEN'T we ever hung out?"

I look up from my spot behind the cash register to see Jill standing there with her newly dyed hot-pink hair, which has now been cut into a short pixie cut. That's the funny thing about Jill; you never know what she'll look like. She is always changing her hair, so you never know the style or color she'll come in with next. I once asked her why she does this, and she gave me one simple answer: *Life is fun with some mystery.*

"I don't know. Do you want to hang out?"

"Yeah. I do."

Honestly I never really thought about it. Are Jill and I friends? We talk a lot when we're working, and I do always love when she is here. Laurie is cool too, but she's not the kind of girl someone would *want* to hang out with. She's so quiet that she disappears into her surroundings. But then again, I'm not exactly the most talkative person either. The only reason people know who I am is because of the small love affair I had with a blade, and gossip travels fast.

"Yeah. Let's hang out, then."

This might be the most awkward plan making in the history of the universe. But then again, I haven't met any aliens out there; so maybe for them it's always awkward. Or maybe it's just me making the situation awkward. I can't help but think of what Adam would do. He would probably smile that big smile of his, the one that shows too much teeth. He'd probably bounce around and start making plans on the spot. How does he do that? I wish I could be like that, happy and light and free.

So I do what Adam would do and I put up a smile and add, "It'll be fun." I don't want to make it sound like I'm going through torture to hang out with her. I like the girl, I really do. I just hardly know her. She's never been more than the feisty girl with the weird hair I work with. The only friends I really have right now are Tommy and Alex. Why not make some more?

That is what healthy, sane people do. They make friends and hang out. I want to be one of those healthy, sane people. Adam deserves that, but I think I do too. I deserve to be happy and sane, right? I want to think I do.

I recite my number, and I watch as she plugs it into her phone.

"Saved."

Jill is smiling, and she brushes her hand through her *very short* hair, the many silver bracelets on her wrist jangling together, sounding like a wind chime outside someone's house. I hear the door open.

"Hi th-th-there."

I can't stop the smile from blooming, and I turn around to see Adam. He is bundled up in a peacoat and scarf. The late November air is quite brisk today.

"Hi."

He seems to be feeling better, judging by how he looks. He goes to hug me, but I've never actually been with Adam in front of people I know. As weird as that sounds, it's kind of awkward for Adam to hug me in front of Jill. I see the growing smirk on her face, as I finally become a normal human being and I hug him back.

"So is this your boyfriend, Jess?"

Not even Tommy or Alex knows about him. My family saw a passing glance of him, but they were never actually introduced to him.

I back away from Adam, and as I look up at his confused look, I know I shouldn't feel awkward about this… but I just do. I'm a private person, and I don't like anyone really knowing about the intimate details of my life.

"Yeah," I sheepishly answer.

He goes to grab my hand, but I move both my hands into my pockets. He looks down, and I can see the rejection in his eyes.

"I-I'm going to, to, um, l-l-look around…."

He walks toward the aisles of the bookshop, leaving me alone with Jill and my regret.

"He's cute."

"Yeah…."

"Don't be embarrassed. You're like a total catch."

"I am?"

How does she see that? She obviously doesn't know me at all.

"Well, duh. You're totally adorable. You have the whole sexy brooding thing going on, plus your dark hair really compliments your pale skin… and do I even need to start on your eyes? You might as well have sapphires in your eye sockets."

"Are you complimenting me or trying to ask me out? I don't really go for girls, Jill. Sorry."

"You're not my type, skinny boy. I like a guy with a few more piercings and tattoos. Now go find your boy…."

"Adam."

"Go find your boy, Adam."

I nod and walk through the small labyrinth of bookshelves until I find him in the music section looking at songs he can play on the violin. Where else would he be, of course?

"Adam… hey."

"Hey. J-Jess, be honest. Are, are, are you n-n-not okay with us, um, d-d-dating?"

"I'm okay. I'm *more* than okay. I'm just not used to it. I just need to learn how to be a boyfriend, because I've never been anyone's boyfriend before."

I've always thought it would be so simple to be someone's boyfriend. You just are together, and that is it. But there are so many factors that come into play, and one thing to not be is an awkward dork, that's for sure.

"I'm sorry for being crazy," I whisper.

"H-hey, don't s-s-s-s-s-say that. You-you're not. I l-l-like you."

He wraps his arms around me, and he bends down to place a kiss on my lips. It's a good thing his arms are around my waist because I would definitely not be able to stand up right now. I'd turn into a puddle on the floor.

"I'll let you w-w-work. T-text me, me later."

"Will do."

I watch him walk out the door, and Jill goes "D'aww." I give her the middle finger before blowing her a kiss, and she just laughs.

"You wish, boy, you wish."

"No, I really don't."

Well, if I was into girls, maybe. She is a cool girl, I guess. Work goes on by, and when Peter comes out of his office, he walks right past us and leaves the building.

"I'm pretty sure the boss isn't legally allowed to do that."

"Probably not," I agree.

"What do you think his problem is?"

"He's an alcoholic," I answer. It's pretty obvious.

"Duh, I mean *why* is he that way?"

I shrug. "I have no clue."

A part of me would love to know, but honestly most of me would rather stay in the dark about it all. I don't want to get to know Peter. I have my own issues to worry about; I don't want to see his as well. I know that makes me sound terrible, but it's the truth. I just don't care to know about Peter's problems. He's just a dumb alcoholic. Nothing more.

"I swear I'll find out one day, even if it is the last thing I ever do." She almost sounds maniacal as she says this. Maybe she's a cheesy villain from a terrible action movie. If I learn she's trying to take over the world, I would not be shocked. I only hope that she spares me. I'd totally work as her henchman.

Peter comes back in with a bottle of whiskey, and I feel only disgust. No pity. I never feel pity. Jill sympathetically shakes her head and says he's a poor man. I don't know what she sees because all I see is a pathetic old man.

When work finishes, Jill and I close up, and Peter walks home, mumbling to himself. She offers me a ride home, but I tell her I'll just walk. The night isn't as bitter as usual.

Walking home, I take notice of all the houses decorated with many colorful lights for Christmas. I don't know why, but it just doesn't feel like it's that time of year. It just hasn't been on my mind. What is it about Christmas that makes everyone go crazy? Many say it's because it's a time of year for families and friends to be close with one another. To that I call bullshit. It's all materialistic garbage. People love the holiday because they love to get stuff from others. Granted, I love getting presents too, but I at least admit it and don't pretend I love Christmas for the *togetherness*.

Am I supposed to get Adam something? I didn't get my family anything, but that was because they told me not to. But Adam, this is our first, maybe of many? Christmases together... so I feel I should get him a little something.

But now I just feel guilty for wanting to buy Adam something when I didn't even get my family anything. Once again, I must ask what is wrong with me? In this time leading up to Christmas, maybe I'll be like one of those crazy last-minute shoppers, and do some crazy last-minute shopping.

As I come up to our undecorated house, I pull out my key and unlock my door. My family has never really been one for decorations. I know my mom and sister always want to every year, but my father doesn't want to be left with the hassle of cleaning up. He thinks it is a waste of time. I would usually agree, but that was depressed-single-lonely-angry-bitter Jess. Now I am taken-somewhat-happier Jess. A couple of Christmas lights could be nice.

What exactly does one get for their boyfriend? I think maybe a sweater, but I quickly push that idea away. I want to keep away from adding *shirts* to his wardrobe, when he looks perfectly fine without them. I'll think of something. I never was a fan of the holiday, even as a kid. Depression just never makes anything fun.

As I curl up into bed, I grab my phone, and I want to text Adam, but I have to text someone else first.

Hey Tommy, are you okay? I haven't heard from you.

The truth is, I haven't heard from Tommy since that night. I texted him the next day, but heard nothing. I decided he needed room to just breathe and feel better, but that turned into a few days, and I still haven't heard from him. If he doesn't answer, I'm going to stop by his house tomorrow.

I text Alex as well, who instantly responds.

No, I haven't seen him either. His father did a number on him this time?—Alex

Yeah.

I wish I could help him.—Alex

Me too.

I feel guilty knowing that Tommy is going through such hardship, and yet here I am finding something good with Adam. I feel as if I'm being selfish, like I should be unhappy with him too. Tommy deserves happiness in his life.

I'm going to go see him tomorrow. You want to come too?
Yes, please—Alex, he responds pretty quickly.
I'll text you when I leave. I'm going before work.
Thank you.—Alex

I never know why he always ends every text with his name. I've constantly reminded him he doesn't need to do that because the ID on my phone tells me who it is, but he still does it anyway. I wish him good night and then text the other person, the one that just won't leave my mind. The one who brings a smile to my face every time I think of him.

Hello Adam!
JESS!!!!!!!!!!!!!!!!!! :)
Happy to hear from me?
YES!!!
You're funny.
You're cute, he responds.

This time I don't freak out. Well, if I did, my family would just think I lost it again because I'm alone in my room, and they would think I was screaming at nothing. At least there are no uncontrollable tears. That got annoying before the hospital. If there is one thing I hate more than anything, it's crying.

Shut up.
And there you are with your beautiful lovely sentiments as usual. I like you too :P
Dork.
You like me! :)
Shut up.
Jesse Holbrooke liiiiiiiiiiiiiiiiiiiiiiiiikkkkkkkkkkkeeeeeessssssssssss me!

How can someone so immature be so cute? That must be one of the mysteries of life. Also, how can he be twenty-two years old? He is more like twelve.

I do and I'm questioning why right now.
:(
I SAID I like you!
Oh.... Very true! :D

This goes on for the rest of the night. Nothing life-changing is said. Just some fun and romantic banter back and forth. It eases my mind, and it's just nice to do something that makes me forget about everything else. I was never much of a flirter, but I definitely like this flirting. When we finish, he tells me to have sweet dreams and that he can't wait to talk more again tomorrow. I realize that we haven't gone a day without speaking or texting one another since we switched numbers. It's kind of amazing. Neither one of us is bored of the other; well, he isn't bored of me yet. But what if he starts to get bored of me? What happens to me, then?

There goes my mind once again trying to sabotage my own happiness. Can't my mind just shut up for once? I grab the only thing that can shut my mind up: my pills. I swallow them, and soon I'm off to bed.

THE NEXT morning I wake up early to shower and get dressed and I text Alex to let him know I'm ready. Soon I hear his car pull up outside, and I'm sitting in his passenger seat. We say our hellos, and we're off. The car is silent as I'm sure all his thoughts are on Tommy right now. Maybe I should tell him about Adam? That's what normal people do with their friends. They tell their friends about their boyfriends, right? I want to be normal.

"So, I met a guy," I say.

"Oh, is that so?" he asks. He has a small smile on his lips. A part of me wants to tell him, but another part wants to keep Adam just to myself. I want him to be my own little secret that no one needs to know. I also don't want to be that annoying guy who always talks about their boyfriend nonstop.

"If you don't want to hear about it, it's okay."

"No, tell me. You can't spring that on a guy and then not go on with the story."

He looks over quickly and gives me a bright smile.

"His name is Adam. I met him at therapy."

"Is that the entire story?" He sounds disappointed.

"Yeah." That's all I want to say for now. It's a start at least. Dr. Wheeler says I need to start opening up to people, so I'm trying. I really am.

"I start school again soon. I'm not ready yet. I'm really enjoying the time off. I mean I've friends at school, but no one like you or Tommy. Plus I have less time to spend with Nick."

Who the hell is Nick?

"Wait... who is Nick?" I ask.

Alex's eyes widen. "Oh wow, I've been all over the place. He's this new guy I met," he says with a blush.

"You started seeing a guy?"

"Yeah. We met online, like every other couple these days." His smile widens.

"I am happy for you, Alex."

"When can I meet him?"

"He's visiting his grandmother for a couple weeks. He actually went to high school with us. He was two years ahead."

For the rest of the car ride, Alex tells me about what he has planned for Nick and himself. It's a pretty romantic date, where Alex wants to have a small picnic outside in the park where they can cuddle on a blanket and drink hot cocoa. It actually is pretty cute, even I have to admit, but that's Alex for you. Ever since we first met Alex, he's been a hopeless romantic. He's been waiting for love to enter his life all these years. He hasn't found it yet, but he tells me he believes Nick can be the one he falls for. I hope so.

I don't tell him what I truly think. He and Nikki broke up only a few weeks ago. How can he have moved on so soon? Sometimes his heart ignores his brain.

We reach Tommy's house, and Alex is the one to pull out his cell phone, but Tommy doesn't answer. He tries two more times, until we just decide to try the doorbell.

"Why isn't Tommy answering?" Alex mumbles under his breath.

I sneak around the small one-story house, as Alex follows behind me.

"Jess, what are you doing?"

I ignore Alex as I find myself outside Tommy's window. I knock on the window, and I see a lump underneath the blanket. It doesn't move, so I knock even louder. The lump finally moves, and Tommy erupts out of the nest of blankets. He walks over to the window and slides it open.

"What the fuck do you guys want?"

"We're worried. You haven't been answering any of our calls or texts," Alex responds.

"I've been busy."

"Bullshit," I spit out.

"I just haven't wanted to be around anyone."

"Even us?" Alex sounds hurt when he says this, but I know how Tommy feels. It's like when I'm in my dark place, I don't want anyone around me.

"Especially you guys."

"But why?"

Alex refuses to give up. He's trying to be a good friend, but I think we should back away. That's exactly what I do. I back away from the window, but Alex stays put. He stares Tommy right in his eyes. The two of them are like two warriors going into battle. I'm just the spectator on the sidelines, where I've always been. I've been on the outside watching my entire life, and I stay here as I watch the two of them.

"Just for once, Alex, please fuck off. I'm not in the mood."

Before Alex can say another word, Tommy slams the window shut, and Alex walks away, all the disappointment visible in his body language. Betrayal is written on his face, and I don't say a word. We get into the car, he drives me home, and I watch his car disappear.

Inside the house I'm met by my mom, who is in the living room reading a book. I got my love of books from her. When I was a kid, she used to read *Peter Pan* to me; I was obsessed with it. It was all I wanted to hear, so every night before bed, she'd read a chapter and then tuck me in. Oh how I wish I could be Peter Pan and just stay forever young and innocent.

"Where have you been?" Anger drips from her voice.

"I went to see Tommy this morning with Alex."

Her anger disappears. "Oh… how is he?" she asks with genuine concern. That's the one thing you can always trust about my mom. She is always genuine about her feelings. Most people are fake when they are concerned about others, but when my mother is concerned, she honestly means it.

"He wouldn't see us."

She shakes her head, and her lips become a straight line on her face.

"That poor boy."

I nod in agreement. *That poor boy.* That is the kind of thing you hear people say after someone has been murdered or goes down a terrible downward spiral in life. That is what people say about me. I don't want Tommy to head in that direction. I want to get him help before it's too late for him. What if he ends up in the same place I was eight months ago? What if he succeeds where I failed? I can't let that happen.

"So, Mom… is there anything you want for Christmas?"

She looks up, putting her coffee mug onto the table. Her blue eyes are wide in surprise. Am I so selfish I never buy anything for anyone else? Although I guess I'm usually preoccupied by my own insanity.

"You know you don't have to buy anything for your father or me."

"I know. I'm just asking."

"Isn't it a bit last-second to be buying gifts?"

"I'm a last-second kind of guy."

After the surprise finally leaves her eyes she says, "So what brought this upon all of a sudden?"

"I felt like doing something nice this year. I never buy anything for anyone, and this year I want to. You all went through so much having to deal with having a crazy son."

"*Don't* ever call yourself crazy. How many times must I tell you that, Jess? You're *not* crazy."

I nod, even though I don't agree with her.

"Is this about that boy—"

"Adam," I finish.

"Adam?"

"Not totally. I would like to buy him something, though."

"So is he your boyfriend?"

"Yeah," I answer. Even the mention of his name causes a large smile to grow on my face. I just cannot hide my feelings for him, even around my own family. As usual my own emotions betray me. My mom's smile grows along with mine, and I can see the happiness on her face. If I didn't know any better, she might be happier than I am.

"You really like him, don't you?"

I do, I really do. Never have I felt so much for a guy. It's like there is a lightness in my stomach that was never there before.

"Would you like to help me get him a gift?"

"Yes," she answers delightedly.

I haven't spent a day with my mother in years, not since I was a young boy before the depression got truly bad. I could use a day with my mom. To feel like a child again, to return to that innocence... now that would be lovely.

Mom and I walk around town, commenting on all the things we see and ignoring the stares around us. We just pretend like the last ten months or so never happened. Sometimes it's nice to pretend things are different. A game of make-believe can go a long way. Sometimes I wish my whole life could be one big game of make-believe. I'd be someone the exact opposite of myself. If I could pretend to be a happy person for just one day, I would take it. I imagine I'd be a college student with great grades and tons of friends, but I would love to keep Adam as my boyfriend, because he is one aspect I am happy about in my actual life. But I guess there are rules to starting a new life: you have to keep everything the way it is or change everything.

I want to keep Adam.

Mom and I continue walking through the small town, ending up in an area dedicated to little shops and boutiques. Most of them sell antique items. My mom got her favorite gold necklace here. It apparently belonged to Princess Diana years ago, or it's just costume jewelry, and my mom was ripped off. I call the latter, but hey, it makes her happy to think she has something beautiful and special. My mom loves those special items, whether they're special to her or were to other people. She is really into antiquing, and in her bedroom there is a glass case just dedicated to small statues and tea sets and anything else that may have had some kind of value to her or someone else. She likes to document everything and loves to keep as many memories as she can. She keeps a scrapbook of memories in her closet, and it's constantly growing with new pictures. She has this anxiety where she is afraid of getting Alzheimer's so she hopes all of this will allow that to not happen, or if it does, it will help her gain her memories back. I don't want to be the one to tell her that none of that will work. If you get it, you get it. Nothing you can do to change that.

Mom is the one who notices that a new shop sits in between two antique shops. It's small, and the outside is painted a sky blue. It's pretty hard to miss. Only a blind person wouldn't notice this store, and even that is a maybe.

Mom and I walk into the small shop. Knickknacks cover the shelves of the store. I feel as if I have walked into Wonderland. The store is called Knickety-Knacks. Everywhere I look I see something that would match Adam's personality. Old antique teacups, black-and-white photographs of older movie stars, comic books, and paintings. There are typewriters and old hardcover novels. The store's walls are painted a lavender color, with landscape paintings on them. On the back wall is a mural of a cloud wearing a rainbow as a scarf, and it has a giant smile on its little puffy face that looks like cotton balls. This store rivals the cuteness of little puppies and kittens, but not quite otters. I love otters.

I decide on the spot that I like the store.

"Well, this is cute."

"Mom, that is the understatement of the year."

Between the bright colors and pretty pictures, this shop makes me want to live on a rainbow or something cheesy like that. Mom heads toward the antiques, and I walk away toward the small movie selection. I end up walking past the cash register, where a perky woman sits smacking her chewing gum.

"Hello, darling. How are you?" She speaks in this regal way, as if she is trying to fake a British accent, but she is really bad at it. She blows a bubble and lets it pop.

"Hey."

"Speak up, sorry."

Oh great, we're going to have a problem here. People always have trouble hearing me because of how low I speak. I clear my throat and repeat myself, trying to sound a bit louder. I think my voice just ends up sounding higher pitched instead.

"How are you, darling?" Every time she says "darling," she draws it out. She really is trying way too hard.

"I'm fine," I squeak out.

"Wonderful. Are you looking for anything?"

"Nope."

"My name is Esther if you need anything."

"Thank you, Esther."

Before she can say another word in her fake voice, I head toward the movies. The DVD collection is small, but they're classic films. Some good ones too. Not too many horror ones, sadly. I look around to see that the store is small but still rather organized. She tries to keep the things together. After the movies, I head to the books, also a pretty small selection. They are all classic novels, which is fine by me. I'm not prejudiced against classic literature. I see an old-fashioned hardcover copy of *Jane Eyre*, and when I look at the price, I see it's only two dollars and fifty cents… score. I grab the novel and put it under my arm.

I find my way toward the jewelry, most of it cheap-looking knickknacks, but they don't lie at least. The prices are all pretty low and the objects are cute. There's one necklace that is a small white kitten on a long silver chain. I could see Jill from The Book Revue wearing that. A light brown wooden box catches my eyes, and my fingers run over the smooth wood. It feels nice under the tips of my fingers. I lift the box up and open it to see a long, thin brown leather band attached to a small brass watch face. The numbers are roman numerals, and the hands of the tiny clock are fancy, seeming like they should belong to a classy grandfather clock. I lift the watch in my hand, holding it very delicately, almost afraid it will break. It's beautiful.

"It's beautiful, isn't it?"

I almost jump out of my skin as the older woman stands next to me. Where the hell did she come from? She stares at me like some old witch. Is she always this creepy?

"Yeah," I respond.

"It came all the way from Germany. It was made by a homeless girl in a factory. This was the last watch she made before being overcome by the terrible disease her tiny body was stricken with."

"Sure…." I find that all very hard to believe. They probably make a million of these in a factory somewhere.

"Turn it over."

I turn it over to see a small inscription in the back, three little words in a beautiful cursive.

Immer und ewig.

"What does this mean?" I ask the elder woman.

"*Immer und ewig.* It's German for 'forever and eternally.'"

She's right, this really is beautiful.

"How do you wear it?" I ask. The leather band is so long, it must be too long for a wrist.

"May I?" she asks holding out her long, thin boney fingers. Her hands are wrinkled and veiny.

I hand her the watch, and she grabs my wrist. I hope this isn't some way for her to get off, her touching my young nubile flesh and all.

She lays the face of the watch on the top of my wrist and wraps the leather band once around and then a second time, so the face is in between the two sides, and she buckles it in.

"There."

I can't take my eyes away from it. My wrist seems to turn into Adam's, and I can picture this watch on his wrist. It's beautiful, and he deserves something beautiful.

Afterward we trek to the supermarket because Mom needs food and supplies. Her favorite holiday was just around the corner, Thanksgiving.

THANKSGIVING COMES, and I wake up to the smell of cooking turkey and mashed potatoes. After pulling on my clothes, I walk downstairs into the kitchen and find my mother in her robe at the stove, her hair in a messy bun. Clara is making the stuffing. I let out a yawn, sit down, and watch as the sounds of clanging pots and pans clatter all around the kitchen.

Every year, Mom makes a big deal over this holiday. But this year, she is really outdoing herself. I've never seen so much food in one room in my entire life. I see different kinds of puddings, pies, cakes. There are soups, bread. Enough food to feed two armies, the navy, and the air force, and it's not even noon.

"Wow, Mom. This all looks amazing."

She turns around and smiles. Strands of hair stick to her sweaty face. She's doing this all for me. How can I thank her for all of this?

"Do you need help?" I offer.

She nods and soon I'm at work right beside her, cracking some eggs and breaking chicken cutlets. Mom, Clara, and I sit around in the kitchen and we laugh and talk. Dad is asleep in his armchair while the parade is on television.

No one comes over to our Thanksgiving feast. At dinner, we each go around and state what we are all thankful for, and my mom says she is thankful to have me back home. Everyone says they are thankful to have me home, and I want to believe them. I want to be happy in life. I want to be normal.

I *need* to be normal.

CHAPTER THIRTEEN

A MONTH goes by, and I wake up on Christmas morning with a smile on my face. This is the first time in years I've been excited for the holiday. I turn over to see Adam's gift wrapped up and a card lying on top. We made plans to have a small minicelebration tonight. After dinner with my family, I will walk over to his apartment, and we're going to be together. My first Christmas with someone, and it's exquisite. Only my favorite word seems about right. I like this new happyish me. It's much better than the morose, sullen version that I've always lived with. Today is just a wonderful day, and I am glad to be alive.

For the past month I've been happy, and it feels so nice. I feel like I'm almost a human being. Clara went back to school for a few weeks, after Thanksgiving, but now she's back home once more. It seems like she just can't stay away from her family.

I've been spending every free moment I have with Adam. I start off every day with a text from him and then we meet up when we can. Every little moment we catch is pure magic.

The rest of the morning goes along superlatively. Superlative is the word of the day. I think it goes along pretty well with how I'm feeling right now.

Superlative; adj.

Excellent, magnificent, wonderful, marvelous, supreme, consummate, outstanding, remarkable, fine, choice, prime, unsurpassed, unequaled, unparalleled, unrivaled, preeminent, wicked, brilliant.

Antonyms: mediocre.

For example: Adam makes me feel superlative. And it feels damn great.

I finally get myself out of bed, and I find my way downstairs into the living room, where a few gifts are stacked in a messy pile. There isn't a ton, but it's a decent amount for just the four of us. Mom hands me a cup of tea, just the way I like it, and I thank her. I take a seat on the couch right next to my sister, her long hair kept back in a ponytail. She rests her head on my shoulder, and I throw my arm over her shoulders.

"Merry Christmas," she says in a sleep-filled voice.

"Merry Christmas, Clara."

"What did you get me?" she asks with a small smile.

"Nothing," I say with a laugh.

"Bastard."

She grabs a pillow and hits me against the chest.

"Bitch."

"You deserved that one, Jess."

Mom sits on the couch on the other side of the room and she sips her own cup of tea. The taste of my tea is soothing to my insides, and especially my mind. I need my mind to be at ease because I hear my father's footsteps walking downstairs, and then he appears at the entrance to the living room. He sits on the couch next to Mom.

"Who wants to open their gift first?" Mom asks us.

"I want Jess to open mine."

Clara jumps from her spot on the couch and grabs a rectangular gift from the pile of presents. My name is written in a beautiful cursive along the wrapping paper.

"I hope you love it."

I unwrap the gift to see a novel. It's an old-fashioned hardcover novel, my favorite kind. They are always so classy, in my opinion. I run my fingers over the silver words etched into the novel.

"Thank you so much, Clara."

I pull her into a hug, catching her by surprise. I'm never one to start a hug. She hugs me back and smiles.

"I saw it and immediately thought of you. An old-fashioned novel screams your name. I know it isn't anything much—"

"No." I cut her off. "It's perfect. Really, thank you."

The gifts are exchanged, and it's just a good morning that leaves me content. My family is surprised and happy when I hand them each a gift. I don't get them anything much, but I wanted to do a little something after all my craziness they've had to put up. My mom gets an antique teacup I saw her looking at when we were in Knickety-Knacks. I went back later that day to buy it. I bought my father a DVD season of *Law & Order: SVU*. That show is his obsession. He smiles and tells me he loves it. I smile as my sister opens her gift—a silver chain necklace, with a small heart pendant. She seems so happy when she opens it, and she has me put it on for her right away.

For the first time in years, we seem like a normal, happy family. I pretend like none of this past shit has happened, and it just feels great. I feel like a new guy, living a new life. It's nice to just be with my family. For once, we can celebrate Christmas. Last Christmas was a disaster. I just sat in a corner quiet all day and wouldn't say a word. The Christmas before that, I wouldn't leave my room. I want to stay like this. I want to keep my parents happy. Everyone seems so happy, and right now it seems like one of those picture-worthy moments you always see. You know, those cheesy pretaken pictures in frames that can be sold at your everyday Target or Walmart.

I look at my parents as they sit on the couch. They smile at each other, and I watch as my father kisses my mom. When he is around her, his tough exterior seems to disappear. My mom used to tell me when I was a child that they were soul mates. For me those are like the idea of fate.

Soul mates. Fate. The universe. I just don't know. People always talk about the idea of someone having *the one*, but is that possible? Is there really only one person for each of us out there? If so, then shouldn't there not be any divorce, or do most people make a mistake the first, second, third, whatever time. People say that it's in the stars and that God brings us together. The universe is so expansive, that if there *is* a God, which I doubt there is, why would he care about any of us? And especially about whom we date?

What happened to me being happy and wanting to stay that way? I really kind of suck at doing this whole happy shtick. Adam is always so happy; I should take notes from him and see how he does it.

As we all sit down to breakfast I laugh and joke along with the rest of my family. I try to get away from my dark feelings. I just don't get why it's so hard for me to escape them. Everyone else I know has such an easy time being happy, but with me I might as well be dragging a two-ton boulder up a steep mountain. I think that would be easier to keep doing. No matter how good everything is, that darkness always manages to seep its way through into my light. It is like it's ripping through to say "Hello. Fuck you."

"Jess?"

I look up to see everyone staring at me. Each face is concerned. "Yeah?"

"I was calling your name before," Mom says.

"Oh sorry, I was thinking."

I see everyone's faces turn white. Me thinking is like an atomic bomb waiting to go off, and my body is just Japan waiting for the effects to take over.

"Don't worry. I don't have plans to off myself again," I joke. I awkwardly laugh, but no one makes a comment afterward. "Too soon?"

Everyone ignores me. Geez, if we can't joke about this, then what can we do?

"I was wondering if you would like to invite Adam over for dinner?"

"Tonight? Me and him already sort of made plans."

"Not tonight, but one night soon. I would like for us all to really get to know this boy you've been seeing."

It never crossed my mind that now that Adam is my boyfriend, he'd be meeting my family. I guess it's about time. I just hope I don't do anything to embarrass myself in front of everyone. Most people are afraid their family will embarrass them, but not me. They are normal; I'm not.

"Yeah, I'll ask him. It could be cool."

"Lovely." Mom seems so happy. I like when I can do that to her.

I really do like how she is trying to be respectful and appreciative of my newfound relationship. I think she might just be happy that I actually met someone for a change. My mom has told me that all she wants is for me to truly be happy in life. That is all I want too, Mom.

That is all I want too.

Breakfast comes to an end, and we all sit together in the living room and watch a movie. Every Christmas morning we watch *A Christmas Carol*, the 1951 version with Alastair Sim. We don't have a lot of traditions. We don't decorate, nor do we put up a tree, but every year we watch the same film, and that is the only tradition we have. And every year, later that day, I go up to my room and watch my personal favorite Christmas film, a slasher film from 1974 called *Black Christmas*. Who doesn't love some terror mixed in with their Christmas joy?

As the movie comes to an end, I watch as Mom wipes a tear from her eye. No matter what, she always tears up at the end, even if she has seen this movie a billion times. You would think it would lose its emotional resonance after a while. Oh well, my mom is an emotional person with movies.

I've caught her many times late at night sitting in the living room and watching her DVD of *Titanic*. I think a part of her wishes she could have a time like that again, before I went totally insane. A time when I was innocent and looked at her like she was God. After all, every child thinks of its mother as God.

The rest of the day passes by, not feeling anything like a holiday. I bring my opened gifts—all clothes and books—up to my bedroom. I hang up the clothes and add the books to the piles of books sitting around my room. This has been a nice Christmas… well, compared to the many years of Christmases that felt like I was already locked up in a hospital before I actually was.

That's the thing about depression; it's not that you're just sad. It's like you're locked up inside yourself with no escape.

It ruins lives.

I am not the only one who is having a good Christmas, though. Two days ago, Nick drove down to see Alex, and they spent the day together, and I know Nick slept over as well. I hung out with them for an hour, and Alex just radiated happiness. He and Nick held hands the entire time and even kissed every once in a while. It made me long for Adam to share a secret kiss with as well. I'm just happy for my friend now. When you see Alex's smile even at the mention of Nick's name, it's like there is nothing but pure happiness inside his body. He's always been one to fall fast. It's the problem of being a hopeless romantic.

The next morning, Nick drove back to his grandmother's.

I sit in my room and read the new novel my sister has bought me. It's not bad but might be a little too melodramatic for me. It's one of those classic love stories, but everything is so damn perfect, and all these characters have such great lives with no obstacles. It's boring. I don't want to read about perfection. If I want to read a romance, I want to read about the obstacles they must overcome to get to one another. Life is hard, and while novels are supposed to be an escape, I still want to see the hardship of life in there. Maybe I should be a writer. I at least know the basic functions of writing. I used to write short stories as a kid, and my mom and sister loved them. They were all these fantastical little things that could only come from a child's mind. They were all pretty much the same. There was always a young handsome knight who fought off evil witches and dragons and had to go through a castle full of evil henchmen to get to the princess he loves. It was basically *Super Mario Brothers*, but with more sword fighting and a less annoying princess. Seriously, what is up with Peach? To get kidnapped that much, she just isn't worth it. She must've been good in bed or something for Mario to always go back for her. I don't really have any of these stories anymore, but I think Mom kept some of them. Knowing her, she probably scrapbooked them or put them in a photo album.

When I was in high school, I took a creative writing class with Alex. It was Mr. Hartwell's class. It wasn't very big, and he was the only person who taught the class. Wilshire High School didn't exactly have a big elective program. Creative writing seemed the most fun to me, and I actually did love it for a semester. I got really into writing some of those stories, and the teacher even admitted that some of them were pretty damn good. He said I *showed real talent*.

He also thought my stories were fantasy. Most of them were about a young man with a mental illness. He never once assumed the characters were based off me and my batty life.

I close the book and place it on my nightstand. It's okay, but the perfect lives of the characters are starting to annoy me now, more than it did before. I just want to strangle them and tell them to shut up. Geez.

I hear my phone go off, and I look to see a text from Alex.

Merry Christmas—Alex

I wish him a happy holiday, and I also text Tommy. He doesn't respond, so apparently he still doesn't want to talk to Alex or me.

Ho ho ho! Merry Christmas!!!

Adam's text comes in, and it's dorky and cute as usual. I love how even in text, his personality completely shines through his words.

Merry Christmas, Adam! I text back immediately. I never like to waste time when it comes to texting him.

How is your holiday?

Mine is well; how is yours?

Great! I'm with my Uncle Martin now. He says hello! He can't wait to meet you.

What do I say to that? When I finally meet his uncles, what will they think about me? They're probably not even going to think I'm good enough for their nephew. I mean, I'm just this insane guy who got out of the hospital. Who wants *that* dating their family member? I know exactly what Adam's uncles will think the moment they meet me: *Who is this guy dating my nephew? He's not good enough.*

I know they'd be right too. It's what I think of myself all the time. Sometimes I wonder what exactly Adam sees in me. Not good enough.

But it's not just Adam. My family too. My mom and sister have always taken care of me, but I never really am able to show anything back. How do they put up with me? Not good enough.

Not good enough.

Are we still on for tonight? :)

Yes.

Are you okay?

Fine.

What is wrong with me? Jess, just be happy. I feel the internal struggle inside my body as my two halves battle each other. The darkness wants to take me back, but my other half wants me to feel the happiness.

I'm excited to see you tonight, I send him.

:) Me too! Is 8pm good???!!!

Haha, yeah. That's great.

YAAAAYYYYY!!! :-D

Sometimes I really do think I might be dating a child, but hey, that childish attitude of his is a big reason why I like him. I just want to be good enough for him. He's so sweet, that he deserves someone who isn't moody like I am.

I spend the rest of the day only wishing for it to be 8:00 p.m., and when it finally rolls around, I hear the sound of his car pulling up outside my house. I grab his small wrapped gift, and I walk to his car with a skip in my step. He's standing outside the car and opens the door for me, like the gentleman he is.

"Hi."

"Hello," I greet him as well.

He walks around the car and sits behind the wheel. I see that his hands are shaking. He blows on them, trying to warm them up. I take them in mine and rub them together between my hands. He smiles down at me.

"Th-thanks."

"Of course."

"S-s-s-s-s-so are, are you r-ready for the b-best n-n-night of your life?"

He smiles really big and wide, and I see the red in his cheeks from the bitter cold outside. He almost looks like a Disney prince right now.

"Yes, I am. Thrill me."

The car ride is spent in silence. He keeps his eyes on the road, and I keep mine focused on the falling snow as it dances through the sky. The snow is so peaceful and beautiful. Watching the snowflakes fall is like watching your own personal ballet. Each flake is just a dancer of the sky.

His car pulls up to his apartment building, and he leads me to his door. As he unlocks the door, I take in the sight.

"You have to be kidding me... again?"

Inside the living room, he has built another blanket fort. He certainly does love these.

"Th-th-they're c-c-c-cool."

I look up at his big blue eyes, and I feel my heart beat. At this moment I desire to feel his body against mine, our hearts beating together.

"You're a loser."

"I'm your l-l-loser."

"You're my loser."

I like the sound of that. He's mine. I could live with that.

I take off my shoes and my coat, and I follow him into the blanket fort, his laptop inside, once again set up to the virtual fireplace. Two mugs of tea sit inside. It's a good picture of what the last fort with him was like. I lie down beside him as he puts a fuzzy, warm blue blanket over us and wraps his arm around my waist. He pulls me close to his body as I lay my head on his chest. I feel his heart speed up as I wrap my arm around his waist.

"I-I-I've been th-th-thinking about this all, all d-d-day." His voice is low, barely an audible whisper. He sounds like he is in heaven.

"Me too," I admit.

I close my eyes, and I listen to the wind blowing outside and the sound of his beating heart. I listen to his even, rhythmic breaths. He runs his fingers through my hair and the touch of his fingertips on my scalp feels soothing.

I remember the small box in my coat pocket. I tell him I'll be right back, and I rush to my coat to get it. I bring it back into the fort.

"Merry Christmas," I tell him with a sheepish smile. I really hope he likes it.

He smiles wide, and he carefully unwraps the gift, pulling out the watch. His eyes seem to widen, and his mouth slightly falls open. Oh gosh, he must hate it….

"I l-l-love it."

I did something right. Nice. He turns the watch over in his hand and sees the inscription.

"What d-does this mean?"

"It means forever and ever…." I hope it isn't weird that I gave him a watch with that inscription. Maybe it's too soon in our relationship for something so romantic like that.

"That's b-beautiful, like, like you. P-p-put it, it on f-f-for me."

I look away, unable to stop my smile. I don't know what he sees in me, but I like that he does see something. He makes me feel beautiful, like he always tells me. No one has ever made me feel this way. I take the watch and wrap it around his wrist, making sure to touch his skin as much as I can with my fingertips. He looks down at his watch and smiles.

"Forever," he states under his breath.

"And ever," I respond in a slight sigh.

"I-I-I got you s-s-s-s-s-something too."

He reaches around and pulls something out from behind the pillow he is leaning against. It's a long, thin box, not wrapped. He lays it on my lap, as I sit cross-legged.

"I-I didn't know, know what t-to get you, s-s-s-s-so I hope you l-like it."

I take the top off the box, and I pull out a long silver chain. At the end of the chain is a long silver key. It looks like a shiny, classier skeleton key. It seems to glow even in the dim orange light of the fake fireplace. The only word that could be used to describe the necklace would be amazing. It is beautiful.

I'm at a loss for words, and when I look up into Adam's eyes, he has a huge goofy smile on his face, and I smile right back.

"S-s-s-s-so I did g-good?"

"You did fantastic."

I put the necklace over my head, and I allow the key to dangle down. It falls to the middle of my chest. The chain is cold on the back of my neck, but right now I feel so warm that I am able to ignore the chill against my skin. Adam pulls me close to his body, and we lie back down underneath the blanket, so close he might actually be trying to meld our bodies together.

"I'm s-s-s-s-s-s-so glad we-we met."

I nod.

"I-I-I mean we-we m-met s-s-s-s-so many t-times in, in one d-day."

"Don't you find it weird, how many times we met by accident that first day?" I finally say, asking him the question that always plagues my mind.

"N-n-not at all. I think, I think it w-w-w-was the world g-g-getting us to-to-together, like we were s-s-s-s-s-supposed to, to be."

"You believe in fate?" I ask him.

He nods. "Yes, d-d-don't you?"

"No. I believe in coincidence."

He stops rubbing my head, and he looks down into my eyes. He looks so serious, and I wonder if I upset him with my pessimistic outlook on life. I just don't see how fate can exist.

"I d-d-d-don't th-th-think anything is-is a coincidence," he remarks.

He gets up and walks away, leaving me alone in this dorky little blanket fort. I feel a chill run through my body without his warmth beside me. I take a sip of the hot tea. He really did a lot to make this all so cozy for us. It makes me feel good to know how much he cares about me. It's different and unusual, but I'm learning to live life with a guy caring about me. He returns with a ball of red thread. I hope he isn't going to actually try and sew us together or anything? That would really put a damper on this whole relationship.

"Do you just keep that lying around?"

"G-g-give me your, your hand," he orders, and I follow suit.

He begins to wrap the red thread around my fingers. "There is, is this ancient p-proverb that I l-l-l-love. It g-g-goes like this: 'An in-invisible r-r-r-red thread c-c-connects those who, who are d-d-destined t-to meet, r-r-regardless of t-t-t-t-time, p-place, or cir-cir-circumstance.'" He continues to wrap the thread through our fingers, tangling it as much as he can. "'The thread m-may s-s-s-s-stretch or t-tangle, but it, it w-will never b-b-b-b-break.'"

When he is done talking, the long red thread is wrapped around both our hands, and he clasps his hands in mine. The thread is tangled between our fingers. Right now it feels as if we are one. With his hand in mine, as we are tangled in the thread, I, for the first time in my life, believe that maybe something did bring us together. Maybe there is such thing as fate, and maybe Adam and I are meant for one another.

"I think the w-w-w-world brought m-m-me you, Jess. S-s-s-s-some things a-a-a-aren't c-c-coincidence."

CHAPTER FOURTEEN

THE DAY after Christmas I spend with a smile on my face. The memories of the night before and the mystical red thread stay in my mind. We kept our fingers tangled with one another and our hands caught in the thread like that for hours. It just felt nice to feel that much of a connection with someone. Never in my life have I felt something so strong for a person before. After only a few weeks of knowing Adam, I can officially say he is someone so incredibly special to me. I don't want him out of my life.

Bzzzzzz. Bzzzzzz.

I look over to my nightstand as my phone vibrates. Why is it that when my phone is on vibrate, it sounds louder than the actual ringtone? When it's settled on a table, it almost sounds like an entire construction crew is trapped inside my phone.

Hey sexy boy

Hey, Jill.

The usual. Same shit, different day yo!

I never understood people's love of using the word *yo*. It's a weird word if you really think about it. Yo. It reminds me of a child's toy, the yo-yo, so how did that get turned into a cool phrase for people to say. When I hear a word that is reminiscent of a child's pastime, I don't usually think "Hey, that'd be a cool phrase to say."

Do you want to do something today? I know you're not working

How did you know that?

Peter was passed out in his office, so I took a peek at the schedule book on his desk

Oh, that's not creepy at all.

I wonder how Peter does the schedules, I respond, trying to ignore her stalkerish personality.

Oh he makes Laurie do it

Makes sense. Yeah, let's hang out.

*Awesome sauce, send me your address and I'll pick you up in an
hour. Get dressed Sexy*

I quickly dress in a sweater and a tight pair of skinny jeans and
tie on my pair of beaten-up low-top Chucks. I brush my teeth and run
a hand through my mop of messy hair. I'm not even going to bother.
I just allow the hair to fall into my eyes as I put on my glasses with
their thick black frames.

A little over an hour later my phone vibrates in my pocket.

Get your cute ass outside

Today should prove to be an interesting day. I've never actually
spoken to, let alone hung out with Jill outside of work before. I wonder
if her personality is as flamboyant as her hair indicates she'd be.

I look outside my bedroom window to see a silver Volvo sitting in
front of my house. Music is pounding from the speakers, the vibration
traveling all the way into my room, and suddenly it's as if I'm in that
scene from *Jurassic Park* when the two kids are trying to eat Jell-O.
Now the image of a Tyrannosaurus rex driving a car with its tiny hands
is stuck in my brain. I grab my coat and walk downstairs. Dad is at work
already—his job doesn't believe in extended vacations—but Mom is
sitting in the living room watching television: *The People's Court*. She
is addicted to her court shows. I swear if there is a new court show, my
mom is in high heaven. My father hates these shows.

She puts the show on mute. "Who *is* that?"

"That is Jill, a girl I work with."

Mom and I look through the window to see her hot-pink hair and
her giant gaudy purple sunglasses, which seem to cover half her face.

"She looks… nice," Mom states, unsure how to describe her.

"She is, I think."

"You think?"

"I think." I mean, I'm pretty sure at least. Again, all I know
about her is what I've gathered from the times we've worked together.

"Oh God. Be safe."

"She's fine, Mom. Don't worry."

"Again, you think."

"I think."

Is it bad I'm finding this moment kind of humorous? I want to place bets on how many more times we can use the term *think*. Where are gambling addicts when you need them?

She kisses my cheek and tells me she loves me, and I walk to Jill's car.

"Hey, sexy," she greets in her low raspy voice, which if I was straight I would admit would be pretty hot. She sounds like she could be an old-time jazz singer. I wonder if she can sing.

"Hi, Jill."

"Dude, you need to speak louder, show some confidence. Show everyone your bad self, yo."

I simply nod, not knowing what to say. She puts her foot on the gas and races away from my house. If I consider Tommy's driving unsafe, then Jill's driving is downright hazardous. She doesn't even give me a chance to buckle my seat belt, so I'm fumbling around to get myself buckled in. I don't feel like dying today. Well, that's a new idea.

"Where are we going?" I ask her, a little bit scared.

"To the mall."

Sad, but true fact of life: Wilshire has never had a mall. We must be going to the next town over, Newton, which is a bigger town than ours and has more life than ours. Newton is usually a half-hour drive, but Jill does it in less than twenty minutes. When we reach the Newton Mall, my hands are clasping each other so hard my knuckles are whiter than usual. I never knew my skin could be any paler until today.

"You okay?" she asks.

I can't find the words, so I just nod once again. I'm almost afraid to step out of the car, fearful I might just fall to the ground after that paralyzing experience. I follow her into the mall, and soon we're going from store to store, like shopping is going out of style. The way Jill drags me around, one would actually think she must shop to survive or she would die otherwise.

After our seventh, or possibly eighth shop (I've lost count), we stop, and I am thankfully able to catch my breath. Jill holds three bags in her hands—two boxes of new shoes, a bunch of clothes from some girly store I've never heard of, and underwear from Victoria's Secret. She keeps asking for my opinion on everything, expecting some sassy gay answer from her gay friend. I'm as far from feisty as one can get. I can be sarcastic sometimes—a lot of times, apparently, or so I hear—but that's about it. Every time she asks, I usually say the same thing: *Yeah, it looks good.* Like what exactly does she want me to say, give her a full analysis on how well a certain dress fits her shape and how the color suits her quite pale skin tone?

I'm pretty dumb when it comes to women's clothes. I don't know anything about them. I mean, I know what I like on me, but that is because it's on me. When she dragged me into one store, she actually told me I was no help, with a pout on her lips. I feel that every girl is looking for a gay man as an accessory to help them shop and talk about boys or whatever. Like, geez, we're people, not things you buy in the store.

"So anywhere you want to go?" she asks.

I shrug. I'm not much of a shopper.

"Come on, there has to be at least one store. You have nothing, and now I'm looking like some rich bitch."

She bites her lip, and I can almost see the lightbulb above her head as she has this aha moment. She grabs my hand and drags me through the mall. Maybe I should tell her I'm not an accessory. I just hope she doesn't take me home and hang me in her closet, which I'm sure is full of colorful clothes.

She pulls me into a random store that I don't catch the name of. Looking around it seems to be a fashionable little store with colorful clothes, cardigans, ties, and nice pants and jeans.

"I'm going to find you clothes. I swear on my life."

"Jill, it's okay."

"Nope. Maybe I'll find you some sexy outfit you can wear for that boy of yours. By the way you have *fantastic* taste. He is one fine piece of man candy. I need to find myself a man half as hot as yours. Nice job."

I can't stop my smile because I have to admit I'm feeling a bit proud of myself. Someone is actually envious of my boyfriend.

"Jess Holbrooke has his charm," I joke.

"That you do," she flirts with a wink.

Just like the rest of the mall, she pulls me around and pulls out random clothes and throws them into my arms. After I have what feels to be about twenty pounds' worth of fabric, she pushes me into a dressing room.

"Now you better model your hot self for me to check out, stud."

I have to say, she is good for the self-esteem. Maybe I should be the one using her as an accessory. She's chosen nice skinny jeans; some are kind of cool colors.

"Ow-ow," she shouts, as I model the bright red skinny jeans. "I'd kill for that ass."

I blush as the store associate looks over. I hide my face and walk right back into the dressing room. The rest of the try-on session goes the same. She's picked out button-ups and T-shirts and sweaters and even some cardigans, all which seem to show off my lithe frame. It's all a little too vibrant, but she won't hear me out.

"Are you going to buy any of that?"

"I don't know. It's a lot."

"But you look so hot in all of those clothes. Imagine what your man will think?"

I can see his smile right now in my mind as his arctic-blue eyes light up at the sight of my clothes. Jill really knows how to persuade me.

"Fine, yeah."

"Sweet deal. When was the last time you bought something for yourself?"

"Ummm...." Actually I don't remember. "I mean I bought myself a book recently?" That counts, right?

"That's what I thought. Now let's pay and get some food. I'm starved."

I pay for *some* of it, as she rolls her eyes as I pull out a red zip-up hoodie. She tells me I don't need to own another hoodie, but I disagree. I love my hoodies and cardigans. I politely refuse the bow ties. They look adorable on Adam, but they're not for me. Even when I don't pay for half of the clothes she forced me to try on, I can still say I'm not going to be shopping for a long time, that's for sure. I end up buying the bright red skinny jeans as well. We walk to the food court as she links her arm with me. We sit down to lunch—cheap pizza, but it hits the spot. She offers to pay for me, but I hate when others pay for me. Then I feel like I have a debt to pay back.

The rest of the day seems to go in the same fashion, and I would be lying if I said I didn't have fun. Jill makes me feel like a normal guy for a change. In Newton no one knows me, so no one stares at me. She makes me laugh, and we just have harmless fun. There are no deep conversations, and not once does she ask about my stay in the hospital, nor does she ask about my suicide attempt. It feels good to be normal.

SHE DROPS me off at my house, and I tell her I had a good time. She wants to hang out again soon, so I tell her I'll see her tomorrow at The Book Revue. I walk into the house to see that my father is home from work, reading a magazine about cars.

"Hey, Dad."

"Hey, kiddo. How was your day?"

I hold up my bags. "Good."

"Looks like you spent a lot of money."

"Yeah, but it was my own. Don't worry."

"I'm not worried."

A cold, awkward silence fills the air as we both look everywhere but at one another's eyes. It's becoming a bit of a game. It wasn't always like this, though. I remember how he and I used to laugh over the cars he'd let me help him fix up. I miss those days. Why did he stop doing that?

"Dad?"

"Yeah?"

"Why don't you fix up cars anymore, like you used to?"

He shrugs, and I see something in his eyes—longing. What does he long for? His passion of cars? His son?

Or possibly the past.

"Just lost my reason to."

"And what was that reason?"

"You're curious tonight."

It's my turn to shrug. That's the kind of guy I am. I prefer a shrug to actually forming a phrase. My father stands up and sighs. He puts a hand on my shoulder and passes by me. He stops at the staircase and looks at me with his dark brown eyes.

"You were the reason, Jess."

And just like that, he leaves and heads up the stairs. Me? I was the reason he stopped messing around with cars… it was my fault, then. How can I apologize to my father for messing up his big love? Hey, sorry for fucking up your passion in life. Here, let me bake you a cake? It's not that simple. Although, my father does love cake.

I find myself in my bedroom thinking about all the wrong I've done. My mother is always thinking about me; my sister puts her life on hold for me; my father… he gave up his passion in life because of me. What have I given back to them? Anger. Aggression. Depression. Instead of being the son they deserve, I've only given them heartbreak and pain. What guy does that to their family?

I am a monster.

CHAPTER FIFTEEN

MONSTER; NOUN

Brute, fiend, beast, devil, demon, barbarian, savage, animal, rascal, imp, wretch, devil, horror, scamp, tyke, varmint, hellion.

That's exactly what I am.

Monster.

The word continues to circulate through my head.

I ruin people's lives.

Is that all I am? A monster? I stand in front of the mirror, and that is all I see now. I already am nothing more than just a pathetic, sad man. I have been my entire life.

I look over at my nightstand and open the top drawer. I dig underneath my underwear and pull out a small black bag. I dump it open onto my bed and pick up the straight razor I have kept hidden from the world. I hold it in my hand, and I imagine the sensation of it running over my wrist again. I almost lick my lips at the forbidden lust. The razor is the apple to my Eve. A part of me longs for that feeling of the razor, and a part of me is frightened of it. It has such a strong hold over me. I am pain's slave. I throw the blade back into the bag and hide it in the back of the drawer. I hide it away from everyone, the world, and especially from me. I know I should get rid of it, let it disappear from my life forever… but it seems to keep me prisoner. I can never throw it away.

I dress, and it's like I'm going through the motions as I am walking outside. I don't actually feel myself moving, but it's almost as if I'm just an outside viewer watching everything.

The star of my own fucked-up movie.

I WAKE up to the sun shining through my bedroom window. After my walk last night, I went back home and passed out. The town is quiet this morning. Only two days after Christmas, and the hopeful feeling of the holiday is already starting to pass on by, like a visiting relative.

Few people are outside, so my body is at least at peace… but inside my mind, it's another story. It's an ongoing war. More imaginary soldiers die in the battle of my internal peace than sperm in their lifelong battle to become people. Gross analogy, but it gets the point across.

After leaving my bed and getting dressed, I leave my house, only to find myself on the empty playground, the same one where Adam and I spent time together. I sit on the swing and just let my toes touch the ground. I slightly rock myself back and forth and allow the wind to bite at my face like a million little piranhas looking for their newest meal.

A little boy sits in the swing beside me and looks up at me. I try to look ahead, but his unnerving stare keeps stabbing at me.

"Shouldn't you be in school, kid?" I ask.

"I'm still on Christmas vacation. I go back tomorrow," he answers in a small, high-pitched voice, which would only be found cute on children.

"Ah."

"So what are you doing here?" he asks in his squeaky chipmunk voice.

"Thinking."

"About what?"

"Everything."

"What's everything?"

"You ask a lot of questions. Don't you have a place to be?"

I really don't want to answer this kid's questions.

"Are you sad, mister?"

I stop swinging, kicking my feet into the snow and dirt. Am I so obvious that even this little kid can tell?

"Why do you ask?"

"Your face. It looks sad. You have the saddest blue eyes I have ever seen."

What is it about children that makes them so honest? And they can get away with it too. If an adult spoke like that, they'd get punched right in the face.

"Oh." I can't find any other words to say. "Okay."

"Why are you sad?" the little boy continues to pry, as he plays with the tassels at the end of his snow hat, which has flaps over both his ears. There is a knit picture of a puppy on there. It's all very *cute*.

I shrug and scratch my head.

"I have a chemical deficiency in my brain that keeps me from having enough of certain chemicals that would allow me to be happier." Or at least that is what one of the doctors in the mental hospital told me.

He tilts his head like the puppy he wears on his hat and looks at me with his big, confused brown eyes.

"What?"

"Exactly. That's what I make of it too, little boy."

"I'm Jacob."

"Nice to meet you. I'm Jess."

He reaches his hand out, and I gently take it, careful of the dirt under his fingernails.

"Are you the crazy boy who got out of the hospital? I heard my brother talking about you. He says you're a 'loony tune.' I like the cartoon. Are you really a 'loony tune'?"

A loony tune. So that is what people say about me behind my back in the comfort of their own houses.

"Yep, that's me."

His smile brightens. "I've never met one before. What's it like to be one?"

"It sucks."

His smile fades. "Oh. Does it hurt?"

"Every moment of every day."

"I have to go home now. Mommy needs me, but I hope you stop hurting soon."

I watch him jump up and skip home.

"Me too."

I look up at the clouds above me and sigh before jumping off the swing. I walk back home and go back to my bedroom, kicking off my Chuck Taylors and throwing my peacoat onto my bed. I close my eyes and think of the little boy. How is it he was able to see something most people never noticed? Or maybe it is just that no one really cares. From the moment he saw me, he knew how sad I was. But before my stay in the hospital, most people never said a word, and many acted shocked at my small stint with death. Locked away, I spent seven months trying to prove to people I was no longer waiting to just destroy myself. But I am starting to think that extended stay was more for others than myself. And I wonder why I went through that whole agonizing hospital experience with all those other mental patients there.

Does anyone actually care about anyone else in this world? Maybe it's all just a ruse. We pretend so much to care about others that we actually are fooling ourselves into believing one of the best lies ever imagined.

A knock comes at my door. I sit up and stay quiet. Maybe if I don't make a sound, they'll make like a Tyrannosaurus rex and vanish.

"Jess, are you in there?"

Well, I guess I can safely assume my mom is not a dinosaur.

"Yes, Mom," I answer in a monotone robotic voice.

I catch myself in my mirror, and I can't move my eyes away from my reflection. I just continue to stare into my own eyes, glaring.

Unmoving.

"Jess, are you okay?" She knows my voice. She knows how I speak when I don't want to be around anyone. I sound like a robot that doesn't know how to show basic human emotions.

I am mechanical.

I am a machine.

"Yes." I try to force a little bit more emotion, but it kind of just sounds angry. Shit. She asks to come in. What can I do? Refuse?

I walk to the door and unlock it. I open the door to see her worried, pretty face. I walk back over to my bed and sit at the edge. Mom follows me and sits beside me, maybe a bit too close for my comfort. Personal space, Mom, personal space. She doesn't say anything at first, so neither do I. We just sit there in awkward silence.

"Jess," she says in a soothing voice.

No matter how upset you are, or how worried they are, a mother can always say your name in the most soothing manner. It must be something every woman is programmed with when they're born, that soothing voice gene. I'm sure some men too. I think my mom could stop an entire race from committing genocide; that is how sweet her voice is.

She smiles at me. "Tell me what's wrong."

"I'm fine."

Fine.

The go-to answer for every person when they are not actually *fine*.

Fine; adj.

Well, healthy, all right, fit, blooming, thriving, in good shape, in good condition, in fine fettle, okay.

Antonyms: ill.

That is the textbook definition my thesaurus gives, but it's not true. No one ever seems to use the word fine for what it really means. People use it to tell the biggest lie anyone can tell themselves and others. Saying you're fine is like signing your own death certificate. Just send me to the morgue now, and let me rot.

So in that case, yes, I am fine.

"Talk to me, baby boy."

Baby boy… that's what my mom used to call me as a small boy when I would lie in bed at night. I used to love hearing those words on her tongue. Now it just sounds like mockery.

"There's nothing to talk about."

"Jess."

"Mom." I can mock right back, Mother.

"I wish you would talk to me. What is going on in that mind of yours? You never tell anyone anything. You always keep your guards up and keep everyone away. Why do you do that? You have no idea how much it frightens your father and me. And Clara worries too. She called once a week to see how you were doing."

I didn't know Clara did that.

"You and Clara maybe."

"Jess, your father loves you. He's just…."

"Just what?"

"Stubborn. You two are so similar." A small chuckle falls from her lips.

Similar? Dad and I? Is she joking, or is she just incredibly high?

"Yeah, right."

"You both are so guarded by your feelings, it's nerve-racking."

Before she can go on with this silly idea, I cut her off. "Mom, what was your dream?"

"What?" she asks surprised.

"Your dreams? Didn't you have any dreams or hopes? You couldn't have envisioned your life as being a mother of a head case."

"First, I told you I hate when you refer to yourself as crazy, and second I wouldn't change this life for anything in the world. The queen of England could offer me her seat on the throne, and I would say no. Patrick Swayze could rise from the grave and ask me to be his wife… although, that one I would probably choose."

I can't stop my laugh.

Mom smiles. "There we go. I like when you laugh."

"But didn't you dream of anything before you had me and Clara?"

She smiles. "Yes, I did. I wanted to be a dancer."

"Were you good?"

"I wasn't bad," she responds. I can almost see her memories, just by the way she smiles and closes her eyes.

"Why did you stop?"

"I met your father, and then I had Clara and then you. My family became my life."

"And you were satisfied with that?"

"More than anything."

"Mom, did I ruin yours or Dad's life?"

Her jaw falls open. "What?"

"Did I ruin your lives? Dad told me he had dreams to open up a car shop, but then my insanity got worse, and he stopped enjoying cars. I ruined his love of cars. Am I a… *monster*, Mom?"

"No. You're not a monster. You're wonderful, Jess. You're perfect."

She throws her arms around me and pulls me close to her and continues to repeat, "You're not a monster." In my mom's arms, I feel so safe and warm. I don't know why, but I begin to cry, and I can't stop the tears flowing as they soak her T-shirt. My sobs continue as she rubs my back in large circles and says, "Mom is here." I know the sight is juvenile, but this is what I needed. Sometimes all a boy needs is his mother. Norman Bates would agree with me.

She kisses my forehead and looks at my tearstained face. "Jess you didn't ruin anything. You hear me? You didn't ruin a damn thing. Your father stopped with cars, not because *that* was his passion. He loved cars because he was able to do it with you. *You* were his passion."

I nod, unable to find the words. It feels like a hand is grasping at my throat, making me unable to speak. So I answer with a low sob.

My way of saying okay, I understand. I hug my mother once more, feeling like a newborn waiting for milk.

"Mom, sometimes I just hate being the way I am. I'm so embarrassed over my condition and—"

She cuts me off. "Jess, you should *never* feel embarrassed or hate who you are. You are wonderful, and you are my son. I am proud to be your mother."

She kisses my forehead and says she'll fix me up a cup of tea. I nod and smile, and she closes the door behind her. I stand up, taking off my thick black-framed glasses and wipe the tears away. I look into the mirror to see my reflection with my red eyes. I look like a fucking mess.

I meet my mom in the kitchen, and she hands me a cup of tea. We sit there in silence and sip our teas. The warmth I feel from the tea and just being here with my mom overcomes me. I pull the hood of the zip-up hoodie I'm wearing up over my head. I love my hoodies. They make me feel safe in some way. They're my own personal security blankets.

It's funny how I sit here with my mom, and it's like these past couple of days haven't happened. I feel good again.

I almost feel whole.

I almost feel normal.

Normalcy is something I've always strived for. I'm close to getting there. I know it. I can feel it. I just wish I could totally feel normal now. I don't want to feel like I'm going to fall apart into a million pieces every moment of the day. Some days, I just want to grab a blade and harm myself once more to stop those thoughts.

When I would cut, it never started with the blade. That was always the destination. It always started with a thought. A million thoughts flying through your mind. Racing, faster and faster. Then that thought turns into an itch. It's like everything is itchy and you just can't scratch it. Your head is itchy and your arms. And you keep scratching until you dig your fingernails deep into your skin. But that isn't where the itch is. It's the mind. Your mind is so itchy, and you can't get to it… so that is when you grab the blade. The blade is the final point of the cutting process. That is when you finally grab the blade and you hold it in your fingers and you bring it to your flesh and cut. You cut, hoping to get rid of that itch finally. You cut to feel something. Or you cut to feel nothing.

The sensation drowns everything out until nothing matters anymore. All that matters is the pain.

That sweet, glorious pain, which you welcome like an old friend. The truth is that pain became my best and closest friend.

Now how do you cut off a friendship like that?

CHAPTER SIXTEEN

CHRISTMAS IS no longer in the air. The other houses have taken down their decorations. Usually after the holiday ends, you can still feel it, but I believe I've caught the last whiffs of the Christmas air.

I am lying in my bed, and I look over to my nightstand to see my cell phone still sitting there. After tea with my mom, I just went back upstairs to my room to relax and think. Usually thinking is bad for me, but now, that is all I want to do. Be alone with my thoughts. But I notice a name on my cell phone, and I smile at the sight of the letters that spell out Adam. I'm getting way too used to seeing this on my phone every day.

I read his text wishing me a good morning. It was sent while I was walking around.

Hello Adam!

Jess, you're finally awake! Let's do something tonight after therapy!

Shit. I forgot that was tonight. Dr. Wheeler will have a field day with me tonight after these two days of an emotional whirlwind.

Yeah, that sounds great.

My uncle Martin is going to cook dinner, and he wants to meet you :)

Oh shit.

Yay!

Oh shit.

It's meet-the-parents time… well, the uncles. This is going to be the night his uncles decide I'm not good enough for their adorably perfect and *sane* nephew.

You don't have to wait around for me after therapy. I'll come and pick you up. This is SO EXCITING! :D

I'm excited too, I will my fingers to type.

I'm such a fucking liar. My heart is beating so fast that I'm afraid I might actually go into cardiac arrest. And it's still early in the day. How the hell am I going to make it through the day to survive tonight?

Geez, my mind is a strange place. One moment I'm having a near–mental breakdown (again), and then the next moment I'm worrying over meeting my boyfriend's—still gushing—family. What is wrong with my mind? Well, at least this is a normal freak-out. I strive to be normal, and this is what normal people think about.

I tear through my closet realizing that I have nothing that is good enough to meet a boyfriend's family. All I see are T-shirts, hoodies, and cardigans. I grab a new button-up shirt I bought with Jill and pair it with a nice cardigan and a pair of my cleanest skinny jeans.

As the day goes on, my fingers fidget, and I play with my hair. I just can't get it to go right, so I end up grabbing a black knit hat— my favorite one—and I let it slouch in the back. Tommy would call this my pretentious hipster look, especially with my glasses. It's been days, and I still haven't heard from Tommy. I've tried texting and calling him a few times, and not once has he answered. Alex has had the same problem. I just hope he's okay. Sometimes I'm so selfish about my own problems and my illness, I forget about other people's problems. I can be a real shit friend.

I grab my phone and dial his number, but I am met by the ongoing ringing. At least his phone is on, so he must want to answer. If he truly didn't want to speak to anyone, wouldn't he turn his phone off and send every message straight to voice mail? I do end up there, and I leave a message, hoping this will be the time he finally calls me back. I've called him thirteen times, and I've sent him thirty-three texts since I last saw him with Alex. Not one has gone answered.

I pocket my phone and sigh. How do you get someone to talk to you, when all they do is pretend to be tough? Tommy and I are so much alike in that aspect. He pretends to be so tough like he needs no one, and I pretend like I don't care. Of course we need someone— maybe more than anyone else out there. I know it. But neither of us would ever admit it aloud.

I guess I know what I'm talking about to Dr. Wheeler tonight. But is it bad that my mind instantly goes back to Adam? No matter how much I think about other problems, my mind is like a rubber band. You stretch it and stretch it, but it flies right back.

By the time I need to leave for therapy, I've brushed my teeth four times and have had six cups of tea to get my nerves to settle down. My mom used to say: "Nothing a good cup of tea can't solve." Well, Mom, this is one of those times. My nerves are racing faster than a NASCAR track.

I sit in the office, with Dr. Wheeler in her seat. Every session begins the same—us in silence for about thirty seconds before she finally asks what my thoughts and feelings were for the whole week. It never gets easier for me. This is so much harder than it sounds, because she believes that if we can track our thoughts and feelings, we may be able to pinpoint the exact moment our depression kicks in or gets worse. My depression, I have no idea what it stems from. I'm just always sad and always have been. Trying to pinpoint why I'm depressed is like trying to find the hipster in a room full of the homeless. So every time I'm stuck here with nothing to say. The therapy and the pills help, but sometimes I do wonder if it is a waste of time.

"You're quiet tonight, Jess."

I look up and shrug. My mom says shrugging is a bad habit, which I should learn to stop. I always shrug in response.

"A lot has been going on."

"Like what, Jess?"

That is one thing I notice she does. She uses my name a lot. I guess it's her way of trying to make me feel comfortable. Honestly, the amount she uses my name just makes me feel like I'm going to vomit.

"I still haven't heard from Tommy."

"Why do you think that is?"

"I don't know. He just won't talk to anyone. Something did happen with my dad, though."

"What is that?"

I go on to tell her everything that took place inside my head, detailing every whirlwind of emotion that slapped me across the face. And as I finish, she asks the million-dollar question every therapist asks many times until you want to take the question and bury it alive to die a slow, painful, agonizing death.

"How did that make you feel?"

Really? What is it about that question that pisses me off so much? Is it because the answer is usually very obvious? Or is it the way she asks? Or maybe it's just a stupid thing to ask. Every time I hear that question, it just sounds so condescending. How does that make you feel? Really? How the hell do you think it makes me feel? Obviously I feel grand that I felt like I ruined my father's favorite hobby.

"I'm okay" is what I say instead.

Dr. Wheeler is a good person. She's just aggravating sometimes with the way she speaks and questions everything. I get that it's her job and all, but geez.

"Just okay?" she pressures on.

I shrug. "Yeah, I guess."

"What are you hiding? You know these sessions are to help you. They aren't for me, Jess."

Except you get paid a hefty paycheck, but I don't say that.

"I know. I feel guilty, I guess."

"Why do you feel guilty? Is it because of your father?"

"Yeah, of course. I basically ruined something he loved doing."

"Your mother said that he loved cars because of his time with you. He lost enjoyment not because you ruined it, but because he was worried over you. I think your father just wanted you to be okay."

She sounds like my mom now. I know they're right, but I still feel guilty. I can't stop that hand of guilt crushing me until I feel like I'm nothing but dust. How is someone supposed to just forget what they did to their own father?

"Does that make sense?"

I nod.

"How is the medication working? Is it still helping?"

"Yeah, I believe so."

"Any thoughts about harming yourself again?"

Yes.

"No."

Liar.

She looks at me, and I can see from her look that she knows I'm not telling her something. It's not that I've harmed myself. It's normal for someone to still think about it—right? I think back to the blade, which I still keep hidden in my nightstand. No one knows about it, and no one will ever find out about it. After my stay at the hospital, I told my mom I threw the blade out. The truth is I kept it for just in case. A part of me cannot be without it. I feel this gravitational pull to it. It's like I need it.

"Jess, if you ever feel the need to harm yourself again, do you have anyone to talk to?"

"Of course. Loads of people I can talk to."

Well, not really. Most people don't understand.

She grabs a piece of paper and quickly writes something down. I take it and see ten digits. I'm going to take a wild guess and say this isn't her social security number.

"If you need someone to talk to, you can call me anytime. That's the number to my cell phone. I always have it on me. Good night, Jess, and I really do mean you can call me anytime."

"Thank you."

I leave the office and find my father in the waiting room with a book. He looks up and asks how it went, and I say fine. The usual conversation between us. In the car we are always silent.

"So your mother says you're seeing that friend of yours tonight?"

Usually silent.

"My *boyfriend*. Adam is my boyfriend. Yeah. I'm going over to meet his uncle."

"Are you excited?"

"Yeah."

"He seems nice. I hope he makes you happy."

I look over at my father, who keeps his face so stiff.

"He does, Dad. Thank you."

He pats my shoulder, and we spend the rest of the drive home in silence. Outside on the front porch, Clara sits in her winter coat and has her cell phone plastered to her ear. She looks serious, and as I get out of the car, she whispers into the phone and puts it down.

"Hey, Jess." She smiles.

"Hey, is everything okay?" I ask, pointing at the phone.

"Oh yes. Don't worry."

Yeah, right. Telling me not to worry is like telling a zombie not to eat flesh.

"Okay."

I enter the house, and I hear my sister start talking again before Dad shuts the door. I wonder who she is on the phone with. It sounds like something is wrong, and now I hope I haven't been so selfish to not notice something is going on with my sister as well.

I sit on my bed with my door open and it feels like forever before I finally hear Clara walking up the stairs, even though I know it's only been about twenty minutes. She stops at my door and smiles, her long dark hair falling in waves past her shoulders.

"Everything okay?" I ask.

"Of course. I was just on the phone with a friend. He's having a problem."

"That's all?"

"That's all."

She enters my room and sits on my bed, putting her arm around me. I rest my head on her shoulder. She strokes my hair, something she used to do when we were children. It used to relax me. Good news: it still works.

"Mom tells me you're going out with your *boyfriend* tonight," she says. She can't contain her smile as she drags out the word boyfriend. I can't stop my smile either as she mentions the word.

"She seems to be telling everyone."

"I think she is just as excited as you are, honestly. She was telling me about it as you were out all night."

"Oh my gosh."

But then I laugh, and so does my sister, and it's a joyous moment. A free moment, one of the few I have. I don't think of the blade or my pain or my sadness. I can only think of my family and how good I feel.

The sound of the doorbell resonates, and Clara's smile grows.

"Go get him, Tiger."

I smirk at her and run downstairs. Before Mom can open the door, I'm there, and I tear it open. Before me stands Adam looking as adorable as ever. His light brown hair is nicely styled, and he wears a button-up shirt with a nice vest, which clings to his toned body, and a pair of tight jeans.

"R-r-r-ready to, to go?"

"Yes."

As I look up into his gray-blue eyes, all my anxiety and fear just seem to evaporate, leaving only excitement and fondness. He smiles that famous smile of his, and he takes my hand in his.

"Have fun," my mom calls out.

"Thank you," I respond.

I stop and let go of Adam's hand, and I run back, throwing my arms around my mother. She stands there stunned and finally hugs me back.

"I love you," she whispers into my ear. "Now go have fun."

I smile at her, and I return to Adam's hand, having already missed it after being gone for a few seconds. He opens my passenger door, and I slip in, noticing that my family is still watching from the window. I shoo them away with my hand, but they don't listen. I just hope Adam doesn't notice.

"They, they s-s-s-s-seem ex-excited."

A deep red-hot blush rushes to my cheeks, and I try to focus on something, anything to erase my embarrassment. I end up focusing on the strawberry scent of his car. I've always loved the smell and taste of strawberries. As a kid I was strange. I never liked the taste of chocolate, but I loved fruit, and strawberries are one of my main weaknesses. Now I'm wondering if Adam knew this or if this is some random, wonderful coincidence.

The drive takes a bit longer than usual, but then I remember we're not going to his apartment. We're going to his uncle's house. We drive in silence, but it's a comfortable silence. He keeps one hand on the wheel and the other clasped in mine. I smile at the feeling of his warm hand and at the beautiful sky outside. It's a clear night, so I am able to see every star and every constellation. To be honest, I've never been able to understand how some people could just point out constellations. I've never been able to find one in my entire life. I look up hoping to find one, but they are all just a bunch of stars, millions of beautiful glowing dots in the sky. They're so beautiful and are always just there, with no worries or pain. I'm envious of the stars.

The car finally stops outside a small one-story house toward the edge of town. We get out, and he leads me to the front door. His hand never once leaves mine and as we stand at the front door, the panic begins to set in once again.

"Ow."

I look down to see that I'm crushing Adam's hand so tight it's turning white.

"Sorry."

"Ner-nervous?"

I nod, not wanting to say how I'm feeling.

"D-don't be. He'll love-love you."

He turns to the door and knocks. I'll be fine. It'll be fine. What am I so nervous about anyway? I'm meeting Adam's uncle. I'm just meeting his uncle. I'm just meeting the family that could despise me and ruin all my chances with Adam. I'm just meeting the man who may make Adam realize I'm not worthy enough of his affection.

Yeah, I'm not fine.

The door opens, and a man in his early fifties stands there. He has a sweet smile on his lips, and has dark brown and gray hair. His thin face kind of reminds me a bit of an older Anderson Cooper, if he had still had some color in his hair. He wears a nice button-up shirt and a pair of khakis.

"You must be Jess. I'm Adam's uncle, Martin Anders. Come in."

He steps aside, and Adam leads me into the small, simple home. Pictures of Adam and their family decorate the walls. I see one of a young boy, obviously Adam. You can tell by the big lopsided grin on his face, which shows too much teeth. He sits outside on a park bench with two attractive people. They are all smiles, and you can tell they're midlaughter. He looks like the woman in the photo, but he has the man's smile. I know these are his parents.

Martin leads us into a living room, where the walls are painted a light green and the carpet is a cream color. We sit in front of a nice brick fireplace, where a fire is already roaring on. Adam takes my coat and sits beside me on the matching green couch. Martin sits in an armchair on the other side of a mahogany coffee table. He puts one leg over the other and continues to smile.

"So Jess, Adam was telling me all about you."

Oh gosh, I hope not.

"Oh, yeah? He talks a lot about you too, Mr. Anders."

"Martin, please call me Martin."

"Martin," I say with a smile.

There is something comforting and warm about him. He reminds me a bit of my mom. I don't know if it is the way he talks with that soft voice or his welcoming smile, but there is something about him that makes me feel less scared.

"So Jess, you work in a bookshop I hear?"

"I do. It's nice."

"Do you love it?"

"I do. It's incredibly quaint and lovely. I love to be around books. It's like I'm at home there."

"That's fantastic. My partner, Max, used to work in a bookshop when he was younger too."

"That's nice," I respond. "Which one?"

"Oh it was years ago, back when he lived in New York. It was in the early eighties."

I smile as he begins to tell the story of how he met his partner. They've been together since 1993 and met while they were both waiting in line for coffee. It's a cute story that brings a smile to my face, and as I look around the home, I can easily envision my future life like this. Maybe with Adam by my side?

"So where is Max?" I ask.

"Oh, he's visiting his parents for the night. His father had a bad fall, so he wants to be with them for a little bit. He's the one who usually cooks, so I attempted cooking earlier, but sadly I've made a mess of the whole dinner. Would you boys like to order Chinese food?"

I laugh and tell him that's okay. Chinese food is my favorite, so I'm definitely more than okay with this. We order tons of Chinese food in little white boxes, and we just eat and talk at the kitchen table. I can't state the amount of laughter that escapes me over the course of the evening. Adam's uncle is one funny guy. He tells us all these stories about when he was young and all the crazy things he would do. When he was a teenager, he once followed a band across the entire country. His parents were so angry with him when he got back, they grounded him for an entire year. Underneath the table, as his uncle speaks, Adam takes my hand in his, and the moment is pure perfection.

Neither my illness nor my stay in the hospital is ever mentioned, and I am thankful for that. I just don't want to be forever known as the man who stayed in a mental hospital. I always ask to be normal, and this night I finally get my wish.

As we finish dinner, we vacate to the living room, where Martin puts another log on the fire.

"Jess, do you plan to go back to school?"

What did Adam tell him? Did he tell him the entire reason I dropped out?

"Maybe, I don't know. I'm figuring everything out with my life to be honest right now. I'm at a weird fork, and I just don't know which direction I should take. One is telling me to do one thing, while another is telling me to do the exact opposite." What is it about Martin that makes it so easy to open up to him?

All he does is smile and say, "You'll figure it out in time. We all do."

"Thank you."

The door opens, and an attractive man, probably in his forties, with light sandy blond hair and beard stubble walks in. He is about my height and wears a pair of wire-framed glasses and a nice tailored suit. He walks up to Martin and kisses him on the lips. I'm going to go out on a limb here and say this is Max.

"I'm so happy to see you, Adam, and you must be Jess. It's a pleasure to meet you. I'm Max." He shakes my hand and smiles down at me.

"Nice to meet you, Max."

He sits down on Martin's legs, and I can't stop my smile; the way they look at one another, it's like they couldn't imagine anyone else ever in the other's place. All I see is pure happiness. I've always wanted to know what it is like to be happy, and now I finally see what it looks like. This is what I aspire to be in life.

Happy.

AFTER DINNER, Adam takes me to a small bedroom that his uncles keep for him for the occasions he stays over. The bed is a small twin-size one with *Doctor Who* sheets, and his light green walls are riddled with all different science-fiction movies and television show posters.

"Cute room," I state with a smirk.

"Sh-sh-sh-shut up."

He has a huge smile on his face, which just seems to radiate with gaiety. He brings me over to his bed, and we sit as close to each other as we can, without actually sitting on one another's laps.

"I like the *Doctor Who* sheets," I jest. "I thought your uncle only moved here a couple years ago. This looks like you've been here since you were a child."

Adam blushes. "He d-d-d-did only m-m-move here a c-c-c-couple years ago. I'm v-very c-c-c-cool, you know."

"Sure. And you still are," I say before I break out into a laugh.

"Are you ha-having a good n-night?"

"Definitely. Your uncles are amazing, Adam."

"They are, are my entire f-f-family."

"Adam, what happened to your parents?"

The moment the question falls out of my mouth, I berate myself. Stupid, Jess, stupid. The smile on his face drops, and he looks away, casting his eyes on the ground.

"You don't have to answer. I'm sorry. I didn't mean to ask. It was stupid and personal, and I don't want you to be uncomfortable. We can talk about something else. So I see you have a *Doctor Who* poster. That's fantastic."

"It's o-okay. They, um, they d-died in, um," he starts, but then it's like his words fall into nothing. Oblivion. He looks away, but I catch a glimpse of how destroyed he looks.

"Oh, you don't have to go on. I'm stupid."

"It's okay. I-it w-was a c-c-ar accident. I-I was f-f-four. I w-was the only s-s-s-s-survivor of-of the crash."

"I had no clue. I didn't mean to bring it up. I'm so sorry. I feel like a complete asshole. I'm sorry, Adam. I really—"

Before I can finish my long apology, which he deserves, his lips are crashing onto mine, and we're kissing. I just close my eyes, and I focus on the feeling of his warm lips and his hands on my back, where his fingers play with the hem of my shirt, and I shudder at the feeling of his touches there. His fingers trace lines up and down my spine as if he is writing out words or playing connect the dots with the freckles on my back. Each finger feels like a magnificent artist's brush, and I'm his canvas.

A moan slips from my lips as the kiss deepens, and his tongue sneaks into my mouth. Damn, his lips just feel too good. Between his hands and his lips, I might just lose it too soon.

"I-I r-r-really like you, J-Jess," he whispers as he finally breaks the kiss.

"I like you too."

He holds me close, his hands still under my shirt, and we fall back onto his bed, which just forces us to cuddle up close. I look over onto the small nightstand by his bed to see a tiny pile of books. Right at the top is *Peter Pan.*

"This was my favorite story as a kid. My mom used to read it to me all the time. It's so sad."

"S-s-s-sad? *Peter Pan?*"

"Well yeah," I say. "It's about a boy who basically runs from his problems and won't face them."

"What d-d-do you m-mean? It's s-s-s-such a fun s-s-s-s-story of adventure and s-s-s-s-strength."

"*Peter Pan* is the ultimate tale of running away from your problems. I mean, just look at it. This young boy doesn't want to grow up, so he runs away to Neverland, a world where he never has to deal with everyday problems such as age or taxes. He gets to be young forever, and he gets to have fun and never get wrinkly or old. He never has to do adult things like pay his bills or get a job... or get married."

"What's wrong w-w-with marriage and, and l-love? That can be f-fun... b-b-beautiful, even." Adam responds back. He looks at me with those big round eyes of his, and I get lost in them. His childlike innocence always amazes me.

"Love is the most painful part of being an adult."

Love is what can hurt someone. Falling in love or having my heart broken can ruin me and force me back into the darkness, and then I might never ever be able to escape.

Adam looks at me sadly and kisses my forehead. "The w-world is a, a place of pain, trust m-me I know. I-I lost a lot, but l-l-l-love is worth it. Even if, um, it does hurt in the end, everything b-b-b-b-before it is, is w-worth it."

It's at this moment I realize love is like a novel. It's all these words and pictures and little marks that are thrown together. It doesn't make sense until you read the whole thing and then it all comes together. I know that, because that is what I'm feeling right now.

I am in love with Adam Foster.

CHAPTER SEVENTEEN

AFTER ADAM took me home, he kissed me good night at the door, and I was met by my mom and sister on the other side. They both asked me a million questions about how the night went, and I told them everything. Well, almost everything. They don't need to hear about the mind-blowing kiss we shared or the fact that I'm in love with Adam.

I'm in love with Adam. I spend all this time trying not to get attached, and here I am attached to the most wonderful man I've ever met. I guess it doesn't matter if you try to run from your feelings, because they always catch up to you.

And now I'm lying in bed, and I can't stop thinking about everything that transpired last night, from learning about his parents to his wonderful uncles and especially down to that kiss, which might have literally taken my breath away.

But am I really in love with Adam? Or do I only think I am? I mean, I have never actually been in love before, so I could just think I'm in love. That happens to people all the time. It once happened to Tommy when we were in high school. He was hooking up with this girl, a hot blonde, and he thought he loved her. She ended it with him, and he said he was heartbroken but then a week later he was into another girl. Is that what this is?

I finally get out of my bed and dress in a tight green T-shirt and my favorite blue hoodie. I put my hood over my head, and I tell my mom I'm going to work. The sun is already shining outside, and it feels good. I'm able to walk outside with my hoodie open and with a smile on my face.

The feeling of *possibly* being in love is new to me. My heart is beating a million miles per minute the moment I think of Adam, and it's both glorious and utterly frightening.

The bookshop has a small group of people, and Laurie is working behind the cash register with her curly, dark hair tied back in a ponytail.

"Hey, Jess," she says with a little shy wave.

"Hello, Laurie. How are you?"

"I'm well. You seem like you're happy."

"Oh that I am. I'm exquisite."

I really am too. I'm not *fine*. I'm honestly doing well right now. Right now, my favorite word needs to be used, because I am exquisite.

The bell jingles, and I see Alex come in. The last time I saw him was the failed mission to see Tommy. I wave to him, and he walks over, a frown plastered to his face.

Oh no.

"What's wrong, Alex?"

"Still no word from Tommy?"

I shake my head. "You?"

"He hasn't been home in two weeks."

"Two weeks? What? How did you find out?"

"I tried calling his house, and his father picked up, drunk as usual, and I quote 'that no-good son of mine hasn't been around in a week and a half.' I'm getting really worried. I went around to his usual hangouts, but I haven't seen him. No one seems to know where he is, or at least no one will tell me where he is. Jess, I'm really freaking out here."

I put my hand onto the desk with the cash register, because if I don't I might fall to the ground. This can't be. This isn't the first time Tommy has run from home. When we were sixteen, he was gone for over a week. It turns out he took some of his father's money and was riding from train to train and sleeping in them and then exploring by day. He told me about all the towns he went to and how no one knew who he was. In each town, he would tell strangers something new. Each day he was reborn and a new person was alive for twelve hours, until he died and another man took his place. I remember being envious of his adventures.

And now I'm frightened.

Where has Tommy run off to this time? He is always searching for action; I just hope he didn't find it from the wrong place or people. Images of him stabbed to death outside a seedy bar spring to my mind, and now I hope these images don't come true.

"Jess, I'm sorry to spring this on you all of a sudden. I just felt you should know too."

"You just don't want to be the only one worried to death."

"That too."

We stand there in silence. That's the first time I realize Laurie has quietly slipped away. Another great thing about Laurie is that she never pries into other people's business. If something doesn't involve her, she always slips away without a sound. She should really consider being a spy or something. She is so small and unassuming; no one would expect her to be one.

"Well, I have to go. I'm helping my parents out today with chores, and I need to buy a new broom. I haven't seen you in forever. I miss you, Jess. I'll text you soon. Promise."

And just like that, he is out the door. I know he's been avoiding me as much as he can. Alex won't tell me the truth. I might be crazy, but I'm not an idiot. I notice things. People never seem to realize that with me. My mom has been trying to make my stay at home so much easier and happier, but she definitely sugarcoats everything. If something is bothering her or something bad is going on, she'll make sure to keep me out of the loop, even if it is something as trivial as not having enough money for something. Hiding things won't protect me; it just hurts me more. I already know how unfair the world can be. I've lived through it all.

The world is a fucked-up place.

Yeah, I tried to kill myself, but that's only one person. There are genocides going on in other countries that no one talks about, and murderers get away each and every day. In school systems children are being bullied so relentlessly they turn into me, and people are raped out there all the time. Innocent people are hurt, and the bad get away. So yeah, I know how the world works.

It's a shame they don't tell us from an early age how much the world and other people can ruin you. Or how much you can destroy yourself. I know that last lesson way too well.

"Hey, are you okay?" Laurie asks in her birdlike voice.

"Yeah, sorry. I got lost in my thoughts."

"Okay. You can talk to me, if there is anything you need."

"Thank you, Laurie."

She gives me a small smile and says she'll do the cash register. It turns out Peter is in his usual place, the office. Laurie tells me how she saw him with a full bottle of Jack Daniels this morning, and he hasn't come out of his office since then.

The workday goes by pretty smoothly. We get a steady stream of customers, and I am never bored. Laurie and I manage to converse and laugh while she is ringing people up. I spend most of the day texting with Adam, who is playing around with his violin. That is not a euphemism. I still need to see him play. Again, not a euphemism, although I don't think I'd mind that.

Jess, get your mind out of the gutter.

Images of Adam shirtless run through my head. I can feel the sweat trickle down my neck as I think of his strong, muscular body and those biceps. I don't get how it is possible for someone to look that good and be that sweet. If God is out there, then he really broke the mold crafting such a beautiful human being. I used to spend my days thinking about my favorite words or how to get further in *The Legend of Zelda*—never did beat the game... any of them, actually. I'm quite awful at video games—and now all I have on my mind is Adam, beautiful Adam.

Sweet *and* beautiful Adam, the man who is perfect for me. Even the thought of him brings a dopey grin to my face. The idea of Adam could get me through the worst pain manageable. He could help me survive being lost in the woods for weeks with little food and water and fighting against savage cannibals, all because he gives me strength.

Day turns to night, and the customers become sparser. I end up sitting in the corner and reading toward the end of my shift. When it comes time to close up the shop, Laurie counts the money, and I start cleaning up the shop. Sometimes I wonder why I bother cleaning up. It's only going to get trashed again the next day. People have no respect for those in retail or for the merchandise. The worst is when I'm organizing the shelves of books and a customer is watching me do that, and the moment I walk away, I see them go through the books and place them in the wrong order. It's sickening how some people treat literature.

Laurie finishes counting the money, and I finish cleaning up the store. We're getting ready to lock up and leave for the night when the sound of mumbling catches our ears. We sneak toward the office to find the pathetic sight of Peter on the ground crying and talking to no one. A fallen bottle of Jack Daniels sits by his side as he lies in the pool of alcohol, and the stench of urine stains the air. A big wet spot is drawn down the leg of his jeans. I have to hold back the bile in my throat as I gag at the wretched smell.

"Oh my God, we need to take him home." Laurie's voice is soft, and she shows no hint of disgust on her face. Then there is me covering my face with the collar of my shirt, because the smell is just too much, and the sight is just too awful. I guess that is what makes her a good person and me a bad one.

There goes Laurie, showing her compassion. One thing I love about her is that her compassion isn't forced or fake. It's completely true. Laurie looks on and sees someone in need of help, while I look at this creature and see nothing more than a pathetic old man in need of a shower and a good shave. A haircut would be good for him too. His stringy hair is getting long and looks full of grease.

"I'll take him home," I respond. I don't want her to have to deal with taking a drunken man home. She is too good for that.

"Are you sure?"

"Yeah, Laurie. You go home and get some sleep. I'll deal with the issue at hand."

She hugs me good-bye, and I try to lift the fucker up, but he is just a pile of sweaty fat on the floor. Gross.

"Geez, Peter. Where are your keys? I'm driving you home."

I hate driving, but no way am I going to walk him home. I bite back my disgust and go through his pockets until I pull out the silver ring holding his keys. Even his keys smell of piss and liquor. I try to lift him up.

"Come on, Peter."

And I have him follow me into the car. Well, it's more like I force him to the car. I'm holding him up with all the strength I have got. I'm a skinny guy with *very* little muscle, but I think I just got the best work out of my life. Trying to give me directions to his house is no less of a chore. We pull up to a small one-story house with chipped yellow paint, and I fumble with his keys to find the one for the front door. I hear Peter begin to sob in the car.

What is wrong with him now?

"Peter, what's going on?" I ask him.

He doesn't answer. I pull him out of the car, and I get him into the house. The house is a complete mess, but pictures cover the walls. The pictures are of a young girl. I wonder who she is. Is this girl a family member of his? She is a cute girl, very young, with long, straight pale blonde hair and a pair of big, light blue eyes. Her smile seems to take over her face, and in one picture she wears a pink dress with a picture of a fairy on the front. She looks so innocent and happy.

Peter takes one look at the pictures and he falls to his knees. "My Sharon. Oh God, why?" He brings his hands to his face and sobs. I am shocked at the sight. Not of Peter drunk and crying, but him crying over the young girl. What is her connection to him, and why does he care so much? That is when it clicks with me. Sharon… is his daughter. She looks no older than six years old in the photos, and I have no idea what happened to her, but I know she isn't with him anymore.

"Where is she?" I can't stop my mouth.

Stupid, Jess, stupid. I berate myself as Peter crumbles apart even further than before. His whole face seems to be melting away.

"She's in heaven with the angels and the Heavenly Father. Her mother left me shortly after… she couldn't handle my grief. It's like she didn't care about our baby," he says through choked sobs.

I can't form any words as his sobs drown out the silence of the night. I close my eyes and cover my ears to stop the noise, but even his sobs can pierce through my manufactured barrier. I open my eyes and cast them down on him. He brings his hands up to his face and just continues to cry. The disdain I had before washes away, and sympathy takes its place. He lost so much and has so little. I would be the same way.

But aren't I the same already?

As I stare down at the man on the floor, I no longer see a pathetic old man. He isn't pathetic… he's me. He's incredibly sad, and like me he drowns his sorrows, although he takes a different path than I once did… but this could still be me. I no longer pity the man, because how can one pity someone for being sad? I am a sad man. In ten, twenty, thirty years, I could be him.

Just a man living so deep in pain, he becomes lost in his own sorrows.

Not being able to take the sight, or my own feelings anymore, I help Peter to his bed and tuck him in, making sure he is on his side in case he vomits. I don't leave his house right away. After placing his keys on his dresser top, I look around at the pictures in his bedroom. I don't recognize the man in any of them. In them is a man years younger than Peter. There is no sorrow or pain on his face. There is only life and happiness. In all the photos, Peter smiles brightly, and he is with a beautiful woman and an adorable young girl. It's weird how much bereavement can affect a person. It changes you. It changes everything about you.

Before leaving, I place a water bottle by his bedside and a small note, just as Alex once did for me. Walking home, my thoughts stay on Peter. Is this what my future will become? Will I become *that*? The image of me crying drunk and pissing my pants in public places makes me want to vomit and cry right here in the middle of the cold street.

Then my thoughts turn to Richard, the old man who I promised to see again but failed to do so. Again, I'm a terrible person. He's probably still waiting for me to sit down and drink tea and eat scones with him. But he's just like Peter and me. Each one of us has had a tragedy in our lives, and each one of us has reacted differently. Peter took to drinking after his daughter's death and the divorce with his wife, while Richard took a happier path after his wife's death. He tries to live life for her and looks at each day as a blessing, while I took to cutting and suicide because of my mental illness when it became too much for me. But what is it about us that made us choose our paths in life? Why did Richard take a happy route, when Peter and I went the darker way? Peter and I gave into our darkness, while Richard was strong enough to fight it and succeed. What is his secret? Everyone in town thinks Richard is so crazy, but he's not. He's happy, and for many people happy just is not something you see or feel every day. Many pretend to be happy, but Richard really is.

I want to be like Richard.

I FINALLY reach my house, and the first thing I need to do is wash my hands. After holding on to Peter, I still smell his odor on me, and I scrub as hard as I can to try to get rid of it. I finish and walk up to my bedroom and sit on my bed, letting out a long yawn. It's been a lengthy night.

I strip off my clothes and get under the covers and swallow the pills that bring some balance to my life. Most people have God to thank for their well-being, I just have a doctor who prescribes me medication. Bless the medication-friendly doctors of today.

I close my eyes and relax, happy to be in bed after today. But my relaxation doesn't last too long, because my phone begins to vibrate. I ignore it. They can call me back tomorrow. When the phone comes to a stop, I feel the pills taking effect, causing me to become drowsy, and then my damn phone starts to vibrate again. I sit up and grab the phone off my nightstand. A name shines brightly on my phone.

I am stunned and unable to move, but the phone continues to vibrate in my hands, and then I remember you have to hit answer to actually talk to someone.

"Hello?"

"Yo."

CHAPTER EIGHTEEN

I CAN'T believe it. After all this time, Tommy has finally called me back. Does Alex know Tommy is connected with the world again?

"Tommy, where are you? I've been trying to reach you. Alex and I have been worried sick."

"Don't worry, Jess. I've been staying with a friend. I had to get away from my father's house. I ran and took a break from life."

"Who's the friend?" I'm almost afraid to ask.

"That guy, Markus Stills."

Now I'm sorry I asked. Markus Stills is Wilshire's resident, and pretty much only, drug dealer. He is the guy who always supplies Tommy with his pot, and I don't know if I actually trust Tommy staying there with him.

"Markus Stills? Why him?"

"Because he wouldn't ask any questions. He doesn't give a fuck about anyone, and that is what I needed. I love you and Alex, but you guys would ask me too many questions to the point I was uncomfortable. I just needed to disappear for a while, man."

I nod. I know he can't see me, but I understand what he means. Sometimes it's good to disappear and pretend no one knows who you are. I can't state how many times I've wished I could do that in my own life.

"Yeah, I get you."

"Good."

Silence.

"So, how are you? Any dark days?" Tommy asks.

"Only a couple."

"Are you okay?" Fear drips through his words.

"Well, I'm here, aren't I?"

"Yeah, good point."

More silence follows. I know there is so much left unsaid right now, but I won't force him to talk, just like how he never forced me to talk.

"I want to see you soon," I tell him.

"I'll text you the address tomorrow. Good night, Jess."

And then I'm met by silence. I plug my phone in and fall back into my bed. Everything in life is just going crazy. I'm in love. My best friend has run away to a drug dealer's house... what is going on with the world?

The nonstop thoughts make it harder to fall asleep this night, but soon the pills push the thoughts away and allow everything to just become a blurry haze that fades into darkness.

IT'S MIDDAY, and I still haven't received a text from Tommy about his whereabouts. It's been fourteen hours since the phone call, and it has been only silence since. My hands are fidgety, and my foot won't stop tapping. Why hasn't he texted me yet? I hope nothing happened. What if he overdosed last night while with Markus?

I grab my phone and dial his number.

"Hello?" Tommy asks, obviously fatigued.

He just woke up?

"Hey, you never texted me the address."

"I've been asleep. I'll text you it in a moment. Bye."

He hangs up. He's never been a guy you want to wake up. He's been known to be a monster in the mornings. A text finally comes in with the address, followed by a second one: *Let me sleep asshole*

I do just that. I don't text him or call him or bother him. I just let him sleep. He deserves to rest. I slide my phone into the tight pocket of my skinny jeans, and I lie back onto my own bed. I woke up incredibly early and couldn't fall back to sleep, anticipating Tommy's text. I just really want to be there for him. He is a great friend to me and he always knows what I need, so it's time for me to pay back the favor to him. It's time for me to become selfless and to stop using my disease as a reason to ignore others.

I get up and finally leave my bedroom. It's about time. I've been dressed since 9:00 a.m. I find Clara in the kitchen, making herself a late lunch.

"Hey, little brother. Want any lunch?" she asks from the stove.

"What are you making?" I smell blueberries.

"Blueberry pancakes."

I sigh. I don't get the love people have for pancakes.

"Isn't that breakfast?"

"I was craving breakfast for lunch."

"Yeah, I'll have some." I don't want to disappoint her.

"Good. I was planning to make you some anyway. Now make yourself a cup of tea, and sit your butt down at the table. I'm treating you to a *gourmet* lunch today." She holds up her spatula, and I can see the batter sizzling on the pan.

"Yes, *very* gourmet," I say with a smirk.

"Shut up."

We break out into giggles, and I grab my favorite teacup and get my kettle settled beside her pan. When my tea is finished I take it to the table, and Clara hands over a plate of delicious-smelling blueberry pancakes. I haven't had these in months, not since before my stay in the hospital, and damn I missed even the smell of them.

"Thanks, Clara."

"Of course. I was craving them today."

I take a bite, and I almost orgasm from how good they are. Yeah, they're *that* good. I thank her again, and I basically inhale every last bite.

"Where's Mom?" I ask, when I notice I don't hear anyone else in the house.

"Oh she went to the store to buy some groceries. I thought you and I could spend the day together. Or are you working?"

"Not today," I answer.

Honestly I don't remember if I was working today, but I figured after last night I get a free shot at skipping work today. I don't want to face Peter after what happened.

"Marvelous," she shouts in enthusiasm, "I have such a grand day planned. I was hoping you'd say yes."

Technically I didn't say yes. I just said I wasn't working, but I don't say any of this out loud. I haven't hung out with my sister in so long that it actually sounds exciting. I mean, she won't be home for vacation forever. She does have to go back to school at some point in the next few weeks. I should take up as much time with her as I can before she is back studying for exams and writing nonstop essays again. She should be paid to be an academic, because she is honestly brilliant at it, and she actually loves school. If she could, she would probably do it for the rest of her life instead of getting a job. Getting paid to go to school sounds like a pretty good gig to me.

We finish up lunch, and I tell her I just need to finish getting ready before we head out. I try to brush my mop of hair but quickly give up. There's no point in trying to do anything to it. My hair has a mind of its own and will do whatever it wants. Tommy is the one who told me I have constant sex hair. I always look like I've just finished having the best sex of my life. If only.

I grab my beaten-up Chuck Taylors and my peacoat, and I'm out the door with my sister walking beside me. The sun seems to have melted most of the snow outside, and it doesn't feel like I'm walking on constant slush. I know winter has its fans, but I just want spring to get here already. I've had enough winter to last a lifetime, but I think that every year.

"So where to?" I ask my sister after following her down the sidewalks for a bit.

"I thought we'd just go to the park. We can play that game we used to play."

"The one where we made up stories about strangers?"

Clara and I had this game where we went to the park every week just about, and we would each pick one stranger. We would go on to tell the most elaborate story we could about that person, trying to give them as much backstory as we could and where they were headed in life. It was a fun children's game.

"That's the one. You always were such a good storyteller, Jess. Mom and I used to think you would grow up to become some great novelist."

"Really?"

"Yeah, we did. I still think you will someday. I wish you didn't stop writing. You were so good."

"I was mediocre at best."

I really wasn't that good. I always think about how cool it'd be to be a writer, but I don't even know what I'd write about. I can create a short, lousy story about a stranger in a park, but my imagination isn't grand enough to create an entire novel. I could always write about my life, but that'd just be boring. Who'd pay to read that?

"You were *good*. Now listen to your sister, because she is always right."

"Did you just refer to yourself in third person?"

"Maybe."

"Yeah, I don't take advice from people who talk in third person. It's just plain weird."

"That crazy woman who used to live next door," she starts.

"Margo," I cut in.

"Yes, that's the one. Margo used to do that all the time, and it was so strange. Dad used to say the rudest things about her behind her back."

"He would always call her a crazy old loon who should be put in a home."

"She was nice, though," Clara says.

We come to the park and take our usual seat on the same bench we always sat on as children. The park isn't too crowded. That's what you get for going on a weekday, but I'm okay with that. I prefer not to feel claustrophobic. Sometimes I get overwhelmed when too many people are around. It'll become hard for me to breathe and I sweat profusely.

A woman in her early thirties, and her small dog walk by us.

"You go first," I tell my sister.

"Okay, um, so she is a socialite. She has traveled here all the way from Russia because she has dreams to become a model. She stopped off in Wilshire, though, because her sick cousin is here, and after this she is off to New York to try to live her dream. Her cousin is the heir to a chocolate fortune because his ancestor is the man who invented chocolate." She stops to laugh at her own joke. "And now she is here… but soon she will meet a man who will change her ways and make her a good person. The end."

I give a little clap and see Mrs. Rattree walk by. I haven't seen her since that day in the bookshop when Jill told her off. That was a beautiful moment.

"She always looks so mean," Clara states.

If the Wicked Witch of the West existed, it'd be Mrs. Rattree. She looks like her in the early part of the movie before Dorothy goes to Oz. Now where is a house when you need it?

She looks over, and her fake overzealous smile grows.

"Shit."

"What?"

"She saw us," I answer.

Before anything else can be said, Mrs. Rattree is standing before us. I look up at her old, wrinkly face.

"How are you, Mrs. Rattree?" Clara asks.

"I'm fabulous, my dear," she answers.

"That's good."

"It's nice to see you out and about, Jess. You look healthy. Are those meds of yours doing the job?"

I grip the wooden bench beneath. I need to hold on to something to stop me from pushing the bitch down.

"We're actually having sibling bonding time, I'm sorry, Mrs. Rattree," Clara states in a soft voice. It's a good thing she's here, because I wouldn't be afraid to tell Mrs. Rattree off.

"Oh that sounds wonderful. I always wished I had a sister. I would always have someone to gossip with," she annoyingly says.

Yeah, gossip about me. I wish she would just go.

She looks at her watch and lets out an overdramatic gasp. My guess is that someone punctured a hole in her and she's letting out air. Mrs. Rattree is just a giant bubble of hot air.

"I must go. I have so many things to do. Au revoir."

"Bye," I say, trying to use the harshest tone I could muster.

Mrs. Rattree walks away without looking back. She doesn't even notice how much we didn't want her here. In her imaginary world, no one could ever dare dislike such a "noble and sophisticated" woman like herself.

She can go screw herself.

"Well, she's always an interesting woman."

"More like an annoying woman," I spit out.

Clara seems to almost choke on her giggle, but she regains her composure. Her smile disappears.

"Sorry, that was mean of me to laugh at that."

"Clara, she's a mean woman," I tell her, unable to see how she can ever feel bad for Mrs. Rattree. I don't think anyone in Wilshire cares for the woman.

"I know. I still feel bad for laughing, though."

My sister is always kind to everyone no matter how much of an asshole they are. I pull her into a hug and rest my head on her shoulder.

"You're too nice sometimes."

"And you're too cynical."

"I guess we even each other out," I say with a smirk, and we break out laughing once again. "So I guess it's my turn to pick a stranger now."

I look around the park to find someone good. My eyes focus on a man in a nice suit holding an expensive-looking cell phone up to his ear. I point at him and tell Clara to stay focused on him.

"Okay, his name is John, but it's not his real name. The name is ordinary and plain, because he is on the run. He refuses to tell anyone his true name, in fear of his enemies finding him. He is married, and to protect his wife, he got her into hiding, and now she is safe somewhere in the mountains. He is an ex-spy, and after moving on, one of his enemies is back and is trying to finish the job. 'John' is hiding in this small town, because who would expect him to hide in a small town. He is on the phone with an old spy buddy of his, and he is making plans to meet him tonight to help him out, because tomorrow he's going to go after his enemy so he can see his beautiful wife once again. The end."

Clara quickly claps and smiles. "That was amazing."

I stand up and give a mock bow, laughing. "It was okay. Unoriginal, but it's been a while since I've played."

"It is still much better than what I could ever come up with. Bravo."

We spend the next hour like this going back and forth telling stories, each one getting more ridiculous than the last. When it seems like we have made up stories about everyone, our speech turns into silence, and I just watch the people going about their business. They all seem so into their lives. Some of them have smiles while others look determined. But each person has his or her own life. I always forget that there isn't just one world; there are millions of worlds. Every person lives in a universe of their own making where they are their own god.

"Remember when we were kids and we would go apple picking with Mom?" Clara asks, breaking the silence.

"Yeah. That was fun."

We haven't been in years, though, not since I was in middle school.

"I used to be so terrified of bees," Clara continues.

"And I would tell you to stop being such a baby," I add onto her story.

"And then you got stung by one and you cried. We were forced to go home because of that."

My cheeks grow red. "Yeah, I like to forget about that part of the story."

"But it's such a cute story."

Me being immature, I stick my tongue out at her, and she just laughs. How dare she laugh at my pain. I give her the middle finger, and Clara just continues to laugh, and soon my laughter joins with hers. It's nice to be carefree sometimes.

After our laughter dies, she stands up and looks down at me. She puts out her hand. "Come on, let's go."

She helps me stand, and I walk beside her out of the park.

"Where to now?"

"It's a surprise," she answers with a coy smile. What does she have planned now?

"Oh gosh."

"Don't be scared."

"Can't help it," I respond.

Clara drags me along through the quiet town, keeping a death grip on my wrist. I might be incredibly skinny, but I won't blow away. I run my free hand through my hair and let it fall wherever it wants. Clara halts abruptly, and I almost collide with the sidewalk as I come to a quick stop. Clara lets go of my wrist, and I massage the small ache away. Damn, Clara really has a tight grip.

"We're here."

"Home?"

We stand outside our two-story house with the white paint and blue shutters. Um, okay?

"No. My car. Get in."

"So bossy today."

I get into the car, and she starts driving. She turns on the radio, and each station is playing some tarty blonde pop singer, who uses way too much auto-tune. It's not music; it's pain to the ears. Clara seems to agree because she pulls out a CD and puts it into the small slit above the radio. A soft melody plays out, followed by a sweet voice. This is much better.

"So one semester left," I say to start conversation.

"Don't remind me. It's depressing."

"Aren't you going to grad school?"

"Yeah, I am. Art education."

"You always have everything planned out, don't you?" I ask.

"It's how I am. I don't like being spontaneous. I feel lost when I don't know where I'm going, especially with my life. I'm excited though because next semester I'm going to be student teaching."

"Let's just hope you don't get a classroom of little monsters."

"Jess, shut up. They could be amazing." She has a giant smile on her face, and I know she is imagining something along the lines of *The Sound of Music* where she teaches wonderful children how to sing, or well, in her case, paint.

"You forget how children are. They're cruel little fuckers." And then there is me, ruining all of her dreams about what teaching will be like. I'm good like that.

"You really are a cynical bastard, aren't you?"

"Yeah, I am."

It's true too. I've always been this way. People have always given me a reason to be distrustful of them.

"So where are we going?"

"No matter how many times you ask, I won't tell you."

We pass a sign reading "You Have Left Wilshire." I like where this is going. Where is Clara taking me? I hope this isn't some elaborate plan to murder me or something, because that would really put a damper on this exquisite day.

"So do you like the theater?" she asks in a fake British accent, which is actually quite good.

"Yeah, I do."

"Well, look in the glove compartment."

I open up the small gray door to find two white tickets, and I pull them out. I read the name on them, and it's a play I've never heard of. Something called *The Cause of My Pain.*

"What is it about?"

"I don't know. I read about it online, and it sounded good, so I ordered two tickets for us the other day."

"What if I was working?"

"I would've asked a friend, then, but you were my top choice."

"I feel so special," I kid.

"Oh you are, little brother."

We spend the rest of the car ride singing along to the music and laughing until we finally pull up to a small brick theater. It looks like one of those old-timey movie theaters with the white marquee at the top. *The Cause of My Pain* sits high above in black letters, and I follow Clara inside the building to learn the cause of this unknown person's pain. I wonder if this is a play about torture.

We find our seats in the theater, which isn't too packed, but that is what you get for going to a show at an odd time in the middle of the day. The lights dim, and the people come out onto the stage. A woman sits alone on stage, and she is silent. She just looks at the audience and sighs before erupting into a monologue about her sad and lonely life.

THE PLAY comes to an end, and the small cast is lined up on stage and taking their rightful bows. My sister and I clap in our seats. It's safe to say the play was *not* about a person getting tortured, but it told the story of a woman with depression and how her life just spirals out of control. She loses her boyfriend and stops talking to her family, and the play ends with her committing suicide. In the end she gives a beautiful soliloquy about how her entire life has come to this and how there is no way out. The writer comes onto the stage, and he looks like he is only a college student. I clap even harder as he bows on the stage, and I feel an itch on my face. I go to scratch it only to realize I'm crying. How did I not realize I was crying?

"Are you okay?" Clara asks as she looks over.

I nod, unable to speak. The heroine, Johanna, and her struggles, just mirrored my own life. Her pain was my pain. Her words were my own. I look at the actress on the stage, but I don't see her. I only see the character. It's funny how after you see something, you never see the person behind the role anymore, you only see the character, and they become real to you. They become more real than the actual person. I won't remember the actress's name from tonight, but Johanna will be sketched onto my brain for a lifetime.

Clara and I leave the theater and walk back toward her car.

"So what did you think?"

"I'm just glad it wasn't a musical," I quip. Seriously, I really hate musicals. They just annoy the hell out of me. They're so light and cheery, and it just makes me want to vomit.

"I'm being serious."

"Me too," I respond. "It was really good. Thank you for taking me to see that, Clara."

"I love you, Jess."

"Yeah, I love you too."

We drive back home in silence. I listen to the tranquil wind outside as it whistles against the window. I lean my head against the glass and I take in the serene sounds. I let out a yawn and close my eyes.

I ALMOST jump as I feel a hand on my shoulder, and I look up to see Clara.

"We're home."

Shit. I fell asleep? I nod, everything in my mind too fuzzy to make use of my tongue. I follow my sister into the house as she ties her long hair back into a messy bun, with strands falling out all along the sides of her face.

"Want a cup of tea?" she asks.

"Oh my gosh, yes."

She laughs and tells me to sit in my bedroom. She'll bring up two cups for us. I kick off my shoes and throw my coat onto the floor. I think back on the day, and it was great. I don't get too many days like this with my family because usually something is wrong with me, so I try to cherish the moments I get.

Clara walks in with two cups of tea and hands me mine. I take a sip, and the hot liquid soothes my cold body. She sits down beside me and drinks her tea.

"I had such a good day, Jess." She smiles a wide, sweet smile.

"Me too. Thank you again for today. It was amazing."

"For you, anything. I just want you to be happy. You deserve it."

"You're the best, really," I respond. And she really is.

"So when are you going to formally introduce us to Adam? I know you met his family. When is our turn?"

"Oh you know, I'm just incredibly embarrassed of all of you peasants who are beneath men like us. That is all."

"Oh of course."

We laugh, but she says, "I really want to meet him. Mom was telling me about how she invited him to dinner."

"I'll tell him. I will. Promise."

"Good. I need to make sure he's good for my brother."

She kisses my forehead and says to relax for the rest of the day. That is exactly what I do. I drink my tea and sit back on my bed with a book. I look over at my phone sitting on my nightstand, pick up my phone, and text Adam.

JESS!!! I've missed you today :D

I love how Adam always seems to be an excited child.

I was out with my sister. We saw a play.

Was it good?

It was actually pretty great.

I leave out how much I connected with the play, and I don't tell him about Peter. I want to keep this day going in the lighthearted direction because it's nice to just have a day where everything is great. I finally take a deep breath and send a second text right afterward. I hope I won't regret this one....

Would you like to come over for dinner soon?

I almost want to delete the text as soon as I send it. A part of me just doesn't want to share this magnificent human being with anyone because it's like he's mine, and I don't want him to belong to anyone else. Now that makes me sound like a lunatic. I don't mean I'm going to go all *Misery* on him or anything, but it's nice to know there is a guy out there who cares about me and not another guy.

I'd love to :)

Awesome!

I don't know if I should be afraid or excited about this. I love the idea of him coming to dinner and meeting my family, but I'm also terrified about the idea. What if they don't like each other? Or what if they like each other a bit too much and it becomes kind of weird?

Or what if I'm just crazy and overreacting as usual?

Yep, that sounds about right.

CHAPTER NINETEEN

I SIT in the living room as Mom cooks in the kitchen. She has something nice planned for tonight; for this is the night my family finally meets my boyfriend. My leg shakes as it continues to tap against the carpeted floor, and Clara sits beside me.

"Don't be nervous. I promise to not embarrass you… too much," she jests.

"Thanks a lot."

I look out the window. Still no Adam. I fidget with my fingers in my lap and check my breath. I've brushed my teeth three times in the last hour and a half. I clean my glasses on the bottom of my button-up shirt, and then I play around with my cardigan. What about my hair? It's a mess. I mean it's always a mess, but I wish I could get it to do something tonight.

I hear the sound of a car door, and I jump and I'm out the door. Adam walks up to the porch, and he bends down to kiss me, wrapping his strong arms around my waist.

"Hello," he says as he breaks away from my lips.

"Hello yourself," I whisper, only an inch from his face.

We step apart, and I see that Adam is holding a bottle of red wine.

"I hope th-they, um, like r-r-r-r-red wine. My uncle gave me th-this to b-b-bring over."

"You did good," I reassure him.

I take him in with his bright yellow bow tie and matching sweater. I used to always think bow ties were for children and nerds, but he makes a bow tie sexy. That's the pro of being one of the beautiful people. You can make anything work. He could show up in overalls and still look breathtaking.

I open the front door, and he follows me into the house. My entire family seems to be gathered around the door. Adam fidgets with his bow tie, and I see a tiny spark of nervousness on his face. I grab his hand, and I slightly squeeze it, and it seems to lessen the tension because a tiny smile appears upon his perfect lips.

"Hello, Adam," my mom greets him, walking out of the kitchen with the brightest smile I've ever seen on anyone's face.

"N-n-nice to, to s-s-s-s-see you again, M-Mrs. Hol-Holbrooke." He holds out his hand, but my mom pulls him into a hug, and I can see the surprise on Adam's face. My mom has always been one for hugs. She loves them. My mom seems to find something very intimate and innocent about hugs. I guess I shouldn't tell her I think about hugging Adam naked. That's not so innocent, is it?

She pulls away, and Adam hands her the wine. "Thank you so much, Adam. This is lovely. And please call me Christine."

Clara is next in line of introductions. She doesn't take Adam by surprise with her hug, for she is much more gentle.

"Hello, I'm Clara, his older and wiser sister," she says with a smile and a shake of his hand.

"N-nice to, to m-meet you a-as well."

When Adam flashes his dazzling smile, I'm pretty sure Clara is close to melting to the floor. His smile has a tendency to do that. I've known him for a short while now, and it *still* gets me every time.

Mom turns to me and says, "Your father called before, and he should be home from work soon. He had to work a bit late."

I nod. "Okay. When should dinner be ready?"

"Fifteen minutes?"

"Great. I'm going to show Adam my bedroom real quick."

"Be good," my sister calls as I pull Adam along behind me up the staircase. I'm glad he can't see me because my cheeks are bright red.

I take a deep breath before opening my bedroom door. I don't know why I am so nervous about showing him my bedroom because I've spent the entire day cleaning to make sure it looks good. It's pretty neat, I guess.

"I l-l-like your, um, p-posters."

"Thank you," I say dragging out the "you." Sometimes when I'm anxious, or just being awkward, I have a habit of drawing out words and adding further syllables.

I fiddle with my cardigan as I watch Adam peer at my DVDs and the *many* books lying everywhere in piles around my room. Adam doesn't say anything, and now I'm wishing I had put my books somewhere else. It makes my room look like a mess. Geez, Jess. I look around the room noticing all the spots of dust I missed and that my closet door isn't completely shut, where you can see the mess of clothes I threw onto the floor in there. I did a shit job cleaning, that is for sure.

"You have good t-taste in ho-horror f-f-films."

"Thank you."

Adam turns around and walks up to me. He stands so close I can feel the warmth radiating from his body. He puts his hands in mine and looks down into my eyes.

"Hi," he whispers.

"Hello," I say softly.

His hands travel up my arms, sending a chill throughout my body, and he clutches at my shirt collar and pulls me into a kiss. His lips seem to grasp for mine and teeth crash. I wrap my arms around his lower back, as his hands make their way to the back of my head. He pulls away from the kiss and breathes into the corner of my neck. He pulls me close to the curve of his body like two puzzle pieces coming together. As clichéd as that sounds, it's true. Adam is the puzzle piece I've been looking for all along.

"I've b-b-been w-wanting to, um, do tha-that all day." He speaks just above a whisper.

I hold on to his waist as tight as I can because otherwise I might actually swoon all the way down to the floor. That would be pretty embarrassing. I look up into his gray-blue eyes, and I pull his lips down toward mine. I've already started to miss them. His lips taste like strawberries. Did he put on lip balm before? He should put this on more often because his lips taste delicious. Well, more delicious than usual.

"Dinner."

Adam and I break apart, panting for air and laughing.

"Nothing like your mom's voice to ruin the moment, eh?" I say.

He gives me a small kiss on the lips. "You're s-s-s-so adorable. Now let, let's eat. I'm s-s-s-s-s-starving."

"Okay," I say in between chuckles.

I take his hand in mine, his fingers tangling with mine so superbly. Our hands were made to hold each other.

In the kitchen, Mom has set Adam's place right next to mine as Clara sits on the other side of the table. Mom left Adam's bottle of red wine. She really went all out to make it look like we're one classy family, because you know that's exactly what people think when they see us. Classy.

Adam pulls out my chair and why must he always be ever so charming. It makes me look bad. Clara smirks at me, and I mouth for her to shut up. My mom brings over salads to everyone.

"Caesar. I hope you like, Adam."

"Oh, I l-l-l-love it."

"Enjoy," she states, sitting down next to Clara.

My mom doesn't know how to cook too many dishes, but the few she knows how to cook are fantastic. We're more of a takeout family, usually. Again, we're pure class.

Adam takes a bite. "Th-this is d-d-delicious, M-M-Mrs. Holbrooke."

"It's Christine, and thank you, sweetheart."

"Y-you're welcome, C-Christine."

My mom has a way of putting others at ease. Adam looks over and reassuringly smiles at me, like he is proud of himself. Of what? I'm not totally sure.

The front door opens and slams shut, and my father walks in. He stops at the sight of Adam and looks confused. Mom and I have told him three times Adam was coming over for dinner this week.

"Hi?"

Adam gets up and stands straight, towering over my father. He puts out his hand. "It's n-n-nice to, to officially meet you, Mr. Holbrooke."

"Yeah, nice to meet you too."

Mom gets up and brings over another salad and sets it at the end of the table, where my father sits down.

"Thanks, Christine."

"How was your day, Dad?" Clara asks between bites.

"The boss was up my ass all day today," he grumbles.

"I'm sorry to hear that," I say.

"So Adam, how old are you?" Dad asks, turning his strong gaze onto Adam. I think I see Adam visibly gulp. I grab his hand underneath the table and try to tell him it'll be okay. Too bad he can't read my mind.

"T-twenty-t-t-two."

"I see. My son is nineteen."

"Dad," I complain. "He knows my age."

"Jess, I'm just stating, because he's a bit older than you. So are you in school, Adam?"

"I g-g-graduated in May, b-b-but I-I'm applying t-t-to grad s-s-s-s-school."

"What are you studying?"

How do you make him stop? Is there an off switch or an instruction manual? Something.

"I w-w-want to s-s-study education and be-be a t-t-teacher."

"Any specific subject?"

"Music."

"Do you like children?"

I look over at Clara and try to mouth for help. Clara shrugs and mouths what to do back. Anything.

"I l-l-l-love them."

"That's good."

"So, Dad, what was your boss doing today?" Clara speaks up.

Thank you, I mouth to her. She smiles, and Dad goes on to tell a long and angry story about his boss and how much he sucks. Adam speaks up and says something cool and encouraging, which I know makes my father like him—I can tell by the way my father looks at him. When he doesn't like someone, he tends to squint, as if he's judging you like a popular girl in middle school. Rather, he looks at Adam with interest. Like Mom, he never even looks at Adam's stutter as being unusual.

Mom brings on dinner, which is spaghetti with pesto sauce. It has bits of grilled chicken, tomatoes, spinach, and broccoli. Seriously, it looks amazing, and when I take a bite from it, it tastes even more amazing. I think Mom may have found my new favorite dish.

Conversation goes along smoothly, and it just feels so right. Everything feels as if it belongs this way. Adam and I together and sitting at dinner with my family. I don't even remember why I was so nervous. I look around at everyone's smiles and their laughter. I look over at Adam, who has that big geeky smile, and I could spend a lifetime looking at him and being with him.

AFTER DINNER, Adam and I go back up to my room, and we kick off our shoes, and we just lie in my bed. We don't do anything. We just lie there.

Most couples are so quick to jump right to the sex, but this is perfection right here. My head rests on his chest, and I count each one of his breaths, so happy that he exists and beyond content that he is in my life. My eyes are closed, and there is nowhere I'd rather be than here in his arms.

"Wh-what are you, you dreaming of?" Adam asks, pulling me out of my muted state.

I turn my head and look up into his beautiful eyes. They remind me of an angry ocean during a storm. This is one ocean I'd love to drown in, and I'm not just saying that because I am suicidal.

"Nowhere, Adam. I am dreaming of nowhere. I don't need to dream of anywhere anymore, because I am exactly where I need to be."

He smiles and kisses my forehead.

"M-me too," he breathes into my hair as I nuzzle up closer than before.

My phone vibrates, pulling me away from Adam. I look over at my phone sitting there on my nightstand. Adam pulls me back down toward him.

"J-j-just ignore it."

I nod and rest my head back on his chest. I am quite comfortable on Adam. But then my phone vibrates again, and I sit up grabbing it to see a text from Tommy. He would choose now as the moment to text me. My smile disappears, and I'm pulled back to earth like a weight falling to the ground. Everything crashes around me, and I'm forced to deal with my reality once again.

"Is-is everything o-okay?"

I shrug. "It's my friend. He needs my help."

I get up and put on my shoes and button up my coat. Adam grabs my wrist and stops me. I look down into his eyes, enjoying the fact that I'm taller than him for a change.

"Hey, s-s-s-stop. Let me, me help."

"How?" I ask. He can't always be my knight in shining armor.

"Just let me c-c-come with you."

"I'm not going to a good place, Adam."

I really don't think I should bring him to a drug addict's house for a date. If I thought telling him I was in a mental asylum on a first date was bad etiquette, I'm pretty sure taking him to a drug den is taking bad date to the max.

"Even *more* r-r-r-reason for me, me t-to go wi-with you."

He looks at me with pleading eyes, his fingers still gripped around my wrist, and I feel my head nod. He grabs his jacket and shoes and says he'll drive, since he knows how much I hate to be behind the wheel.

"You know how to win a boy's heart."

"That's my g-g-goal."

"You're succeeding."

We leave the house, telling my parents we're going out, but we don't mention where we are going, and then we are in Adam's car. I tell him the address, and we try to find our way there. This guy is at the edge of town, the opposite direction of Adam's uncle's. We drive up to a small, crappy house that looks like no one has lived there in years, but when I knock on the front door, I hear footsteps inside. There is a lot of shouting, and I look over at Adam.

"Maybe you should take off the bow tie, just in case."

He looks at me confused, tilting his head with wide eyes. He looks like a child right now, but then my eyes glance at the bow tie. What if Markus shoots us for looking too gay?

"Take it off," I say again.

He listens and stuffs the bow tie in his pocket, just as the door opens. Tommy is there, with the reddest eyes I have ever seen. Either he has been crying all day, or he is high off his ass. My guess is the latter.

"Jess," he says dragging out each and every syllable. "You're here."

He steps aside and lets us in as he eyes Adam.

"Who is this?"

"Um," I start. Smooth, Jess, real smooth.

Adam takes my hand. "I-I'm his b-b-boyfriend."

"Ah, nice to meet you, Adam. I'm Tommy, Jess's delinquent and fuckup of a friend. Do you guys want anything? We have tons of alcohol, and Markus just brought out his bong."

"You're not a fuckup" is all I can muster. I just don't like being here.

"I d-don't d-d-drink," Adam responds.

"Lame," he shouts at our faces.

He leads us through the hallways and into a den full of garbage, clothes, and alcohol bottles strewn about everywhere. Markus sits on the couch with three other guys I don't know. Each one looks blazed out of their minds. Markus holds a bong in his hands.

"He calls it Belinda," Tommy says.

"Fascinating," I respond.

I just want to get out of here. I feel like I've fallen down the rabbit hole and took a wrong turn, except this place certainly isn't full of any wonder. Tommy tells me each person's name, but I choose not to listen. I don't plan to make any of their acquaintances.

"Tommy, I think you should go now."

"But Jess, you *just* got here. Sit down, and smoke a little. It'll be fun."

"I'd rather not. I'm going to take you home with me, okay?" I try to use my most soothing voice possible, but sadly I didn't inherit that gene from my mom.

I grab his hand, but he pulls it away. "No." His shout echoes through the house, and I almost fall back in surprise. Adam keeps a hand around my waist, but I push it off. What if one of these guys shoots us? I can see Adam's hurt eyes, but I try to keep my focus on Tommy.

"L-l-let's go outside and, um t-t-t-talk about thi-this?" Adam reasons with my friend.

"Who the fuck are you? I don't even fucking know you."

"Tommy, stop it."

"Fuck this. Just get the fuck out of here, Jess. You're just some crazy fucker. I don't need you."

He walks away and sits on the couch with these people who pretend to be his friends, and one of them shouts for us to leave. Adam takes my hand, and I don't feel anything as he pulls me out of the house and into his car. Tommy texted me. I thought he was ready to leave and join the world again, but my mind drifts back to what he said.

Crazy fucker.

Is that really all I am to him? Am I always so wrapped up with my own problems and my illness that I've missed out on everything that has happened with him? Maybe those people aren't the ones pretending to be his friend. Maybe it's me?

"Jess, are, are you o-okay?"

I shrug in response because there is nothing to say. I don't know how I feel at the moment.

"D-do you w-want me t-t-t-to t-take you home?"

I nod.

He frowns, and a crinkle appears between his eyebrows.

"I'm sorry," I say.

"It-it's okay."

"I shouldn't have let you come tonight. That was a disaster."

"I j-just wanted t-t-to make s-s-s-s-sure you were s-s-s-s-safe."

"Thank you."

"W-why d-did you n-not let me t-t-touch you?"

"I was afraid one of them would pull out a gun and shoot us." It sounds so much dumber when I say it out loud.

He just smiles. "Oh, okay."

"Shut up. It's a serious problem. Who knows how they would react to a gay couple? They're so drugged up they wouldn't even realize what they were doing until they were burying our bodies somewhere where no one would ever find us."

"You're a-a-a-adorable."

I don't say anything because I feel like an awful friend. I left Tommy back there. I should have tried harder to get him out of that place.

"So you don't drink?" I say, trying to think about something else.

"N-nope."

"Why is that?"

"I j-j-just don't l-like how it ch-changes your entire p-p-perception. It, it makes s-s-s-s-some people angry and m-mean."

"I see."

The rest of the car ride is spent in silence. He drops me off at my house and walks me to the door. He bends down to kiss me, but I'm not content like I was before. I'm here spending the night with my boyfriend, and my best friend is off somewhere getting high and drunk.

"It'll b-be okay."

I nod, but how does he know? How can anyone know it'll be okay? It's funny how an entire night can change so quickly. Everything was so perfect, and then one text changed everything. I went from being happy to whatever this is. Guilty. Hurt. Numb. Sad. Angry. All of these feelings rush through my veins like a drug, and there is no way for me to stop them.

"Jess, are, are you s-s-s-s-sure y-you're okay?"

"Yeah, I am. I'll text you in the morning, okay?"

"Promise?"

"Promise."

He kisses me once more on the lips, and I wrap my arms around his neck to take in the kiss. At least that still makes me feel good.

"Good night," I say as he pulls away.

"S-s-s-s-sweet dreams."

I watch him drive away, and as I find myself lying in bed, I wish I hadn't let him leave. I just want him here right now so I could go back to before with my head on his chest when everything was wonderful and I was content. I would give anything for a time machine to turn back time and to be in Adam's arms once again. His arms make me feel warm and safe.

CHAPTER TWENTY

THE NEXT morning I end up telling my sister everything about Tommy. I don't know how it happens. One moment she asks how the rest of my night went, probably expecting some juicy details, and the next thing I know I'm telling her about Tommy and the druggie's house. Clara never interrupts me; she just lets me tell my story. As it comes to an end, she is silent.

"Is he still there now?"

I nod.

"I wonder why he texted you. He must want to leave but can't bring himself to."

"What makes you say that?" I ask. That's a lot to assume from my story.

"Well, he texted you, so he obviously wants to leave... but he also can't bring himself to because he doesn't want to face society or his father."

"I just wish I could do something."

"Me too, but Tommy needs to let us help."

"Isn't there anyone we can call?"

"I honestly don't know."

"Why are you going to school for art? You should have gone to law school, and then we would know what to do," I attempt to joke.

She humors me and smiles.

"It'll all work out," she reassures me.

"That's what Adam said."

"He's a smart man."

"Yeah," I agree.

We've texted a bit throughout the day. He's worried about me, and I can understand why. I didn't end the date on the highest of notes, but as usual Adam is outdoing Prince Charming in the act of being charming. I don't know how he does it. He should be angry or annoyed or just plain freaked out, but instead he worries and wants to make sure I'm okay. What kind of guy does that in reality? It's kind of weird. Amazing, but weird.

"I liked him," Clara remarks.

"Me too," I smirk.

"I would certainly hope so," she says with a giggle. "He's very...."

"Very what?" Oh gosh, what is wrong with him?

"Dapper. He's very dapper. He kind of reminds me of an old-school gentleman from the 1960s or something."

"Is that good?" I ask.

"Jess, that is wonderful. I've always dreamed of meeting a guy like that, once I get my master's degree of course, and here you are with Mr. Wonderful."

"Yeah, he is pretty wonderful."

Clara takes a glance at her watch. "Oh, I should head out."

"Where are you going?" I ask. It's not even noon yet; where does she have to be?

"I'm just seeing one of my friends. We'll talk about this later tonight, okay?"

"Yeah, thanks."

"Anytime."

She kisses my forehead, and I watch her leave my bedroom. I need to dress and get ready for work anyway. I've been avoiding Peter like the plague, and I think he's been doing the same. When he walks in, he doesn't look at me. I'm surprised he even remembers I took him home, he was so plastered.

When I get to work, the day is going normally. I'm with Jill today, who is her usual loud self.

"Hey, sexy. How are you?"

"Hey, Jill."

"You won't believe this," she basically shouts.

She starts to go on and on about something, I don't know what. Maybe it's about a band? I pretend to listen the best I can, but her fast talking goes right over my head and she's lost me. She stops talking when Peter's office door screeches open. Peter comes out of his office and looks at me. Right into my eyes. Jill looks on strangely, and I shrug, and I follow Peter into his office. It smells like alcohol, but it's cleaner than last time I saw it.

He sits behind his desk, and I take a chair in front of it. I notice that an unopened bottle of Jack Daniel's sits on his desk. Peter sighs, and I look around the office.

"So…," I mutter.

"Thank you."

"Um, okay."

I really don't know what to say.

"I was a mess, as usual, and just thanks."

"Um, no problem."

We sit there in awkward silence.

"Go back to the floor."

I stand up and leave the room, but I catch a glimpse of him opening the bottle and taking a sip. I sigh and find my way back to Jill.

"What was that about?"

I shrug. "Nothing."

"Weird," she responds.

"Yeah, I guess."

As Jill begins to talk once again, I feel my phone vibrate in my pocket, and my smile grows once I read the name. Adam. I may or may not do a bit of a happy dance, I won't lie.

I miss you. Can I see you tonight? xoxo

Yes, I immediately respond. *What do you want to do?*

I'm going to finally introduce you to the greatest show on Earth!!! :D

Doctor Who?

DUH!!!

I can't wait!

Would you like to spend the night? :)

My smile drops from my face. He wants me to spend the night? Is he trying to tell me something? When most people want you to spend the night, it usually means they want to have, um, have sex….

Sure.

:)

Oh gosh, did I just agree to sleep with him? I don't know if I'm ready for that. But if I sleep over, he's probably going to want to do that. I know I'm not really up to date with how relationships work, but sex is usually involved when your boyfriend sleeps over, right? I'm sounding like a damn kid in middle school who just started puberty.

"Oh, a sleepover… sexy!"

I look up to see Jill reading over my shoulder, and I try to force down the want to push her away.

"Hasn't anyone ever told you that's rude?"

"Yeah, all my life… but how else is a girl like me supposed to learn what is going on around me? It's culture."

"It's creepy," I quip.

I watch as she pulls herself onto the desk next to the cash register. A customer looks over, confused. No one ever really gets used to Jill.

"Shut it. So your boy wants you to sleep over? How cute. Are you going to, you know?"

I really don't want to have this conversation.

"No, I don't know," I say playing dumb. Please just let this conversation die. Is that too much to ask for?

"Oh come on, you know," she says with a wink.

She takes one hand, making a circle, and then uses an index finger of her other hand and inserts it.

"Jill, stop that," I utter.

Her smile grows wider, and she starts mimicking an orgasm, and I'm trying to hold the bile back in my throat. I look around as customers stop in their places and look over at the two of us, and Jill's way-too-realistic orgasm sounds. I try to shrink myself as much as I can, hoping to find a way to disappear. I mean, that must be possible somehow.

"Stop it," I repeat. "Why must this happen to me?"

I think I died and just woke up in hell. I'm way too awkward for this. When it comes to sex, I'm like a prepubescent child. Actually that is a bad analogy, and kind of wrong.

"Fine," she says, but then the smile grows wide on her face. "Wait… are you a virgin?" she asks with way too much curiosity.

"No, I'm not," I lie.

"It's okay if you are. Being a virgin is adorable. It's so rare to find a virgin nowadays, especially among men. For fuck's sakes, even middle-school kids are doing it now. It's revolting. Being a virgin is like a unicorn."

I press my lips together, refusing to meet her eyes.

"You totally are. Oh my God, that is so cute. You're my little unicorn."

"Yes," I whisper, a part of me hoping she doesn't hear what I say.

"Oh my gosh. You are too cute," she shouts, jumping off the desk and pulling me into a bone-crunching hug. Yeah, it hurts as much as it sounds.

"It's not that big of a deal, Jill."

Though it is. It's a huge deal. I'm a virgin, and I'm sleeping over at a guy's house. I'm a virgin and I'm sleeping over at my boyfriend's house. I'm getting flashbacks of our first date when I outright told him I wouldn't have sex with him. I am certainly a catch, that's for sure. Crazy and weird. Adam might as well date a deadite from *The Evil Dead*.

"It'll be so much fun. I want to hear *every* juicy detail."

"There won't be any."

"Sure," she says sounding unconvinced.

I want to say she stops acting like this, but the rest of the workday seems to follow in this fashion. Jill never once lets up with the sex talk to the point it starts making me never want to have sex. Why does sex have to be so complicated? Can't Adam and I continue doing what we do? I'm happy like that.

WHEN MY shift ends, and Laurie comes in, I'm all too happy to get out of there… but the entire walk home my mind focuses on what Jill was saying. I am not totally inexperienced. I have done things but never actual sex, and is it weird the idea of it kind of scares me? I should be turned on or something, but it just makes me want to run and hide.

When I get home, I end up googling sex, and the results I get are interesting. I see more penises than I have ever seen in my life. I end up watching gay porn, and for the first time I don't watch it to get off, but instead I take note of their moves. I watch the thrust of their hips, and I pay attention to everything the guys do. It's all for research of course. I don't enjoy it at all. Not at all. I am so happy I have a lock on my door.

All my research is interrupted by a text. From Adam.

Dress warm tonight :)
That's it? No reason why?
Why?
You'll see!!! :D
Now I'm scared. What does he have planned?
I'll pick you up at 8!
Okay....
:)

How dare he end the conversation on a smiley face emoticon. I spend the rest of the day following my usual predate routine: showering and brushing my teeth multiple times, so that by 7:30 p.m., I'm completely ready. I pack a small overnight bag, using my canvas messenger bag, and at eight o'clock sharp, I hear a car pull up outside. I look outside my window to see Adam's car.

I leave the house, telling my parents I'll be back much later. I throw my bag into his backseat, and I immediately feel Adam's soft lips on mine. Will I be feeling those lips everywhere tonight?

"So am I allowed to know what we're doing now?"

"You'll s-s-s-s-s-see s-s-s-soon." He seems very proud of himself as he speaks.

"I'm scared."

"I-I-I am here to p-protect you."

I like the sound of that. Adam protecting me is a feeling I could get used to. He takes one hand off the steering wheel and grabs mine, weaving our fingers together. I let out a contented sigh, and I just look at him as he drives. His focus stays concentrated on the road. I spend the entire car ride just watching him and that beautiful face of his. I notice the freckles; there aren't a lot, but they sit along the bridge of his nose and some under his eyes. I connect them, playing my own game of connect the dots. I am able to make out a badly drawn seahorse.

The car comes to a stop, and we are outside his apartment building.

"This is your apartment? The surprise was we were coming here?"

"No. I have t-to get s-s-s-s-something from here f-f-first. Wait here."

And so the plot thickens. I watch him skip out of the car, and I swear he actually skips. I look out at the cloudless night. Each star can be made out, and the moon shines full and bright. Adam comes running back to the car with a bag and a couple of large blankets. He throws them into the back and gets back behind the wheel.

"Where to now?"

Adam just smiles and hums and then kisses my hand before driving away. He is really intent on keeping this all a surprise, isn't he? We don't drive for too much longer, though, and we come to a stop outside a small wooded area. Now this is just getting plain weird. He grabs the blankets, and I offer to help, but he says he has got it.

We walk toward the trees. The night is cold, and the wind isn't too strong, but it's there.

"It's a, a p-picnic." He seems to explode, unable to keep the secret any longer.

"Isn't it a bit late to have a picnic?"

He leads me through the woods, and I can't stop the shiver as the night continues to get colder and more bitter. He takes an arm and brings it around my waist, holding me close to his body.

"N-n-never too late," he jovially replies.

I start to shiver worse, and now all I want is to be back at his apartment wrapped up in his blankets with my head on his chest.

"Isn't it a bit cold to have a picnic?"

"I-I'll keep you, um, w-warm."

"I'm holding you to that."

He uses a flashlight to guide our way until we reach a small clearing. We have a perfect view of the night sky, and I have to admit, it is a beautiful sight, even if it is colder than hell frozen over. He unrolls the blanket from under his arm and spreads it out on the ground, putting a rock on each corner. He sits down, pulling me down with him, and throws the other blanket on top of our laps. He opens up his legs and pulls me in between them so I can rest as close to his body as humanly possible, and he wraps his arms around me, taking my hands in his.

"Is this just an excuse to get close to me?" I joke.

I always knew he had a nice laugh, but to feel him laugh against me is a new experience. I feel like I am a part of him.

"I, um, d-d-don't need an ex-excuse."

"Getting cocky now."

He answers by kissing me on the back of my head. Okay, he wins this round. He's lucky he's adorable. He's my goofball of a boyfriend.

I take in my surroundings—the oh so dark and ominous woods, the setting of many of the horror films in my collection back home. Now is the time a masked killer with a machete would jump out and slaughter us or chase one of us until he is the sole survivor. My mind really is weird.

Adam opens the bag and hands me a thermos. I take a sip, and it is English breakfast tea, made exactly the way I like it. I take another large sip, allowing the hot liquid to warm me up, although Adam is already doing a pretty good job of that.

"Any other surprises in your bag of tricks?" I ask.

"Actually j-just the tea."

"Some picnic," I joke.

"I, um, d-d-d-don't like b-b-bugs, s-s-s-s-so I n-never eat outdoors," he admits sounding embarrassed.

"It's okay. I hate bugs. Disgusting little things."

"They f-freak me, me out… to, to the p-point I a-actually m-may s-s-s-scream. It's n-not a p-p-pretty s-s-s-s-sight."

No, it's not a pretty image in my head, but I like that he screams at the sight of bugs. I also like that he makes me feel warm when we're sitting outside on a winter night. I like how he knows how I like my tea. I especially love how he makes me feel. He makes me feel important and special, like I matter. He makes me glad I didn't die that night and he makes me glad to be here with him right now. I want to tell him how much I love him, but I know where that leads a person. Heartbreak. I don't want to have another breakdown, so I plan to keep my declarations of love to myself.

He takes a sip from his own thermos.

"C-c-coffee for me," he says almost sounding proud of himself. Adam, I'm noticing, is a bit of a prideful man. But it's never boastful or annoying. It's cute. Like when a puppy is so proud of himself after performing a trick. I lean my head all the way back so I can look right up at Adam. He smiles down at me, and he brings a hand up, resting it on the side of my cheek, and he brings his cold lips down onto mine. I don't need the tea anymore because this is enough to keep me warm.

I never knew love could be so warm. It is like lava circulating through my veins, warming every inch of my body.

His lips leave mine, and I lean my head on his shoulder and just let myself enjoy the moment. He gets up, and I pout, missing the feeling of his body against mine.

"L-let's go b-b-back to, um, to my place."

"Okay…."

This is where my heart begins to pound. Why am I so nervous? I've slept over at his apartment before, and it was fine. Yeah, I slept over when he was incredibly sick. All we did was cuddle. But tonight, he is going to expect something more. Geez, even my thought process is painfully awkward.

I spend the entire car ride back, all five minutes of it, anticipating what is going to happen next. At the sight of the apartment building, my breathing all but stops. I follow Adam into his apartment, and I welcome the coziness of his home.

"Where should I leave the blankets?"

"J-just put them on the floor," he states while sitting down on the couch. "Now c-c-come here."

He holds out his hands, and I throw the blankets to the ground. I take his fingers in quivering hands, and I sit on the couch beside him. I greet his lips with mine as his fingers slowly glide up my arms, sending goose bumps all along my skin each place he touches. It is like a million tiny magnets underneath my skin attracting one another. A small, electric sensation pulls his body and mine together. We fall over as he leans into me, his body on top of mine. His lips are soft, and his body is warm and so inviting.

"Wait, wait," I say, pulling my lips away from his.

"Wh-what?" he asks concerned.

"It's just…," I whisper, my eyes glancing back to his lips. They're so full and pink.

I bring his lips back to mine. Maybe I am ready. I mean, I love Adam, at least I think I do. My mind and body certainly believe I love Adam, but am I ready to go to the next level? His lips move to my neck, and I have to stop myself from letting out a moan because it feels too good. He starts to suck on the soft flesh, and I fail at keeping my moan in. I feel his smile against my skin. He's enjoying this.

"Wait, stop, sorry," I say again. What the hell is wrong with me?

"What? Are you, you o-okay?"

"Yeah, I'm just...."

"Wh-what?" he pressures.

"I'm, um, notreadytohavesexwithyou...," I say under my breath, too fast for anyone to understand. Everything seems to tumble into one word, creating a mess of dialogue.

"S-s-s-s-sorry, what?"

"I'm not, um, ready to have sex... with you...," I repeat, taking a breath between each word. I feel the angry red blush rise to my cheeks at my admission: I'm a virgin who is not ready for sex.

He leans back and looks surprised, and he is probably angry too. I mean, he invites his boyfriend to spend the night, only for said boyfriend to say he's not ready to have sex yet. That must be disappointing.

"I'm sorry," I say.

I sit up and look away. I feel like I'm putting Adam through the ringer right now. One moment I'm hot and then the next moment I'm cold. Why can't I just be a good in-between warm? Adam grabs my shoulder, and I look up to see his giant smile and his warm eyes.

"We d-d-don't have to, to do anything you d-don't w-w-want t-to, Jess."

"Really?"

"Of c-c-course. Don't be s-s-s-s-silly."

He places his hands on the side of my face and lays a soft kiss on my lips. "I, I really l-like you, Jess."

"I like you too," I say back to him with a large, relieved smile on my face.

My heart finally begins to slow down, and it no longer feels as if I'm about to have a heart attack. I don't know why I was so nervous about this. Of course he'd understand my hesitation; he's Adam. He is gentleness in human form.

"I c-c-can just hold you, if you, um, w-w-would like that."

"Yes," I respond. "I'm definitely up for some holding."

He takes my hand and leads me to his bedroom, but first I tell him I want to change. I take my bag to his tiny bathroom and pull on a pair of sweatpants and a long-sleeved T-shirt. I brush my teeth, because who wants to kiss a guy with bad breath? I find him in his bed with his shirt off—why must he do this to me?—and a pair of shorts on. He opens up his muscular arms, and I slide into his embrace. I feel his strong muscles against me, and I have never felt so safe in my entire life. It's like nothing can touch me as long as Adam holds me close to him.

I close my eyes and breathe in his scent. He smells like vanilla and strawberries. I have always loved strawberries, so of course the world would allow Adam to smell like that. It's like the world is tempting me more and more.

I snuggle up closer, and soon I feel his rhythmic breathing against me. I quietly slither out of his arms and I just look at his rising chest, and my eyes wander over his abs and biceps. I still wonder how I got so lucky. It's not just because he's good-looking—but goddamn, we can admit it: he's just plain hot—but he's so incredibly nice and caring and just so dorky. Every time I'm around him I have to stop myself from turning into a puddle on the floor. He makes me feel like goo every moment of the day.

I grab my meds from my bag and swallow them, grimacing at the feel of the pills going down my throat. I'm too lazy to get myself water. I turn the light off in the bedroom, and I find my way back into his arms, doing my best not to wake him. I hear him sigh, and I allow myself to relax beside him.

A small voice in my head seems to speak up: *He will break your heart.* Shut up, small voice. What do you know? *More than you know. All love does is hurt you.* Adam won't hurt me. *As long as you get close to him, he will hurt you. They all do in the end.* I tell myself to shut up because this is getting weird now. I'm creating a conversation in my own head. I just want to allow myself to be happy, but my mind never seems to want that.

Geez, I'm arguing with a voice in my head now. Dr. Wheeler would have a field day with this. I'll file this into the folder of things I will *not* be telling Adam anytime soon. That's not exactly the thing someone wants to hear about their boyfriend.

I try to calm my thoughts, and I just let myself fall asleep.

I SMILE as I wake up to see Adam's sleeping face next to mine. He looks so sweet and happy, and his hair is in a wavy mess. I notice a tiny bit of drool at the corner of his mouth, and I can't help but marvel at the childlike image before me. He moves closer, wrapping his arm around my lean waist.

"You're w-warm," he mumbles against my neck.

His lips create a warm sensation on my bare skin.

"I am going to make some tea. Do you want some?"

I feel him nod, and then he looks up and stares right into my eyes, and he gives me his famous dorky lopsided smile. Seeing it makes me feel like I'm about to float, like I'm a bubble in the air. All thoughts from last night seem to drift away like petals in the wind.

Looking into my eyes he says, "I'd l-l-love s-s-s-s-some tea."

I stare into his eyes as his hair sits in a mess on top of his head. The sheets are tangled between his legs, and sweat dots his chest.

"You're the most beautiful person I have ever seen in my life." This falls right out of my mouth. I can feel a blush rushing to my cheeks, but as I turn away, I feel his strong hands on the sides of my face, and he looks right at me.

"You're am-m-mazing, Jess."

I kiss him and tell him to stay in bed. I want to do something nice for him, because he always seems to be playing the role of perfect boyfriend. I find my way around the kitchen, and after a lot of fumbling—seriously, I couldn't find anything—I bring two steaming hot mugs back to his bedroom.

"S-s-smells delicious. Thank y-you."

We sit in bed sipping our teas, and I silently pray to whomever is out there that Adam keeps his shirt off. Yeah, seeing him shirtless makes me feel incredibly flawed, but I still like looking at his muscles. I'm a hormonal guy after all. I can't help it. It's like in my nature or something to have thoughts like that.

"D-do you have w-work today?"

"Nope," I state quite proudly. No work for me today.

"W-would you like t-to s-s-s-s-spend the day t-together?"

"Of course."

I mean how else would I spend it? Probably alone on my computer reading blogs about horror movies or something. I'd go on Tumblr and see people talking about their favorite ships. I live an exciting, fast-paced life, so be jealous.

"Yay." And he literally says "yay." Could he be any more adorable?

We both dress, and I take my time, trying to get my hair to stay down. Yeah, no luck. Why do I bother with it? My mom used to tell me I needed a haircut, but she has recently given up because she knows it's a losing battle. While it annoys me, I like how my hair falls into my eyes. It's my shield. When I don't want to deal with the world, I just throw my hood over my head and let my hair cover my eyes, blocking everything from my sight.

I find Adam in the living room with his jacket on and keys in hand.

"I f-f-forgot to sh-show you *D-Doctor Who*," he states, his disappointment obvious.

"We can watch an episode now… if you'd like?"

His smile grows, and he throws his keys and jacket onto the couch. He grabs my hand and pulls me into the bedroom like a small child dragging their parent. He all but throws me down onto his bed, not sexually at all, and grabs his laptop. We kick off our shoes, and he cuddles up close to my body, setting the laptop on top of his stomach.

"Are, are y-you excited?"

"Yeah," I answer. I mean, the show should be good. I hope.

He starts it up, and a man with a bow tie is introduced.

"Is that Doctor Who?" I ask.

"J-j-just the D-D-Doctor," he responds. "He's the, the r-r-r-reason I s-s-s-s-started wearing b-bow ties."

If this show started that adorable trend for him, it can't be all bad. And for a forty-minute show it wasn't bad. I was involved enough, and by the end I wanted to see what happened next.

"S-s-so what d-did you, um, think?"

"I, uh, liked it. It's weird." It's *really* weird. "But, yeah, I liked it."

"Yay," he shouts.

"Calm down," I giggle.

"S-s-s-s-sorry, I'm j-just s-s-s-so happy you l-liked it."

We watch another episode. I half do it to make him happy, because I love seeing that smile, and the other half of me actually wants to see more of the show. After watching three more after that, we finally put the computer away, and I listen to him as he tells me the entire history of the show. I can't help but smile as he goes on and on and on, but he does it with such enthusiasm that it makes me enthusiastic. I can't even be bored because of how adorable he is right now.

"I'm confused," I tell him… and goddamn, I'm confused. This show's history is longer than the last *Harry Potter* novel.

"It's o-okay. You w-w-will learn. I sh-sh-shall t-teach you."

"Cool."

"C-c-cool," he repeats with a sly smile.

"Cool," I say once more.

He takes my hand and rubs circles with his thumb over my knuckles.

"C-c-can we g-go outside?" he asks, with the most pleading puppy-dog eyes I've ever seen.

"Yeah, sure. Where do you want to go?"

"L-let's go t-t-to the park."

"The one where we sat on the swings that night?" I ask.

"Th-that's the one."

After only dating a short while—I'm a terrible boyfriend. I don't remember the exact date—we're going back to one of the places we first met. Well, one of the three. Technically we would have to go back to The Book Revue to relive that again.

We grab our coats, and we decide to walk. We clasp hands as we make our way through the neighborhood, and I like the image of it: the two of us holding hands walking around. We really are a couple, aren't we? The last time I got this close to a relationship was when some guy I met online pretended to like me just because he wanted to fuck me. That was two years ago.

The day is warm, and I love it. The snow has completely melted, and the sun is bright. I'm even able to keep my coat open. The only way it could be better is if it was actually spring. We come up to the playground, and we see that the swings are still empty. We jump onto them, and before I know it, we're swinging as high as we can. I'm soaring through the air, feeling the wind on my skin as it brushes through my hair. I look over to see Adam smiling, and I hear his giggles. I laugh at the image of us—two grown men swinging and giggling like schoolchildren. It's ridiculous, and I love it. We stop swinging, and we just laugh.

I don't know how long we laugh, but it's like every bit of anger or disgust is leaving my system. I feel free of the darkness. I am no longer trapped in that place that has so long held me prisoner.

I am here.

I am alive.

I feel wonderful.

"You l-l-look happy," he says.

I look over at him and smile. "That is because I am. I never knew I could be happy like this, but I am happy."

His smile grows, and I can't stop mine. Happy. Happy. Happy. I am happy. I am exquisite. I am ecstatic to be alive, and I'm joyful at the thought of being here with Adam.

"I'm g-g-glad we're t-t-t-together," he admits.

I just smile and nod. I don't want to ruin the moment with my awkwardness, so I just stare at him. I'm amazed someone so wonderful could ever exist. I don't want to be self-deprecating, but who am I kidding? When am I not? I am honestly amazed he could like me. He must be some sort of masochist.

A little girl and her mom walk onto the playground. Her curly blonde hair is done up in a small updo. She wears a little fake tiara and a long blue costume gown with a pair of plastic slippers. A hot-pink Disney princess backpack sits on her back.

"How c-c-c-cute."

"Yeah, she is," I agree.

"*C-C-C-Cinderella*. I love that movie."

"What?"

Then I realize, the little girl is dressed as the famed Disney princess. Adam would love that movie. I look over at him, but he has jumped up from the swing, and I watch as he bends down in front of the tiny girl so he is at the same height as her.

"Oh m-m-my gosh. I have n-n-n-never s-s-s-s-s-seen a princess before. May I, I have your autograph?" Adam asks with such excitement in his voice.

The little girl's face lights up like a Christmas tree.

"I don't have a pen," she answers in a high-pitched voice.

"W-wait here."

Adam runs over with a wide smile on his face. Before he can even ask, I pull out a pen and a small pad from my bag. He smiles and heads back. I always keep a small notepad and pen in my bag for just in case. You never know when you'll need it, such as your boyfriend asking a tiny little girl for an autograph. Her mother stands to the side, a pretty woman, not too old. Possibly early thirties. Her dark hair is held back with a clip, and she has a smile on her face.

Adam hands over the paper and pen, and she quickly scribbles something, and Adam thanks her, and the girl skips away to the sandbox. She takes off her backpack and pulls out a bunch of Barbie dolls. And I mean a *ton*. It seems like she just keeps pulling them out, one after another. Each doll is dressed up like a Disney character.

Adam sits back next to me. His smile is so bright, and he holds the paper in his hand. It's just a bunch of scribbles with a smiley face next to it. The mom walks over to us. She speaks with a light, honey-sweet voice.

"Thank you. I think you made her life. She just got that dress. She wanted me to make her look like Cinderella today."

"Sh-sh-sh-she looks like a p-p-princess."

"That's my little girl for you. Do you plan to have kids?"

"Oh we just started dating," I respond.

"Oh sorry. You two just look so comfortable together. I thought you've been together for years."

"We do?" I ask.

"You can always tell. Yes, some couples may kiss all the time and show their passion, but it's not a true relationship. Sometimes you can just see on their faces and through the way they are together. You two seem like you have something real."

Adam takes my hand in his, and I feel his thumb rub circles on my skin. She walks away, and I look over at Adam. He looks so happy, like he's just floating on a cloud.

We sit in silence before I say, "So every New Year's Eve my family orders way too much food, and I was thinking maybe you could come over and help us eat the food. I mean, I'm sure you have plans or something, but before or after you could stop by. That's if you'd like to, but…."

"Sh-shut up. Yes, I'd l-l-love to c-c-come." He jumps off the swing. "Now let's g-g-get s-s-s-s-s-some food. I'm s-s-s-starving."

I follow him off the swing, and he takes us back to his apartment where he cooks and I just imagine a future like this. Maybe one day we'll have our own house, one with a wrap-around porch. Nothing too big. It could possibly be a sweet little cottage. It'd be painted yellow and have blue shutters. There'd be a garden with the most beautiful flowers, and nearby we'd overlook the lake. It would look like a house from a fairy tale. We'd be married, but we'll be that disgustingly married couple who is so in love everyone hates us, and we'd have a kid or two.

And some animals, of course. I could not have a future without animals. When I was a kid I had a dog. He was a Shih Tzu named Snuggles. Not the most original name, but the name was true. He was the most snuggly, adorable dog ever. He passed away when I was sixteen, and I was utterly destroyed. I didn't get another dog because I felt no other animal could live up to my baby, but in my future I'd love some animals. Maybe a lot of animals.

The more I picture this fantasy the more I want it, because every time I picture a future with Adam, it looks more and more like a fairy tale.

CHAPTER TWENTY-ONE

NEW YEAR'S has passed, but I stand in the kitchen, which has been invaded with food. Mountains upon mountains of food. A six-foot hero sits on the table along with salads, macaroni and cheese, baked ziti, meatballs, and just so much more. I never understand why we do this because we don't invite a lot of people over. It's like my parents, or really just my father, are pretending to be a normal family. My sister has a couple of friends here tonight, and my father has two guys over from work. I tried calling Tommy and Alex, but neither would come. Jill is out with friends getting drunk, but Adam stands beside me. He wears a nice shirt with the top few buttons open, revealing part of that muscular chest I love so much, with an open cardigan over that.

We're celebrating the holiday a few days late, so no ball dropping or midnight kisses as we ring in the New Year. With everything going on, my family and I have been scatterbrained. My parents want everything to be perfect this year since I'm home, so all the planning required an extra few days.

My eyes remain on the exposed flesh of his chest. I try to look away, but I picture my fingers opening each button one by one, taking my time to run my fingertips slowly over his skin.

"Jess, are you okay?"

I look up to see my mom's worried look, and I instantly blush. Okay, my hormones need to calm down. I'm not some young boy anymore. I'm a man. I'm nineteen years old.

"Oh yeah, totally," I halfheartedly respond, my eyes staying on Adam. He smiles at me, slightly sticking out his tongue. I break out into a laugh, and my parents and Clara turn to me. They all look confused and somewhat scared. They're probably worried I'm about to have another breakdown again. Nope, I'm just in love. Although I guess falling in love is a lot like going crazy.

Are you okay? Adam mouths to me. I nod in return. I can't put into words just how more than okay I am right now. I like that Adam is my date for the small New Year's Eve party at my house. I like that I have someone with me.

"W-w-what's on your mind?"

"You," I answer truthfully.

"Oh? Good s-s-s-s-stuff?"

"The best. This old theater in the next town is having a marathon of all three *Evil Dead* films back-to-back next week. Would you like to join me?"

I mean, I have all three movies on DVD already, but how can I give up a chance to see them all on the big screen? This trilogy is one of the defining moments of horror. It blends together horror and comedy so seamlessly, and it somehow works. Personally I hate when filmmakers try to add comedy to horror. It's like you're trying to scare me, not make me laugh. But *Evil Dead II* and *Army of Darkness* just know how to straddle the line between the two genres without going overboard. Most people would actually consider *Evil Dead II* to be a masterpiece... but I would disagree. For me *The Evil Dead* is still the best. I mean, yeah, Ash—the awesome Bruce Campbell—isn't at his most badass, but the movie is so gory and over-the-top and disturbing... *I love it*.

"I'd l-l-love to," Adam responds. I smile, and I pull him into a hug.

Clara walks over, and she and Adam start to converse about something. Honestly the topic goes over my head, so I totally zone out. I think it is about some musician. I feel my phone vibrate in my pocket, and I look at the screen to see Tommy's name. I jump up and tell everyone I'll be right back.

"Tommy."

"Yo, am I still invited?"

"Yeah, of course. Come over."

"I'm actually outside."

I hang up the phone and run to the door to find Tommy standing on my porch. He wears an old wrinkled button-up and a pair of baggy khakis. His shirt is too big for his scrawny body. The bruises his father left on him have faded away, and now he almost looks back to normal.

He walks inside, and he slowly follows me like a lost child into the dining room where everyone now sits waiting for dinner. There aren't a lot of us, but the chatter is still pretty loud. My mom smiles at the sight of Tommy, and she pulls him into a hug and sets him a place. Dad doesn't say a word. He just nods in his direction. Hey, it's better than nothing.

"Let's eat dinner," my mom states.

We sit down at the rather large table in the dining room. We only eat in here on special occasions, such as Thanksgiving or Christmas, or if we have some guests over... which isn't often. Adam sits on one side of me, while Tommy sits on my other side. Throughout dinner, Adam shovels back as much food as he can, while Tommy quietly eats whatever he takes. In fact, Tommy is quiet throughout all of dinner. He never looks anyone in the eyes, keeping them on his plate, as if he is afraid someone will steal his food if he looks away. Little by little he finishes his food.

"Everything okay?" I murmur.

He nods. "Yeah. Everything's cool."

Do I believe him? Not a bit, but I'll let him live the fantasy for now. I'm just happy to have him here with my family today. After dinner, Tommy, Adam, and I end up in my bedroom... and we sit in awkward silence.

"Hi, I'm Adam, J-J-Jess's b-b-b-boyfriend," Adam states, putting his hand out into the air and introducing himself as if the scene at Markus's house never happened.

Tommy stares down at his hand for a moment, before finally deciding to play along. "Nice to meet you, bro."

"So, Tommy, I'm so glad you're here. What made you change your mind?"

"I wanted some of your mother's cooking."

"I'm being serious," I respond.

"So am I," he fights back with bite to his voice.

Silence reigns once again. Not one of us knows what to say. I can't exactly just say "Hey how goes living with low-life scum?" now can I? That'd be rude, or so I've been told.

"So are you still living with—"

"No," he cuts me off, before I can even finish. A part of me wants to sigh with relief, but the other part grows scared at the thought of where he could be living now. Is he at a place much worse... or is he back living with his father? Both thoughts frighten me. I don't want to see my closest friend living in a place like that.

"Before you ask, I've moved back home. I'm going to find a place to live. I have to."

"I c-c-c-can help."

Tommy and I both look up at Adam.

"How?" Tommy incredulously asks.

"My f-f-f-friend is l-looking for a new r-r-r-roommate?"

"Really?"

"Yes. I, I, I can g-g-give you his number. His n-n-name is K-K-Korey."

Adam grabs a small notepad off my desk and quickly writes down the name and number, handing it to Tommy. This guy might be saving my friend's life. I look over at Tommy, whose eyes are wider than a scared child's.

"Are you fucking with me?"

"I'm n-not *f-f-f-fucking* with you," Adam says. The curse word sounds so odd coming from his lips. When he curses, he sounds like he is saying a foreign word he does not understand. It's adorable. He really needs to make me stop falling for him more and more. It's just getting ridiculous now.

Tommy holds the small yellow lined paper in his fingers. He can't take his eyes away from it. Is his nightmare finally over? Please let his nightmare finally be over. He pockets the small slip of paper, remaining silent—though silent from gratitude or from fear, I have no idea. His life could be heading in a new direction, and a new future may be the result, one he never foresaw coming. I hope for a better future, a safe one for my best friend. I of all people know the world is an unfair place, but maybe it could at least become more bearable if we try.

I look over at Adam, and I can't help but be thankful for everything he is doing. Not only has he come into my life and somehow made it better, but he's also trying to help Tommy. He is lending a hand to someone who needs it, not because he has to but because he wants to. Adam has a rare gift that is absent from many people—compassion.

Tommy's voice grabs my attention. "So I'm going to go before you two lovebirds start making out in front of me."

"You don't have to go," I tell him.

He smiles. "Yeah I do." I tell Adam I'll be right back, and I walk Tommy to the front door. I give him a hug while he does that thing guys do where they have to pat your back. It's like they're enforcing their manliness by doing that. Yeah, I don't get it. It doesn't make a hug any less of a hug.

"I like him, Jess. He's good for you."

"Thank you." I didn't realize I wanted my friends' approval of Adam, but hearing Tommy giving us his blessing warms my heart and makes me feel good. It's like there is this glow inside, which just continues to get brighter. I watch him leave, and I find Adam lying on my bed, his shoes kicked off onto the floor. He opens up his arms, and I leap at him like a fierce cheetah going after its prey. He laughs as I kiss his neck, and I snuggle against his body.

No one has ever made me feel so protected before in my life. When I was a child, I was always so afraid. I didn't even speak until I was three. My parents thought I had a mental handicap, and they brought me to speech therapists, but they said nothing was wrong. I just didn't talk. I finally said my first real word right before my third birthday. It was "I'm hungry." Okay, so two words. I can imagine my parents' faces now.

"Wh-what are, are you thinking a-about?" he whispers into my ear before slightly kissing it.

"Nothing really. Stupid life things."

"S-s-s-s-s-stupid life th-things?"

"Yeah."

"C-c-care to elaborate?" Not really. I look over at him and I smile, lightly kissing him on the lips. He grabs the sides of my face, and he deepens the kiss. Well, that shut him up. I like this technique. It will be very useful in the future. Nothing could stop this happiness I'm feeling right now.

"D-do you w-w-wanna s-s-s-s-spend the night at m-my place?" he asks in a low deep voice. His fingers slide up and down my arms, and I can't stop the resulting shudder. I close my eyes and imagine how those hands would feel on my skin.

"Yes," I answer. I keep my voice steady and strong. I don't sound meek as I answer.

HIS APARTMENT is cold as he takes my jacket. He hangs both of our coats in the small closet right next to the front door. A slight shiver comes over me, and the hairs on my arms stick up. I bite my lip as I take in Adam's round bottom, which looks oh so good in his tight pants.

I watch Adam disappear into the kitchen, and I take a seat on the couch. Calm down, Jess, calm down. My breathing is rapid and my heart beats like a jackhammer. What am I so nervous about? This is Adam. Lovely, perfect Adam. Well, perfect for me. He comes back with two glasses of water and sits down beside me. The clock turns twelve on the wall.

"Happy N-New Year," Adam says as he kisses my cheek.

"It isn't New Year's," I whisper into his ear, nibbling at the soft skin at the bottom.

"T-t-t-tonight it, it is."

New Year's is supposed to be a time of new beginnings where we make resolutions and goals. I made one resolution for this year— happiness. Whether it is with Adam, or just through my own self-discovery, I want to finally find the happiness I have been searching for my entire life.

The kiss deepens, and I don't know when Adam shuts off the television, but we are met by silence. Everything disappears, leaving only Adam and me alone in our own little world. Adam's hands slide up under my shirt, and I feel them stop abruptly. No, please not now. The world we inhabit comes crashing down, and a bus known as reality hits me full force.

"J-J-Jess?"

Don't let this happen. Not now. Not here. Everything was going so perfectly.

He starts to pull up my shirt, but I quickly force it back down, pleading with my eyes for him to stop. I can't let him see me like this. I can't let him see me for who I truly am.

"P-please let me s-s-see," he whispers.

I look away, and I allow him to pull my shirt up, and I hear his gasp. Here it is. Here is when he finally realizes what I'm like and runs away. I open my eyes as he takes in every single one of my scars, each one more disgusting than the last. My body looks like a fucked-up drawing. Little lines of raised pink flesh run up my sides, and he hasn't even seen my arms yet.

"B-b-but why?"

"I told you once. I'm a very sad man, Adam. I'm sorry."

"D-d-d-don't apologize."

He kisses my lips, and I close my eyes as his fingers slowly glide over each one of my scars. Adam takes his time, and he bends to kiss each one of them. He looks at my wrists and places a long kiss on each of my scarred wrists.

"Y-you're s-s-s-s-s-so beautiful."

"You have a fucked-up sense of beauty," I joke.

He kisses my lips, and I feel a weird sensation of comfort. No one has seen me shirtless in I don't know how long. The last person to do that was a doctor who would routinely check my body in the most awkward of manners to make sure no new scars had been added to the canvas, also known as my body.

I allow my hands to slide under his shirt, and he pulls it over his head. I let my fingers roam everywhere from his arms to his chest all the way down his torso. His muscles clench under my touch.

"I love your muscles," I state.

Adam lets out a little giggle. "You're s-s-s-so cute."

Our hands seem to touch every spot of our upper bodies until they rest at the waistbands of our jeans. He backs away, and I feel my heart pound a million miles per hour.

"I, I can s-s-s-s-stop," he states, sounding nervous. I see the sweat building on his forehead. The apartment has suddenly become hotter than an oven.

But I don't want him to. Yes, I'm nervous, but it's not like that time I slept over. It's different now. It's a good nervous. An excited nervous.

I shake my head. "No, keep going."

"R-really?"

I nod and bring his lips back to mine as he unbuttons my jeans. He does it quick, but when I try to do it to him, I fumble and have to break the kiss to use a second hand. I see the peek of green underwear. He slides my jeans down my legs, revealing my blue briefs. Never in my life have I felt so exposed. It's not just because I'm almost naked, but I'm allowing Adam to see a lot of me, almost all of me. It's both scary and exhilarating. He helps me by taking off his own pants. The sight of him in green briefs is a picture that will be forever ingrained into my memory. I look back and just take in the sight. The only way

I could seem more awkward is if I was literally drooling at the sight. I wipe my lips just to play safe. No drool, thankfully.

"You like?" he asks.

"Very much so," I reply. Goddamn, I very much like. I love.

We kiss again, allowing our hands to roam everywhere, and I do mean everywhere this time. I'm not experienced, but I feel like a brand-new canvas, and his fingers are just paintbrushes that paint pictures on my skin. They allow me to forget about the old sketches of my past life.

When our underwear comes off, I feel my entire body shaking. He asks if I'm okay, and I nod. I don't know why I'm shaking, but I don't want to stop what we're doing. Everything feels too good and it all just feels so wonderful to me. All these new sensations. I never want them to stop. He pulls me off the couch and leads me to his bedroom. I lie down on his bed, waiting to feel his body against mine.

We make love that night. It's not like it seems in the movies where it's perfect and everything goes well. I mean, yes, it's beautiful, and I love everything, but there is a lot of fumbling and a bit of pain. The pain does subside, and it does start to feel somewhat good, but we're both so incredibly awkward.

But even with all the awkward and even some embarrassing moments, I wouldn't change it for the world. I'm glad my first time is with Adam.

Afterward I find his head on my naked chest. We lie together skin to skin. There are no layers of clothing, no barriers separating us. For the first real time in my sad and lonely life, I feel like I am one with another.

I don't feel alone.

I WAKE up to the warm sun shining through the room, beating on the bare flesh of my arm, which hangs off the bed. I look over to see a much taller man asleep. His muscular arm is wrapped around my pale waist. I smile as the memories of the night before play back in my head like a fantastic movie. Adam is still asleep. His hair is a mess, and he has a small smile on his face. I have the urge to run my fingers over his cheek, but the fear of waking him stops me. He looks so peaceful, so beautiful. If I could, I would spend a lifetime just watching him sleep. Never in my life have I seen someone so beautiful. It is as if he is an angel sent from above.

He begins to stir, and his eyes try to open. He squints as the sun shines on his face.

"G-good m-morning," he whispers in a barely awake, raspy voice.

"Good morning." Even I can hear the happiness in my voice.

I try to move, but his strong arm wraps tighter around my waist, pulling me closer to his body. The warmth of his skin radiates onto mine. I feel his smile as he nuzzles the back of my neck.

"W-where d-do you think you're g-g-going?" he asks playfully.

"I *was* going to make a cup of tea. Would you like some?"

After a moment of silence, he finally responds. "That w-w-would be f-f-fantastic. I'll c-come to the k-k-kitchen with you, you."

"You don't have to...."

"Sh-shush. I'll h-help."

I turn around and smile at him. "Thank you, Adam."

He kisses me lightly on my lips, and for that second, all seems right in the world. All the pain and sadness I have felt for years erases from my mind for that one moment I am touching Adam.

"You l-l-look happy, Jess."

"That is because I am," I answer.

"You s-s-s-s-sound s-s-s-s-s-surprised."

"That is because I am. This is the first time in my life I have ever been truly happy. It feels so wonderful and odd but...."

I can't find the words. How do I describe this feeling? Am I content? No. I'm not just content. I am something more. How do I explain this happiness?

"P-perfect," Adam finishes.

I smile at him. "Yes. This is perfect. I feel perfect."

He runs his calloused fingers over the side of my face, covered in light stubble. I close my eyes at his touch.

"You're m-m-more b-beautiful than you r-r-r-r-realize, J-Jess. You r-r-really are."

I open my eyes as he stares at me, his hand still resting on my cheek. I pull his hand toward my lips, and I place a small kiss upon the tips of his fingers.

"Shut up." I awkwardly laugh.

"N-no, you r-r-r-r-really are. Trust m-me."

I look into his eyes. There is not an ounce of doubt written across his face. His gray-blue eyes plead for me to believe what he tells me. He runs his hand through my hair and pulls me in for a kiss.

As I ease away, I can't stop the smile from appearing on my face. "Do you want that tea?"

He laughs. "S-s-sure. Let's g-go."

I sit on the edge of the bed, pulling my glasses off Adam's night table, and settling them on the bridge of my nose. I feel Adam's arms around my waist, and his lips are soft on my pale neck.

"If you continue to kiss me like that, we'll never get up from this bed."

"You s-s-s-s-say that like it, it is a b-b-b-b-bad thing," he whispers. I can feel his smirk against my neck.

"Come on."

I jump up off the bed, causing Adam to groan in frustration, and I can't help but laugh.

"Get dressed. I'm hungry," I say as I turn around.

I place a kiss on Adam's lips. He lies on the bed, his naked body looking ethereal in the sunlight that shines through the windows.

"Fine," he says with a pout, sounding like a small child who was just denied a delicious treat.

We find our clothes, still lying by the couch, and Adam pulls on his green briefs and he follows me through the apartment into the kitchen. I pour the water into the empty silver kettle, and I place it on the stove to let the water boil. Adam's arms wrap around my waist, pulling me closer to his bare body. His lips find my neck, and I can't help but close my eyes at the glorious feeling of his mouth on my flesh.

He lifts his lips off my neck, much to my disappointment, and I turn around. I wrap my arms around his neck, and he kisses my lips. He leads me back to his bedroom. We lie back down in his bed. Our underwear comes back off, and we touch one another. I like feeling his skin on mine. I look over to the corner of his bedroom and his violin stares back.

"Will you play for me?" I ask. He smiles as he takes his violin out of its case. He stands there in silence, and then he starts to play. He closes his eyes, and a beautiful sound comes out. He is so meticulous as he plays, and I watch as he sways with the violin. It is like the entire world has drifted away for him, and he is playing a concert for one. I can't take my eyes off him as his fingers move along the strings and the bow beautifully scratches along the violin. Every word that Adam has had trouble saying is coming out fluently through the music.

"I love you." The words just seem to spill out of my mouth. I don't mean to say it, but it just comes out, like my body is ready for Adam to know. I look down in embarrassment, a blush rising through my face. He stops playing, places the instrument on the floor, and he walks back to me.

Using two fingers, he lifts my chin and looks into my eyes. He smiles and says something I have only dreamed I would hear a guy say to me. "I l-l-love you t-t-too."

CHAPTER TWENTY-TWO

A WEEK has gone by since Adam and I first made love… and I feel wonderful. To paraphrase the definitive one-hit wonder: I've been walking on sunshine. Everything about that night was perfect, and now he knows the truth about my past and me. I don't know how to describe the way I've been feeling. The best way is I feel like Glinda in *The Wizard of Oz*. I'm constantly traveling in a bubble, just gliding through the air. Tonight is also the big night of the *Evil Dead* marathon. Adam is picking me up in an hour so we can drive to the next town and watch three awesome movies back-to-back-to-back. Two of my favorite things together: Adam and horror films. What can be better than that?

I grab my black T-shirt, which is snug to my lean body. An artwork of *Evil Dead* sits on the front of the shirt where a badass Bruce Campbell stands there with his sawed-off boomstick, aka shotgun, and a chainsaw for a hand. Yeah, I scream *cool*.

I finish getting ready, grabbing a thin hoodie, and I hear the sound of a car pulling up outside the house. I run to my window to see Adam stepping out of his car. He is nicely dressed as usual. That bastard. I'm outside before he even rings the doorbell, and I lunge into his arms and kiss him. He wraps his arms around my waist, and he laughs into the kiss. The drive to the theater is no more than a half hour, and it goes by smoothly. Adam holds my hand for most of the car ride, and I smile as he sings (quite badly) to the music on the radio.

We make it to the theater, and it's one of those old-fashioned-looking theaters where the ticket booth is situated outside. A young man, around eighteen or nineteen, sits inside behind the glass window. He holds a comic book in his hands and chews bubble gum. A very short line stands outside his booth.

Adam and I park, and he takes my hand as we get in the line. I don't know what is more exciting: seeing all the *Evil Dead* movies again or seeing them with Adam. Adam isn't that knowledgeable about horror films, so I'm excited for him to take these goretastic movies in.

I rest my head on his shoulder, and he wraps his arm around my waist. Yeah, I can get used to this.

I check my watch to see it's only 4:30 p.m. We still have fifteen minutes until the first movie begins. It's funny how many times I can watch a movie, yet each time I get excited like it's my first time watching it all over again. My heart races, and my fingers tap against my side. I am on the borderline of jumping in my spot, feeling like a giddy child. Horror films have always given me a sense of happiness and safety. It's funny to say that about a genre that is notorious for trying to scare you and make you feel unsafe… but for me, it makes me feel welcomed. Every time I watch a horror film, I feel as if I am returning home. It is the exact same feeling that literature provides for me. Two mediums of art, and yes horror films are an art, each very different, but both provide me with fulfillment that is necessary for a person to live a satisfying life.

A group of three young guys, all around eighteen, gets in line behind us. I watch them call out a hello, and the boy behind the glass waves back. So the boy behind the glass has friends. He isn't just there to look pretty. I take them all in with their designer jeans and their colorful polo shirts, with their collars popped. Come on. Who even pops their collars anymore? It's lame, and trust me I know lame. I am the King of Lame. I should make a papier-mâché crown or something.

We get to the ticket booth, and I feel my excitement growing in anticipation for the gory mayhem we're about to see on a big screen. The young man looks up at us with the most vapid gaze I've ever seen. It's as if nothing is going on in there. He pops a bubble of his gum. I start to reach for my wallet, but Adam stops my hand, and he smiles.

"T-t-two t-t-t-t-tickets f-f-for *Evil D-Dead*, p-p-please," he says to the young man.

"What are you? Retarded?"

Everything seems to fall apart, like paint dripping away on a canvas. The smile disappears from Adam's face, and I feel his fingers tighten around my hand. I look back to see the three teenage boys, who are really just children, laughing among each other. They must think they're fucking hilarious.

"Grow the fuck up," I spit, mustering as much venom as I can. I try to keep my voice loud, not to let it falter.

"What? Can't the retard stand up for himself? Or is he t-t-t-too a-a-afraid," one of the boys laughs, mocking his stutter. If I could kill them, I would. Adam isn't responding. He isn't even moving. He quietly takes out his wallet and hands over the cash, taking the two tickets. He pulls me away by my hand, but I manage to flip them the middle finger before disappearing inside.

By the time we're sitting down in the theater, Adam hasn't said a word. I look over, and he just looks like a zombie. He doesn't seem to move or smile. He blinks and breathes.

"Are you okay?" I compassionately ask. "Those guys are assholes who don't deserve our time. They're immature fucktards."

Adam simply nods but doesn't look at me.

"Come on. Look at me. We're supposed to have a good time...." And then the three assholes come in. "Shit."

Adam looks down into his lap, and the three assholes look up at us, and they burst out into a roaring laughter. They want us to see them, because they can't just talk to each other. They have to make their presence known. I had to deal with bullies throughout all of school, and they want you to know when they're talking about you. They want you to feel as miserable as they do. Why else would they want to make some stranger feel awful? They must live some fucked-up lives. At least that is what our parents teach us growing up: that bullies bully because they have their own problems. I do wonder how much of that is true. Maybe some people are just born assholes.

"We can leave," I whisper. I don't want to be here if Adam is going to be upset. He should be happy all the time and smiling.

He looks over at me and gives me a smile, but I know it's forced, and trust me, because I'm the master of forcing faked smiles. "I-i-i-it's okay."

"We don't have to stay here," I reassure him. He doesn't have to be strong for me.

He shakes his head. "You were s-s-s-s-so excited f-f-f-for the m-movies. We're n-n-not going to, to l-leave." He looks over at the three little douche bags. "I'm n-n-not going t-t-t-to let them r-r-r-run us out of here."

I grab him and kiss him. "I love you."

He kisses back and smiles into the kiss. "I l-l-love you too."

"How sweet," an annoyingly high-pitched voice calls out. Ah, how mature. They're trying to mock a stereotypical gay man's voice. Someone should tell them not all gay men sound like that.

"Just ignore them," I tell him. Or maybe I should tell myself this advice, because I've never felt the urge to get up and beat the shit out of someone so badly in my life. Adam is literally the nicest person I have ever met, and now we have these three fuckers feeling the need to harass him.

At last the first movie begins, and Adam and I turn our attention to the screen. The three kids never stop talking or laughing at the movie. They make fun of the cheesy effects and the acting—it's a low-budget film, geez, not to mention it's art—and I just want to duct tape their mouths shut. I still manage to block their voices out and watch the film with wide-open eyes like a child watching a cartoon. The ending is complete chaos, and the gore is just wonderful. When the film comes to an end, I have to fight the urge to stand up and applaud.

"Wow," Adam states. Is that a good wow or a bad wow? "Th-th-that w-w-w-was interesting," he goes on.

"Good interesting?"

Before he can answer, someone screams "Hey retard!" Adam looks down at the ground, and the three guys get out of their seats. They make their way up to us, sitting down right behind our row.

"Did you forget how to talk?" one of them mocks.

"Just leave us alone," I demand, trying to sound tough... but I know the tremble in my voice gives me away.

They all smirk. I want to kill them. I want to kill them all. Watching their smug faces, I feel an intense anger bubbling up inside me. I feel it in the pit of my stomach. It's not like when the sadness pulls me back into the dark place... no, this is something more intense. It's like a volcano is sitting in my stomach, preparing to erupt. I feel the hot molten lava coursing through my veins. Adam remains silent beside me, his eyes cast toward the ground. I watch a tear slide down his cheek, and I want to just kiss it away. I want to make him forget about the pain in life that I feel every day. He should never feel the pain I feel.

I look down to see my hands balled into fists. My hands tremble, wanting to break free and to make contact with their faces... until they feel the soft touch of Adam's fingers. I look up at him. His blue eyes plead with me to let it go… but I don't want to. I shouldn't have to let it go. I can't let these people win. Why does the bad always win?

"L-l-let's go." Barely a whisper, but I hear Adam. We get up, and we walk out in silence, letting the jeers disappear with the theater. The car ride is spent in silence. I don't know what to say. I've never seen Adam look so heartbroken in my life. He doesn't cry, but he just looks so broken. Something has finally cracked his happy exterior.

"Adam," I say finally breaking the silence.

Silence. His eyes don't leave the road. He continues to drive until we're outside my house.

"I w-w-w-will t-t-text you t-t-t-tomorrow," he says.

I watch him drive away. That's it. No good-bye. No kiss. I'm only left with the thought of wanting to take away his pain. I find myself walking through the house, ending up in my bed. I stare up at the ceiling.

I forget sometimes I'm not the only one with darkness in my life. That's a pretty selfish thing of me to think. I guess that just adds to the tragic nature of my well-being. Adam has his own issues too… and I'm not there for him. Everyone has their issues and their pain, but I'm always so stuck in my head trying to get away from mine. Maybe I'd be better off dead….

As much as I try to escape, I feel the tiny hands of the darkness seeping into my life and planting their seeds into my core. I want to stop them, but I feel powerless to them. I am nothing but a slave to my own darkness.

CHAPTER TWENTY-THREE

I WAKE up to three texts from Adam, each one longer than the last.

Hey, I'm so sorry about last night!

Then, *Are you there? I really am so sorry.*

And finally, *If you're ignoring me I understand. I was a real ass last night. I shouldn't have ignored you. It wasn't your fault.*

I grab my phone and I text him back. *Don't worry. I was just asleep. You didn't ruin anything. Those assholes from last night did.*

He quickly texts back. *Okay, good! The moment I woke up I felt awful about my behavior last night. I want to make it up to you. I want to go on a date part 2.*

I smile at the text. *Sure. That'd be great!*

Thank you!

As I smile at the text, something just doesn't feel right. It's like there is a cannibalistic pit in my stomach that is just eating away at my body. It's scratching at my flesh and tearing apart my bones. Adam isn't mad at me... so shouldn't I be feeling good? Shouldn't I be feeling happy?

Maybe I'd be better off dead. The thought from last night still resides in my mind. For a while I've been trying to push those thoughts away, but they never truly go away. They just lie dormant for a little while, just like a volcano. It slowly rises until it is ready to explode. I'm not ready to explode yet, but I feel it just below the surface, waiting. It wants to truly torture me until I can't take it anymore.

I shower and get dressed, and I find myself in the kitchen. My family is sitting down to breakfast, and I hear their laughter. My mom sits in front of my sister. My dad is at work right now. They both turn to me and smile, and I force one out. I can't let them see the darkness in me. They have been nothing but amazing, and I can't let them think I'm slipping once again. I'll just pretend. For them.

I will be happy for them. And for Adam.

I sit and force down some cereal, but the moment it reaches my stomach, I feel like throwing it back up. I try to make conversation, but honestly I don't know what they're even saying. I watch their lips move, but nothing reaches my ears. What is wrong with me?

My phone vibrates in my pocket. It's a text from Adam. He wants to know if I like to ice skate.

Never been, I respond.

Good answer, he says right back. *Be ready at 10pm.*

Why so late?

I have my reasons. Now just be ready and dress warm! We'll be outside.

Okay, I answer. *Sounds like a plan.*

"Who are you texting?" I hear Clara ask. She has a little smirk on her face.

"Adam," I respond.

"Oh, what does he have to say?"

"Nothing."

"Jess, are you okay?" Mom asks me.

"Yes. I'm full. I'm going upstairs to my room. I'm really tired. I'm sorry. I didn't get to bed until real late. I think I need to rest more."

"Okay…."

I get up, and I walk back up to my room, and I curl up on my bed, wrapping myself in my blanket. Can I just stay like this forever? In my own little cocoon? I close my eyes and just imagine my own little world where I'm the only one who exists, and no one and nothing can bother me. I'm untouchable and I'm happy. My own little Utopia.

The vibration of my cell phone rips me away from my dream world, and I answer it to be met by Tommy's voice.

"Yo, man. What up?" He sounds like his old smug self again.

"Nothing, really. You?"

"I'm bored and want to leave. Let's do something."

"Yeah, okay, cool."

I'm dressed and ready by the time Tommy is outside my house. He is smoking a cigarette in his car, and I roll my window all the way down, ignoring the cold air.

"So what's up?"

I shrug. What could have happened in the last half hour?

"So I spoke to Adam's friend Korey the other day. I called him up. He let me stop by the place."

I turn toward him, praying for the story to have a good ending.

"What happened?" I ask.

"I don't know yet. We spoke, and he says he'd get back to me. It's probably a no...."

"You never know, though," I say.

"Yeah, but who knows. With the way my life is right now, I'm not exactly expecting good things."

I want to tell him it'll all work out, but how am I supposed to know? I'm still waiting for my own life to truly work out, so how can I tell someone else to be happy and confident? Tommy tells me it's a nice apartment, small, but there are two bedrooms and a tiny kitchen. The rent isn't a lot, so he thinks he'd be able to manage... now it's just all about waiting. I wish I believed in God so I could ask him to allow Tommy this one thing in his life.

"How is Adam?" he asks.

"He's good," I answer.

"That's good," he responds.

The car comes to a stop, and I am happy to *not* see the warehouse. We are outside Traveling Tunes, the little music store that Wilshire has. It's one of the last remaining places I know that sells actual CDs. Everyone just downloads their music. Tommy has always loved music, so he still refuses to this day to actually get his music online. He likes to own physical copies. We walk into the tiny store where the cashier greets Tommy by name.

He goes through the many rows of CDs, and I just follow him like a pet. He so meticulously handles each CD, making sure to place them where they belong. I could see Tommy working in a place like this, so I tell him.

"I don't know. They're probably not hiring."

"You should ask. It's an extra paycheck along with your garage job." He nods, and I watch him as he walks up to the cashier, named Kirk, as he asks for an application. Tommy and Kirk converse as I start to go through the CDs. I find the classical music section, and I pull out one with a picture of a violin on the cover. It's a collection of songs done on the violin. A small smile comes onto my face as I think of Adam and his love of the instrument. I pay for the CD.

"I didn't know you like classical music?" Tommy asks me.

"I don't. It's for Adam. He plays the violin."

He smiles. "Oh, beautiful Adam." A blush rises to my cheeks as I follow Tommy outside, and we walk toward his car. "I like how he makes you smile. It's good to see my best friend happy."

There is that word again. Happy? Am I happy? It's something I try so hard to be, but can't reach. It's the one ghost that will haunt me all my life. Why is it so hard for me to reach when it comes so naturally to everyone else? Happiness is like a train that continues to pass me by. I come close, but I always miss it.

But Adam... I love him. I really do. He makes me smile, and making love with him made me the happiest I've been in a while, but even that happiness seems to be fleeting. It's all just seeping away like blood from an open wound.

"Jess, you okay?" Tommy's voice distracts me from my thoughts, and I nod. I ask him if there is anywhere else he wants to go, and he says he just wanted to get out of the house. He couldn't stand being there anymore. I nod. Tommy drives me home, and I walk back to my bedroom with the CD. I open it, and I let the music play from my stereo. The sounds from a violin fill my room, starting slow, and I just listen as the music continues to build. By the end everything is swelling, and all is beautiful. I close my eyes, and I pretend that Adam is here listening with me. I can picture his goofy smile as he dances around the room. He takes me into his arms, and he holds me close. I can breathe in his scent, and it sends my body into a whirlwind of hormones and desire. But when I open my eyes, the fantasy dies. I'm alone in my bedroom. No Adam, and the song has come to an end.

The CD continues on, but I stop listening as I lie on my bed, and I just stare at the blank whiteness of the ceiling. It is like when you stare at something for so long, that it almost becomes something more. It becomes something so big that you're afraid to fall in. The ceiling turns into a void. I must not let myself fall.

My mind goes back to Adam, and while he makes my heart skip a beat... if it ends my heart will turn into stone dropping down into my chest, weighing down my entire body. Will that be a darkness I'll be able to escape? All the movies make love look so effortless and happy, but it's false. Falling in love is tough, confusing, and painful.

Sometimes I can't tell the difference between being in love and being insane. They both make my head go in circles.

AS THE day turns into night, I find myself still lying in bed. I haven't moved. The CD came to an end a few hours ago, but I never got up to take it out. I should move, but I just feel so tired. Everything just feels tired. My mind. My body. My heart. I try to get up, but as I walk it feels like I'm dragging a boulder along with me. I take the CD out, and I put it back it in its case, and when I'm in the shower, I turn the water up so it's hot. My skin burns red, and I lean my head against the wall. I close my eyes. Please don't let me slip away again. I want to stay. I don't want to go back to the dark place. All the movies tell you a prince will come save you, but it's not true. The prince comes along, but no matter how long he stays, he won't be able to save you.

I feel itchy. Everywhere. I scratch my sides and my stomach and my chest and I dig my nails into my arms, dragging them. I open my eyes to see slight scratches all over my torso and arms. Some of the scratches on my wrists have little droplets of blood. I run it under the hot water, and I gasp at the stinging, but I let it take me over. I turn my pain into something physical, and I let it release from my body. Sometimes it's the only way I know how to escape the pain.

I turn the water off, wrapping the towel around my waist. I stand in front of the mirror, which is completely covered from the steam of my hot shower. I'm nothing but a blur in the mirror. I'm not a human. I have no feelings. No emotions. I am just a passing blur in the way of life. I take my finger, and I bring it down against the glass, creating two vertical lines. I add a frown underneath. The sad face stares back at me... but something isn't right. It isn't me quite yet. I add a diagonal line to each eye, so now a pair of X's lie where the eyes should be. Now, that's better. A dead face stares back.

ADAM SHOWS up on time, and he smiles at my gift, kissing me on the lips and telling me he loves it. He puts it into the CD player of his car, and the violin fills every spot. I turn up the volume so I don't have to speak. He holds my hand in the car, and it feels nice, but I wonder why. Should I really be letting him hold my hand? I can't let myself fall for him any more. It'll hurt him and me in the end. I know it. *He doesn't really love you, Jess*, my mind tells me. I close my eyes and will the dark place to go away. I can't let it take me over. Not now. Not here. Not with Adam around. I can't let him see me like that again.

When he stops the car, we're outside a darkened outdoor ice-skating rink. He smiles, and he grabs my door, letting me out.

"What are we doing here?"

"We're g-g-g-going ice-s-s-s-skating," he exclaims.

"I don't know how," I state.

"It's o-o-okay. I-I'll sh-sh-show you." He wears a smile on his face, and I want to put my lips upon his. I also want to know how he can find so much happiness in the world. He leads me to the ice-skating rink, and we lace up our skates. He tells me he asked the owner for a favor, as the owner knows his uncle. He leads me onto the ice, and I don't feel steady. He holds me up, but it's no use as I come crashing to the ground. He smiles, and his smile makes me smile, and it feels good to smile. He helps me up.

"Hold on-on-on to m-m-my hands."

"No problem with that." He laughs as I take his hands. Gosh, I love holding his hands. They feel so perfect in mine. He glides backward across the ice, and he moves with such grace. I wonder if there is anything he can't do. I'm not as steady as him. Not even close. I am wobbly and awkward, but I manage not to fall too many times. As long as I hold on to him, I can stay upright. Adam keeps me going.

"You're g-g-g-getting it," he says. And then I fall. Even I have to laugh at this. He helps me back up and kisses me. "I l-l-love you," he states. I smile and tell him "You too." Love is such a powerful word. So many people throw it around, but I don't think many know what it actually means. After one date people will throw around the word, and then the next day love someone else... but I truly love Adam... but what if he only thinks he loves me?

I want to have fun, but something clutches at my heart and my mind and it just won't let me go. I feel the claws of the darkness digging into me, and it wants me back. I tell him I feel tired, and it's not far from the truth. I feel so damn tired. I just want to go to sleep.

"A-are you o-o-okay?" he asks me concerned.

I nod. "Yeah, just really tired. I didn't get much sleep, and then I was running around with Tommy all day."

"O-okay."

He tries to help me take my skates off, but I tell him I can do it, and he takes me back home. He tries to talk to me in the car, but I just smile.

"Take me back to your place," I tell him, and he smiles. We drive back to his apartment, and he leads me up to his bedroom where I throw myself at him. I tear off his clothing, and he takes off mine ever so gently. I'm the predator, and he is my last meal. I want to taste him. We make love again in his bed, and he falls back, smiling, kissing my temple. I lay my head on his chest.

"I love you," he tells me again. I don't respond.

He doesn't really love you, my mind says again. I don't want to believe it. I can't stay away from the thought, though. *No one could ever love someone like you. You're meant to die alone. No one will ever truly love you.* I try to turn my mind off, but it continues talking, and I notice that Adam looks scared and confused.

"Don't," I say.

"J-J-Jess, what is, is g-g-going on?"

"Nothing," I lie, my voice quivering. I close my eyes, and I try to will the world to disappear. I want my mind to shut up, and I suddenly wish for once I was not with Adam. I just want to go away and disappear. I can't do this anymore.

"W-w-why do you p-put up that wall, J-Jess?"

"What wall?"

"This one where y-you w-w-w-won't let m-me in when s-s-s-s-s-something is b-bothering you."

"I don't know."

Liar. I know exactly why. I just don't want anyone to break my heart or to make me worse. From the look on Adam's face, he knows I'm lying too.

"You k-k-keep trying to k-keep the s-s-s-s-sadness and the p-pain out, b-b-but you're also b-blocking all the h-happiness that c-c-c-can come into your l-l-life as well."

I look into his gray-blue eyes, and I realize he deserves someone so much better. He deserves someone who can give him the love he wants. He doesn't need me. If I left, he'd probably forget about me in a moment.

"Just take me home, Adam."

"Jess, t-t-talk to me."

"Please," I plead. I just want to go home.

"N-not until you s-s-s-s-start t-to talk to me. O-open up. I l-l-love you, Jess." His eyes are wide, and I want to believe they're full of love… but it's true, I don't deserve love. He doesn't know what he wants or feels.

"Adam, just take me the fuck home, now." The anger is biting, and Adam flinches.

"Jess…."

His eyes are big as I stare into them. Seeing those big blue eyes just hurts me even more, and I look away. My arms are itchy. So itchy. I dig my nails into my skin, and I scratch.

"S-s-s-s-s-stop that."

"Adam, just leave me alone. I can't be with you. I'm sorry, but I can't do this anymore."

"What?" He looks shocked, but I can't keep doing this to him. I can't keep stringing him along through all my bullshit. How terrible of a person can I be? I jump up, and I pull my clothes back on.

"This," I shout. "I can't keep doing this." I point from him to me as I stare anywhere but his eyes.

"You d-d-don't m-m-m-mean th-that. I-I l-love you, J-J-Jess."

"Well, get over it. We're done. Now fucking leave me alone." He doesn't listen as he takes a step near me and tries to wrap his arms around me, but I push him away. "We're fucking over."

I rip open his apartment door, and I race down those stairs, and I walk along the sidewalks, never looking back. Don't look back. Don't look back. This is for the best. I know it is. I can't let him be with me. All he is going to do is get hurt. Or he'll hurt me. I don't see the point in this relationship anymore. He says he loves me, but is it real? Or is it just an illusion that we all create for ourselves. Maybe love is nothing more than a magic trick our minds perform.

I see the front door of my house. The walk home is nothing but a blur to me. Just an endless array of sidewalk, buildings, trees, and people. All blending in to a mess of a society. I enter my house, and Clara stands by the staircase.

"Jess, I called you three times. What is going on?" She has worry written all over her face, but there is a bite to her words. She is angry that I never responded. Good, let her be angry with me. Let her hate me. Let everyone hate me. I don't even fucking care anymore. None of this is worth it anymore. It's never been worth it. Hating me will make everything easier for them and me.

I ignore her, and I walk up my stairs, and I lock my door. I hear my sister's footsteps race upstairs, and then Clara screams for me to open the door. I just want it all to stop. Shut up. Shut up. Shut up. I cover my ears, but it doesn't stop anything. It doesn't stop the world from moving. It doesn't stop my sister's cries. It doesn't stop the thoughts inside my own head.

"*Shut up!*" I finally scream, unable to hold everything inside. Why won't it just end already? I don't know what happens as my right hand balls up into a fist, and I just watch it punch the wall over and over and over again until the wall starts to dent, and blood stains the light blue paint. Pain shoots up my arm, as I feel it in all my bones, and I fall to the ground on my knees. I am weak.

Please just make everything stop.

You're pathetic. You fuck up everything. All you have ever done is fuck up everything and everyone around you. No one loves you.

The voices continue to scream at me, and no matter how hard I try, they never seem to stop. The little voice becomes louder and begins to drown out Clara until I can't hear anything except for my own mind. Pathetic. That is what it tells me I am. I know I am. The tears fall down my face, and I feel weak. I am powerless to my mind.

"Jess, open the door," Clara continues to cry out.

I hear her footsteps run, and I blast my stereo, drowning out her screams, but the voice remains. *Just kill yourself. Just do it.*

Just do it.

My eyes go toward my many pill bottles.

Just take them all.

Sleeping pills.

No one will care.

Sleep sounds good to me. I can finally be at rest, and this will all be over. Sleep, yes. That sounds wonderfully enticing.

I open the bottle, half-full of pills. I close my eyes, and one by one I take them. One after another. I swallow every single one of them. My body feels like a weight, as I can't stay up straight. I lie back on my bed, and my eyes close. I try to open them, but it just becomes too hard. I'm so tired. I think I can finally sleep.

I think I am.

CHAPTER TWENTY-FOUR

I AWAKE to a blinding white light, and my first thought is that I am in heaven and that I have always been wrong. But then the doctors and nurses around me become tangible, and I see the wires connected to my body. I watch the line on the screen that shows my heartbeat. I don't know if I am more disappointed for surviving (yet again), or if I am more proud to know I am not wrong about heaven (yet). Unless heaven is full of lots of tubes and wires, that is.

A nurse notices my eyes have opened, and she whispers to the doctor. One would think I am already dead. I can hear you, I want to say... but my throat is so dry, and I am so tired. I don't even feel like moving my lips to speak. I will have time to talk later. I'm sure I'll have many nice words to tell everyone. The nurse leaves, leaving me alone with the doctor.

"Hello, Mr. Holbrooke. I'm Dr. Rantzen. You've been asleep for a day and a half. Your sister brought you in."

I can't find any words, so I just simply nod. Dr. Rantzen is an older man in his late forties. His hair is dark brown with patches of gray throughout and a matching beard is closely trimmed to his face. His hair reminds me of a jigsaw puzzle in pieces. His smile is soft, almost fatherly.

I try to speak, but my throat is so dry. "Do you want water?" I nod, and he brings me a small plastic cup of water. He helps me sit up, and my whole body feels exhausted. I down the entire cup, and I feel it go through my body.

"Where am I?" I finally ask in a husky voice. I mean I know where I am, but which hospital? I hope it's not one of the more expensive ones that my parents won't be able to afford. I've already done enough shit to them.

"You're at Westview Hospital." Fuck. That's not cheap. "Your family is outside in the waiting area right now. They want to see you. Is that okay?"

I really don't want them to see me like this. But what is the point? They've seen me like this before. I feel that my story is nothing but a tragedy only existing to repeat itself. Maybe I'm just the tragic hero of some teenage boy's novel, and I don't realize it as he is writing it. If so, he is writing a pretty lame story, isn't he? Where is the action or the horror? Where are the sword fights and bloody deaths? I'm disappointed.

"Jess," I hear my mom's choked voice. I look toward the door, and she and my sister wear matching tear-streaked faces. Dad stands behind them, trying to keep his composure, but I can tell he's not doing a good job when he brings a finger to one of his eyes.

"Hey, everyone," I meekly respond. I don't know what else to say. I feel like saying *sorry for trying to kill myself... again* is out of the question. "Sorry?" Again, what else can I say.

"Don't apologize," my sister speaks. "I thought...." She wipes away her tears. "I thought you were doing better."

So did I. But I guess none of it ever really went away. My darkness was always there; it just was dormant for a while. But it would always come back to consume me. I knew it.

"I'm sorry," I repeat, looking away from the three crying messes. Even my father's tears are finally spilling out like a waterfall of emotion.

"I said not to apologize," Clara says with a small laugh. They all take a step closer to the bed, and they tower over me, making me feel smaller than I have ever felt in my life.

"Why, Jess, why?" my mom asks.

I can't look at any of their faces, as seeing all their tears just brings me guilt. I shrug. I just want to apologize, but how many times can I say that I am sorry?

"Are we not making you happy?" she asks me.

"Gosh, no, Mom. You didn't do anything wrong. None of you did. I just... you know I'm sad. I just wasn't in my right mind, and I wasn't thinking... or no. That's not true. I was thinking too much, and everything became too much. I just feel... I don't know. I'm not doing too well with my words now," I try to joke.

No one laughs.

"Sorry."

"Stop damn apologizing."

It feels nice to talk to my family, but it seems like something is missing. Or someone. Adam. I said so many terrible things to him, and I left him. The last thing he saw of me was my bout of insanity, and now he isn't here.

"Where is Adam?" I finally ask. A part of me doesn't want to know. He probably never wants to see me again.

"He's in the waiting room," my dad answers.

"What?"

"Do you want to speak to him?" he asks.

I simply nod. He wasn't scared away? But why? How? Any normal human being would have run away after my antics, but he stayed? My family leaves the room, and in walks Adam. He wears a plain T-shirt that clings tightly to his muscles. His light brown hair is in a mess and he hasn't shaved for a few days. His stubble is growing in. He even wears a pair of glasses over his beautiful blue eyes.

"Adam… you're here," I state in shock.

"I ha-ha-haven't l-left," he says with a small smile. He walks over to the bed, and I feel the weight of his body as he settles down next to me. I try to sit up, but I feel so tired that it almost hurts. He puts his arm around my waist, and he helps me sit up. He even fixes my pillow to make it more comfortable for me.

"Why?"

"I l-l-love you, J-Jess. When your s-s-s-s-sister called me, me, I w-w-was s-s-s-so w-w-worried. I-I-I don't w-w-want anything b-bad to, to ha-happen to you." That is when I look into his eyes and notice that tears are falling. Even crying, he looks beautiful.

"I love you too. I'm so sorry over everything I said and all that I put you through. I shouldn't have done that to you. You shouldn't have to deal with my shit, Adam."

"Sh-sh-shut up. I w-w-w-want to b-be with you." He touches his forehead against mine, and I close my eyes as he rubs his hand against my cheek. "I l-love you s-s-s-so much."

We sit there in silence, and he holds me, and in this moment life feels good. Even though I'm lying in a hospital bed, after just having my stomach pumped, it feels right to be here with Adam again. After Adam leaves, the doctor tells my family they want to put me back into the mental hospital again. Hearing those words causes my heart to drop, as I really don't want to return… but this time I really need to help myself. I want to be better. I *need* to be better.

CHAPTER TWENTY-FIVE

Two months later

IT'S FUNNY how when you're away, it's like the world just stops turning without you there. But it just keeps on spinning, and people continue on living, even if you're not a part of it. I guess it was incredibly selfish of me to think everything would just pause when I was in the hospital—for a second time—but now that I'm home, everything is still going. Dad is back at his office job. Mom is still worrying about me. Clara is back at school. Tommy is still drinking, and Alex is still going to school to be a teacher. His relationship with Nick is great, he says. They are planning a vacation together to Nick's family's summer home. I'm really happy for him. Peter is still running the bookshop with Laurie and Jill at his side. It's like nothing has changed. In the hospital Tommy visited me a few times, but he couldn't stand the place, so I didn't see much of him. When he did visit, though, he never acted differently. He cussed a lot and talked about girls.

Jill and Laurie brought me flowers and a really nice card, and they both made efforts to see me every couple of weeks. Hell, even Peter visited me while I was at the hospital. Yeah, it was only once, but I was shocked when he showed up. Obviously my family was there as often as they could come, especially my sister. Clara wanted to see me as much as she could before she left for school again.

And Adam…. Adam hasn't left my side once. Even after all the terrible things I said to him, he had every right to leave me, but he didn't. Adam visited me at the hospital every chance he could, and he made sure to let me know how much he missed me every time. He was there multiple times a week, and each time he visited me it felt like I was home again.

But now I am home for real again, and my doctors said I have been making incredible progress. I'm on a different kind of medication, and this one seems to really be helping, but I think the biggest change is Adam. Knowing he is there is making me stronger. I guess that is what love is. Love is strength. Love is finding that person who not only completes you but also makes you a better person and makes you stronger. Adam does that for me. He has helped me find the strength inside me I never realized I had.

And when I can't find my strength, Adam is still always there, ready to help me. He always found it in me, while I had to go looking for it. Even on my darkest days, and I'm still having them, he was there. One of the nights after I got out of the hospital, I was feeling sick from the new medication. I felt like I was going to throw up, and I didn't want to move from my bed. The new meds hadn't taken effect yet. I was lying in bed crying. I just couldn't stop the tears. I cried over my life and my fears. My past, my present, my future. What I knew and what I didn't know. Each tear that I let loose was another anxiety of mine coming free. I had wanted to die in that moment. Adam was there, though. He was in my bed holding me close to his muscular body. His arms were strong as he held me to him and he just brushed my hair and told me everything would be okay. As I cried and wanted to die, he smiled and told me it would all be okay. Sometimes that is all a person needs to hear. That reassurance that there is something in life worth living for.

I'm back at the bookshop, and I'm living at home again. It feels nice to be with my family again and to be back in my world of books. Am I not depressed anymore? No. I'm still ill, and I will always be ill, but I'm learning to deal with my sickness in new and much healthier ways. I'm talking to people about my feelings now, and not just my doctor. I'm starting to let people in. Little by little, I'm allowing my wall to crumble down.

I'm thinking of even going back to school. I have no idea what I want to study anymore. I keep changing ideas, but I need to be the strong person I've always dreamed of being. I want to make a life for myself and maybe even make a life with Adam. I can't think about the past anymore. I can only think of the present, and I can look toward the future. Because that is what really matters. A person's past doesn't define them, and my illness doesn't have to define me.

While in the hospital, I truly learned that everyone's life is like a novel. Each person's life is made up of all these different chapters. And it is true. We go from birth to school to college to work to death. Each is just another chapter and another change. Our novels can't be rewritten, but we are always still writing.

The truth is I may never be happy, but I'm working on it. I really am. And you know what, Adam is still right here by my side. He's seen me at my worst, and he still loves me. He wants to be with me. I always hated myself and berated myself for not being better, but I know now that I am the best person I can be as long as I try. I must try to live. Will Adam and I be together forever? I don't know, but he is here now. I love him so much it hurts sometimes, but he won't bring me darkness. It's only me who can send me to the dark place. My future is nothing but a blank canvas just waiting to be painted. I have all the brushes and paints I need, and now it's up to me to paint the life I want, and I *want* to be there. I think it will be beautiful, and I want to be a part of all the beauty. I know now that there are dark days, but there are also the light days. When those days happen, they are so beautiful, and they almost make the dark days worth it. I know I'm sad, but one day I know those dark days will be fewer and fewer. I think I can be happy one day.

I guess it's time to start writing myself a new chapter.

BRYAN ELLIS grew up in New York and graduated from SUNY New Paltz with his BA in English because all he ever wanted to be was a writer. When he isn't watching horror films, he creates stories inside his head and performs them with Legos, something he's done since birth. Bryan loves horror films, often found quoting them and forcing his friends and family to watch them. As an openly gay male, he feels it is important to give a voice to people who are normally silent. When he isn't writing, he spends his free time with his boyfriend, Alex Maccaro.

E-mail: b.ellis6990@gmail.com
Twitter: @BryanMEllis
Facebook: facebook.com/brybry69

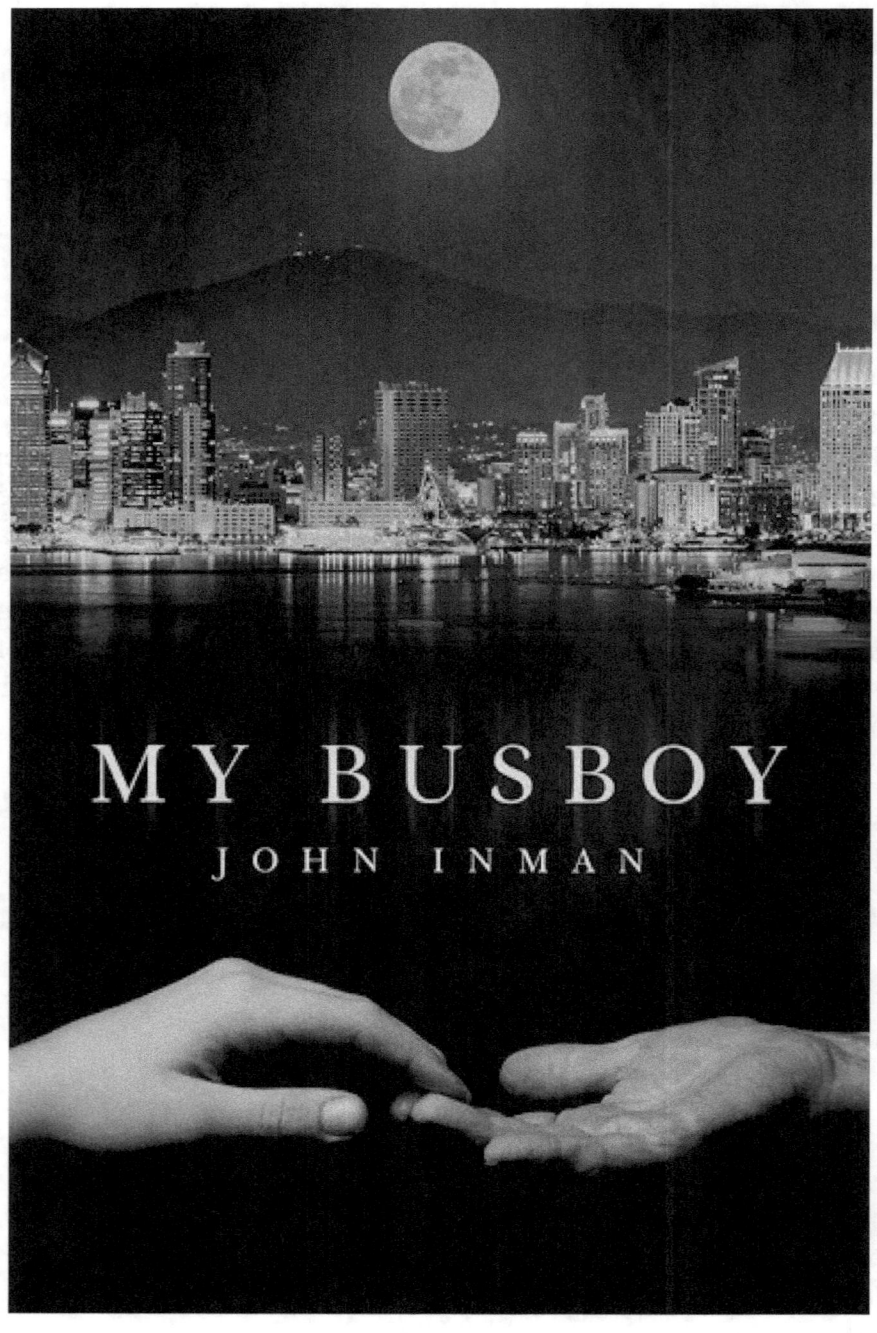

Open Road

M.j. O'Shea